Private Lives

Mimi Francis

Second Chances In Hollywood

MIMI FRANCIS

4 Horsemen
Publications, Inc.

4 Horsemen Publications, Inc.
1497 Main St. Suite 169
Dunedin, FL 34698
4horsemenpublications.com
info@4horsemenpublications.com

Edited by JM Paquette

Library of Congress Control Number: 2021935820

Paperback ISBN-13: 978-1-64450-591-5
Audiobook ISBN-13: 978-1-64450-229-7
Ebook ISBN-13: 978-1-64450-590-8

Table of Contents

Chapter One

CHRIS

The fight was *epic*.

Unfortunately, it was also public, inside a little coffee shop, and across the street from Lillian's apartment.

The café was crowded with people seated inside and out. Chris suspected that was Lillian's intention. Witnesses. Someone recorded it—recorded *them*, making him look like the bad guy, losing his temper and letting loose on poor, innocent Lillian.

Not that Lillian was innocent, not even a little, but she'd kept her calm, sitting with a smile on her face, completely cool while she explained to Chris that she had been seeing someone else, not cheating on him—no way she would ever admit to that—but she had found someone else and as far as she was concerned, she and Chris were finished. His feelings were hurt, crushed if he was honest with himself, but how could they not be? So he'd lashed out, chewing her out, his voice getting louder as her smile widened.

He felt like a fool and that had fueled his anger, pushing him over the edge until he screamed at Lillian, calling her every name he could think of, desperate to hurt her as she'd hurt him. Instead, she'd risen to her feet, thrown her purse over her shoulder, and walked away while he was in the middle of his tirade. Two hours later, the fight had been all over the internet. His publicist was pissed. Again.

His pissed off publicist, Wendy, was the reason he was sitting in a downtown Los Angeles high rise, his hands folded in his lap, being chastised like a child who had stolen from the cookie jar. He picked at the seam of his jeans, his hat pulled down low on his head so she couldn't see his eyes. He didn't want to be sitting here being told how he would ruin his career if he wasn't careful, blah, blah, blah, for the hundredth time. He wanted to go home, lock his door, and hide for a week, mourning the loss of yet another relationship he thought might be the real deal.

"—your therapist, Chris?" Wendy asked.

"I'm sorry. What?"

"I asked if you've called your therapist?" she repeated.

"I don't want to call her." God, he even sounded like a petulant child. No wonder Wendy was treating him like one.

"I think you should," Wendy said. "Call her, talk to her, and get over Lillian so you can go back to work."

"You make it sound so easy." He sighed.

"It is." Wendy shrugged. "You'll be fine." She picked up a pen and scribbled something on a scrap of paper. "I talked to Jack and Paul. They agree that you need a few days to recover. So, Paul called Juan and told him you needed a couple of days off. He okayed it. You are due back to work on Tuesday. Take advantage of the time off."

Chris pushed himself to his feet, shoved his sunglasses on his face, and stalked from the office. An hour and forty-five minutes later, after an impossible drive through Los Angeles rush hour traffic, he pulled through the gate at the bottom of the hill, following the winding road up past the other million-dollar homes, finally parking in his attached garage. He killed the engine and sat in his car, staring out the window.

An overwhelming sense of loss was descending over him again, that feeling that something was missing in his life moving to the forefront of his mind. The voices in his head, the ones that told him he wasn't good enough, that he didn't deserve his career, his fame, his money, were screaming, drowning out everything else. He contemplated turning on his car and letting the engine run, allowing the carbon monoxide to fill the enclosed garage. He could lean his head back against the soft leather, close his eyes, and fall asleep. He could finally be at peace, finally quiet the voices once and for all.

A loud, sharp bark caught his attention, yanking him back into reality.

Chris released a heavy sigh, shoved open the car door, then stepped out. As soon as he opened the door between the garage and the kitchen, a fifty-pound bundle of black and white fur pounced on him.

"Oof," he exhaled, catching his rescue mutt, Oliver—Ollie—in his arms. He succumbed to the face licking from Ollie's slobbery tongue before setting the dog on the floor. "You hungry, buddy?"

Ollie stared up at him with an adoring look that melted Chris's heart. He spent the next few minutes feeding Ollie and refilling his water dish before looking through the refrigerator. Unable to find anything he wanted to eat, he grabbed a beer and made his way through the house to the living room, his furry friend right on his heels. He dropped to the couch, his feet on the coffee table and remote in his hand. He didn't turn the TV on right away, just sat staring out the window at the lights of Los Angeles, wondering when everything in his life had gotten so off track. Before long, he dozed off.

Chris heard himself screaming, losing his temper, the eruption playing in his head while his therapist, Ingrid, watched the video for herself.

When it was over, she shut her laptop, folded her hands atop her desk, and stared at him. "That was quite a blowup, Christopher."

Ingrid always used his full name, something that drove him crazy; every time she said it, she sounded so damn condescending. He'd asked her numerous times to please call him Chris, but she refused, saying it blurred the doctor and patient line too much if she used what she called "nicknames."

"Yeah, it was."

She said nothing, staring at him with that intense look she had, the one that made him squirm. After what felt like forever, she spoke. "Is that all you have to say?"

"Apparently," Chris muttered, his arms crossed over his chest, eyes narrowed. He hated it when she did this; he felt like a child waiting for his mother to dole out punishment for some slight. He hadn't wanted to come at all, but Wendy insisted, demanding he make an appointment with Dr. Walton before he went back to work. She'd left no room for argument.

The whole reason he'd sought counseling in the first place was to quiet the constant noise and chatter in his brain, to quell the crippling anxiety and stress that seemed to be a constant in his life. Since the breakup with Lillian, he'd barely been able to leave the house. He was only here because he was afraid of losing his job.

"Are you purposely being an ass?" she snapped.

He blinked, his mouth involuntarily falling open, guilt making his stomach churn. Ingrid had a very calm demeanor, rarely losing her composure. Her outburst was unexpected.

"I'm not trying to be difficult." He sighed.

"But you are being difficult." Ingrid leaned back in her chair, her pen tapping incessantly on the desk until Chris wanted to scream. "All right, I'll come right out and say it then. What happened? I thought things were good with you and Lillian?"

"So did I. But I was wrong, wasn't I?"

"Christopher, please."

"Okay, okay," he mumbled. He pinched the bridge of his nose, hoping to stave off the headache he felt coming on. "She broke up with me. She was seeing someone else."

"How does that make you feel?"

"Really? How do you think it makes me feel?" Chris scoffed. "It makes me feel like shit. And you know what's worse? I was completely clueless. I thought things were good, that we were going somewhere. She'd just gotten a part in some new TV series, a part I helped her get, I might add. If it weren't for me, she never would have gotten the audition. She gets the part and breaks up with me a week later. She used me. They all use me, Ingrid, every one of them. That makes me feel like shit."

Ingrid fell silent for a heartbeat. She shifted uneasily in her seat and set her pen on the desk. "I'm sorry, Christopher, I really am. I had no idea you felt that way. You've never mentioned it before. It's no wonder your anxiety is out of control. I'll offer again, for what is probably the hundredth time: I can prescribe something for you. Just say the word."

He'd been down this road before, seeing a therapist and taking medication. While seeing a therapist was low on his list of things he wanted to do, taking medication was even lower. It affected his ability to act, put him in a foggy haze that he didn't care for at all.

"You know my answer. I don't want anything."

"Do me a favor and think about it, okay? Maybe temporarily until you get past this."

"I'm fine."

"You're not," Ingrid said. "You know it, I know it, and thanks to that video, all of America knows it. Don't be so stubborn."

"According to my mother, stubborn is my middle name." Chris shrugged. "But I promise to think about it. If things get to be too much, I'll let you know."

"Fair enough," Ingrid agreed.

Chris didn't feel much better when he left Ingrid's office, not that he ever did. He only saw the therapist because his entire management team insisted on it, but also because his mother encouraged it as well. They thought it helped; he knew it didn't. He kept going, hoping maybe just once it would make a difference, make him feel better. But the voices never stopped, never quieted, never gave him peace.

Maybe one of these days seeing Ingrid would help. Unfortunately, it looked like today wasn't that day.

"Jesus, Chris, what were you thinking?"

Chris rolled his eyes. Two days after the video of him losing it on Lillian went viral, Seth had hopped on a plane and flown across the country, leaving his lucrative construction business in the hands of his second-in-command to be with Chris. He'd landed, grabbed a cab, and shown up at the crack of dawn with coffee and donuts, ready to dissect his best friend's behavior.

"I was thinking, 'holy shit, I'm being shit on all over again by a woman I thought loved me,'" he snapped. "Do you know how many times I've been through this, Seth?"

"Too many to count," Seth replied. "I get that, Chris, I do—"

"But you don't," Chris cut him off. "Every relationship I've had over the last seven or eight years has been a joke. It was either a publicity stunt, an up-and-coming wannabe looking to make a name for herself, or someone who couldn't handle my fame. Of course, with that one, I can't really fault anybody. I can barely handle it myself. It's unfair to ask someone else to put up with the constant press, the paparazzi, and the wildly inaccurate speculation about my love life."

"I put up with it." Seth chuckled, bumping his shoulder into his best friend's. "I mean, come on. It's not that bad."

"For you, no," Chris said. "The press and my fans love you. The childhood best friend who keeps his egomaniac, mega-superstar best friend down to earth. But that's you. Any woman that comes into my life gets torn to shreds—how she looks, what she's wearing, the constant 'she's not good enough for him' bullshit on social media. The last two girlfriends I had before Lillian shut down their Twitter and Instagram accounts because of all the hate. That all comes back on me. How's anybody supposed to deal with that?"

Seth could only stare at him and shrug his shoulders. "I guess I never looked at it like that."

"Because they love you."

"Because they love me." Seth nodded. "So, what are you gonna do?"

"Give up," Chris grunted. He scrubbed a hand across his face, scratching at his beard. "I don't know. I'm tired of trying to find someone. Sometimes I wish I could find someone I could just fool around with and then walk away; no pressure, no strings, just two people in a mutually satisfying relationship."

"Good luck with that," Seth snorted. "Everybody in the world knows your face. You'll never find someone like that. Never."

"Exactly," he muttered. "Which is why I just want to give up. I'll be a bachelor for the rest of my life."

Seth shoved half a donut in his mouth. "A celibate bachelor," he mumbled around his food.

Chris threw a wadded-up napkin at his friend. "Don't remind me." He stood up and brushed the crumbs from his hands. "You know what the worst part of all of this crap is? Everybody expects me to get over the heartbreak at the speed of light or something. I get two extra days off work, and I'm supposed to go back and act as if nothing happened. I dated Lillian for almost a year. I thought I might be in love with her, but I'm supposed to suck it up and move on." He pinched the bridge of his nose and shook his head. "I guess I'm not supposed to have any feelings, huh?"

"Jesus. Chris, that's…that's bullshit. I thought maybe you were being dramatic," Seth mumbled. "I'm a shit best friend."

Chris ignored Seth's comment and snatched his dog's leash off the kitchen counter which had the dog immediately jumping and whining at his feet. "I'm gonna take Ollie for a run and try to clear my head. You sticking around?"

"Of course," Seth said. "Gotta make sure the paparazzi knows I'm here supporting my mega superstar best friend." He winked and burst into laughter.

"Fuck you," Chris yelled over his shoulder. Seth's laughter followed him out the front door.

———————————

He and Seth spent the weekend hanging out, like they'd done when they were younger, before his fame and Seth's construction business separated them, one on each coast. They played video games, drank a lot of beer, ate a lot of pizzas, and dissected the last year of Chris's life, hoping to find clues to the misery his love life had become.

Tuesday came far too soon. He took Seth to the airport, dropping him at the curb, but not before embracing his best friend and extracting a promise that he would come back sooner rather than later. He would have walked him inside, but the paparazzi hung around the Los Angeles airport, and he didn't want to be seen, not to mention that duty called; he was due at the studio in an hour.

Chris drove himself to the studio rather than using his normal driver, in part because he wanted to take Seth to the airport, but he also wanted the extra time to himself that the drive gave him. He turned the music up loud, drowning out not only the sound of morning traffic but also the negative voices in his head. He loved being in his car, a brand new, navy blue BMW M760i. It was the only place he didn't feel as if he was under a microscope, everyone staring at him, judging him, watching him. People couldn't even see him behind the tinted glass. It had been the first thing he'd bought after *Hunting the Criminal* was picked up for a second season. It was his most prized possession.

Thanks to L.A. traffic, he arrived at the studio thirty minutes late, yet another thing that the press would use as proof that he had gone off the deep end. All weekend he'd had to avoid the "news" stories about his mental instability and his anger issues, coupled with his diva-like attitude when he didn't show up for work on Friday or Monday. Just once, he wished he could sit down with one of those so-called reporters and tell them the truth about himself.

Stacey, one of the overzealous ADs, pounced on him as soon as he stepped out of the car. "Jesus, Chris, where the hell have you been? Juan's head is about to explode. He's already called Paul and Jack to bitch about you being a diva."

"Traffic sucked," Chris muttered.

"Well, you're here now and we've gotta move. They're filming one of the scenes you're not in, but

Juan wants you on set in twenty. That means hair, makeup, and costume need to get done ASAP." She grabbed Chris's hand and dragged him across the lot, shoving him into the makeup trailer with a grunt. She shouted some vague instructions to Sandy, his hair and makeup artist, before taking off at a sprint.

"Hey, kiddo, how are you holding up?" Sandy asked as he settled into the chair.

Chris tossed his hat on the counter and shrugged. "I've been better. But, you know, I must power on. Work to be done, right?"

Sandy patted him on the shoulder, a cursory touch before she started. Hair and makeup finished quickly, then Stacey returned, her arms loaded down with clothes. Within minutes, fully dressed in Ambrose Whitwood's suit and tie, fake badge, and fake gun on his hip, Chris got the nod of approval from both Stacey and Sandy, along with a couple more swipes of makeup, then Stacey led the way to the sound stage. He endured a few minutes of not-so-good-natured ribbing from his co-stars and the director before it was time to work.

Chris stepped into the shadows, taking a few minutes to get himself settled and in character. He loved acting, loved losing himself in a character, taking on a different persona, building a character from the ground up. He especially loved playing Ambrose Whitwood, a goody-two-shoes police detective and a character that had brought him a lot of recognition over the last few years.

Acting centered him, helped him focus, and quieted the voices in his head screaming that he wasn't good enough for anybody or anything. He'd started acting in high school when the pressures of hormones, puberty, and girls got to be too much for him; it was an outlet. And lately, it was the only thing that kept him sane. It was his one and only escape.

The director had a full day planned for him, trying to make up for the lost time. By the time he peeled off the suit and scrubbed off the makeup, it was almost midnight. He dropped into the chair in the hair and makeup trailer and closed his eyes. He still had the drive home ahead of him.

"Hey, buddy, how's it going?"

Chris sighed quietly. He wasn't in the mood to deal with Brent right now; he'd managed to avoid the pompous ass most of the day, but it looked as if his luck had run out. Brent acted as if he had good intentions, but he was always looking out for number one—himself. He was one of those people who knew everything; he didn't hesitate to give advice, share his knowledge, or correct you if he thought you were wrong. He drove Chris crazy. Thank God he was only on the show a few times a year.

"Brent," Chris smiled weakly. "How are you?"

"Better than you from what I hear." Brent chuckled. "Lost another girl, huh?"

"Yes, Lillian and I broke up," Chris replied. Hearing yet another person act as if the end of his year-long relationship was no big deal was like a rusty spoon digging into an open wound. Exhaustion washed over him, and all he could think about was his soft, comfortable bed.

"You know what you need?" Brent asked.

"Sleep?" Chris joked.

"You need somebody who isn't looking to get anywhere using your celebrity, somebody you can be yourself with, somebody you can hang out with."

"From your mouth to God's ear," Chris mumbled.

"I think I can help you," Brent said, smiling.

"Thanks, Brent, but I'm really not looking to get set up right now."

Brent shook his head and took his wallet from his pocket. He pulled out a black card with simple gold lettering and put it in Chris's hand.

"They're good, and they're discreet," he said. "Call them if you want to or don't. No skin off my teeth either way. But it looks like you need a change, brother. This might be just what you need."

And then he was gone, his bag thrown over his shoulder, the door swinging closed behind him. Chris stared at the card in his hand.

Private Lives. Call (424) 783-5698.

Chapter Two

SOFIA

Sofia pulled into the driveway and shut off the car. She didn't move, not right away. She wanted to soak it in, give herself a few minutes to get used to the idea of being a homeowner.

The thought made her smile. If someone had told her two years ago that she would be the proud owner of her own home—free and clear, nonetheless—she would have laughed in their face. Yet, here she was, about to get out of her car, walk up *her* sidewalk, and into *her* house. Well, a condo, but it was still hers.

She pushed open the car door and stepped out, her purse clutched in one hand, the keys in the other. She'd picked up the keys less than an hour ago and driven straight here, too excited to go back to her apartment. She hadn't even stopped to call Sasha. Probably not a good idea because once her best friend found out she'd come here alone, she would be furious. She'd just have to deal with Sasha's fiery temper later; for now, she wanted to look around inside, see the place without the previous owner's stuff taking up space. This way, she could decide how she would decorate.

The spacious, two-bedroom condominium was in a quiet community about twenty minutes outside of Los Angeles, close enough that work shouldn't be an issue, but far enough away that she felt like she could get some peace from the craziness that was L.A. life. It had taken her five months to find the perfect place, exasperating not only her real estate agent, but her best friend as well during the search process. Sofia had rejected more places than she could count, dragged Sasha to dozens of open houses and viewings, and fussed over every little detail of each listing they'd looked at. She'd about given up hope until they'd stumbled on this place after an unsuccessful visit to a home five minutes down the road. That place had taken the term "fixer-upper" to a whole new level. Sasha's eagle eye had spotted the sign for the condo on the drive back and, on a whim, they'd turned down the road and gone to see it. The second she'd stepped inside, Sofia had known it was the place. She made an offer that afternoon.

She was barely through the door when her phone rang. She pulled it out of her back pocket, smiling when she saw who it was.

"Hey, Sash," she answered.

"Where are you?" her friend of five years asked. "I stopped by the apartment, but you weren't there."

"I got my keys."

"Shut up! I thought you weren't getting them until later!"

Sofia bounced on her toes, her entire body shaking. "Marjorie called and said I could pick them up any time. The painters finished up Tuesday, and they installed the new carpet yesterday. The paperwork is all filed, and the condo is mine, free and clear."

"Dammit, Sof, I wanted to go with you," Sasha scolded.

"I couldn't wait. I'm sorry," Sofia replied. "I'm too damn excited. I mean, come on! I've been packing up the apartment since the previous owners accepted my offer."

"I know." Sasha laughed. "I'll tell you what: I'll come over and help you move stuff in. How's that sound?"

"That sounds great," Sofia said. "Why don't you meet me at my apartment at six? We can load up the cars with boxes and bring them out here."

"Sounds like fun. I'll see you later."

Once they'd said their goodbyes, Sofia shoved her phone in her pocket, locked the door, and started through the condo, imagining exactly where she would put everything. She took extensive notes, putting everything in her phone, noting where she wanted to put some of her artwork.

Eventually, she reached the room where she planned to set up her canvases, the room that was the biggest reason she had fallen in love with the condo.

The glass-walled sunroom had the perfect light, especially in the late afternoon. Everything about it was perfect. Sofia couldn't wait to get a canvas in here and start painting. Or even a sketchpad and a pencil. The tree outside the window was begging to be drawn.

Sofia opened the door leading to the small backyard and sat atop a small set of stairs. She closed her eyes and took a deep breath. For the first time in a long time, she felt at ease.

Her life certainly hadn't gone as she'd planned. Three years ago, it seemed as if things couldn't get any better. She had a coveted master's degree in business, a minor in art history, a good job, and the chance to move up through the ranks of the company she worked for, not to mention a great boyfriend, and a nice apartment with the perfect roommate. But things had taken a turn she hadn't expected, and she'd fallen on hard times. Her student loans—hundreds of thousands of dollars—had come due, her rent had doubled after her roommate unexpectedly moved out to care for her sick mother, her fifteen-year-old car had died, she'd caught her boyfriend cheating on her with her boss's daughter, and to top it all off, she had lost her well-paying, respectable job, thanks to the boss's daughter insisting on her removal from the company.

Unfortunately, Sofia hadn't even been able to turn to her family. Her father had died when she was sixteen, and her mother had fallen apart after his death. Joyce Larson had turned to drugs and alcohol to numb the pain of losing the man she'd loved since she was a teenager, going from casual drinker to full-blown addict in less than a year. She'd blown through the insurance money, wiped out their savings, and lost her job as a teacher. When Sofia was seventeen, she had left home, living with friends while she finished school. She'd earned a scholarship to a good school in California and fled, running from the chaos her mother's life had become, intent on making a better life for herself. It had been years since they'd seen each other, and they rarely spoke, only a few times a year on birthdays and holidays. Seeing as how Joyce could barely take care of herself, it was out of the question for Sofia to ask her for help. Not only would her mother not be able to help her, but calling mom to bail her out would have been admitting she was a failure, and she knew exactly how her mother would have responded to that. Gleefully.

She'd even tried her hand at being an artist-for-hire, painting murals in children's rooms, commissioned artwork, but in a town filled with artistic people, she went largely unnoticed, her hobby not profitable enough to keep a roof over her head. The only work she could get was a temp job as a receptionist at a law firm. The money she made didn't come close to covering her bills.

Desperate, with nowhere to go, no one to turn to, no money, and no job, days from being thrown out on the street, Sofia responded to an ad online offering the chance to earn some money by going on a few dates with men of substantial means. After calling the number in the ad, she'd received an email with an application. Three days later, she'd gone to a plush office in an upscale part of L.A. where she'd met with Georgia Pierce, owner of Private Lives, an elite escort service whose clientele was comprised of men with money to burn who wanted a beautiful, young woman on their arm. Clients were fully vetted, as were the escorts, and both were sworn to secrecy with legally binding, ironclad, non-disclosure agreements. But the best thing about Private Lives, as far as Sofia was concerned, was that she was entirely in charge of each encounter, each date. Everything was on her terms.

Technically, she would be an escort, though the thought of calling herself that made her skin crawl. She wouldn't have to sleep with men for money. In fact, sex was off the table unless she decided differently. She was grateful for that; she would never work for a company that asked her to have sex with strangers. As Georgia explained, Private Lives merely connected young, beautiful women with men who had money to spend, men who wanted beautiful women on their arms for whatever event they might be attending. Sofia would fulfill that role. Companionship was a guarantee; sex was not.

Georgia had been eager to hire her, and at first, Sofia had agreed to work on a part-time basis. The first few dates had paid well, so well that not only was she able to pay her rent, but she'd been able to put some money in savings and pay down her credit card debt. Before she knew what was happening, working at Private Lives became a full-time occupation. Over the last three years, she'd paid off her student loans, bought a new car, and now, she had her own place.

She contemplated heading out to grab some food before meeting Sasha, but her phone rang again. She pulled it out of her pocket and hit the button.

"This is Sofia."

"Sof, it's Georgia."

"Hey, Georgie, what's up?"

"Are you available tonight?" her boss asked.

"You know I am, or you wouldn't have called. But I told you, I'm not interested in taking on any new clients." Her ten or so regular clients were more than enough to keep her busy and earn her plenty of money. Taking on even one more would be overwhelming.

"Please, Sof, I need you," Georgia begged. "This one is big time. And I mean big time. It will require someone who can keep a low profile and do what she's asked. Honestly, I don't trust anyone else with him except you. You're the best. You know I wouldn't ask you if I didn't think it was important."

"How big is big?"

"You know I can't share details over the phone." Georgia laughed. "I'll email you his file. Please, do this. If for no other reason than you love me."

"That's not fair, Georgie," Sofia scoffed.

"Just look it over and get back to me. He wants to set up a meeting for tonight, so you've got one, maybe two hours to decide."

"Fine, send me the file." She sighed. "But I'm only agreeing to look it over, not go out with him. I can back out if I want to, right?"

"Of course. And thank you, Sofia. I really appreciate this, more than you know. The file is on its way."

"I'll call you after I read it," Sofia said. "I promise." She disconnected the call and stared at the sun peeking through the leaves of the tree. So much for settling in; it looked like she would be working.

"Another year," she murmured to herself. "One more year and I'm out."

The last time Sofia had been this nervous was on her first date as an escort. This time might have been worse. Her hands shook and her stomach twisted in knots. She'd been on important dates before with important clients, ones handpicked by Georgia none-theless, but this one—this one might be the scariest one ever. Who would have thought one of the most handsome men in Hollywood, one of Hollywood's most eligible bachelors, would need an escort?

Billy, her driver, parked in front of the hotel and came around the back of the SUV to open her door. She stepped out, her hand in Billy's, and straightened her skirt.

"I'll be right here, Ms. Larson," he said. "If you need me, don't hesitate to call."

"Thank you, Billy." She squeezed his arm before entering the hotel. She checked her phone for the room number before hurrying to the elevators. Luckily, the hotel wasn't busy, so she could take the elevator to the fifteenth floor by herself. She squeezed her hands together and took several deep breaths.

"I can do this," she said to herself. "He's just another rich guy who needs a date."

According to Chris's file, he was thirty-two years old, only five years older than she was, single, and looking for someone he could spend time with, out of the public eye, with no strings attached or assumed. Private Lives had appealed to him because of its promise of complete secrecy. While Chris wasn't the first celebrity to use their services, he was by far the biggest, with his own television show and rumors of a huge movie contract in the works. Georgia had begged her not to mess this up. Having Chris Chandler as a client was a big deal.

She was so caught up in her own head that it took her a second to realize that she was standing in front of the hotel room door. She raised a shaking hand and knocked.

It felt like forever before he opened the door, a shy smile on his face. He was even more handsome in person. He was tall, muscular, with bright blue eyes, and light brown hair. A five o'clock shadow dusted his cheeks. She could see the edge of a tattoo on his upper chest, just visible above his open collar.

"Sofia?"

She nodded. "And you're Chris."

"I am." He gestured for her to come inside and closed the door behind her. "Thanks for coming."

"You're welcome." She shifted uneasily from foot to foot.

"Would you like a drink?" he asked.

"I would love a drink," she said. "Scotch on the rocks, with a twist if you have it."

"I've got everything." He chuckled. "Whatever your heart desires." He quickly made her drink and handed it to her, their fingers brushing.

"Thanks," she murmured, heat rising in her cheeks. She was off her game. She was a professional, for God's sake. She never let her clients get to her, and this one would not be the exception.

Chris opened a bottle of beer and pointed at the sofa. "Would you like to sit down?"

"Sure." She followed him across the room and sat beside him on the plush sofa, her skirt tucked around her legs, her drink clutched in her hands, her purse on the table, open, in case she needed her cell phone. What she really needed was to calm down.

"So—"

"I've never—"

They spoke at the same time. Sofia smiled at him and leaned back, making herself comfortable, while Chris sat forward, his elbows on his knees, picking at the label on the beer bottle in his hands. It made her feel better that he was as nervous as she was. She nodded at him to continue.

"I've never done this before," he continued. "Called an escort, I mean."

"Why now?"

Chris exhaled a shuddering breath. "I'm tired of my relationships being picked apart in the tabloids, tired of dating women who only want to use me for my celebrity. I'm tired of all of it. I want something fun and easy with no expectations."

"So, are you looking for someone to date publicly? Someone to take to events, premieres, whatever? A no strings attached instant date?"

"No." Chris shook his head. "That's definitely *not* what I'm looking for."

Okay. That was not what she'd expected to hear. She hoped her surprise didn't show on her face. "Tell me what you want, Chris," she urged. "Otherwise, I can't tell you if I'm the one for you."

Chris nodded, his eyes on the floor between his feet. He spoke without looking at her. "I'm looking for someone to spend time with outside of all those things, someone I can have an intimate relationship with and not have to worry about all the other stuff. I'm tired of dealing with all the bullshit—the press putting my love life under constant scrutiny, trying and failing to date my female counterparts, which never works out, but more than anything, I'm sick of the damn gossip sites speculating about my every move. It makes every interaction awkward, makes every date feel like I'm under a microscope being examined. I know women all over the world want to date me, but it's not because they care about me, but because they like my money, the prestige, the celebrity. Most days, I feel like there isn't a soul in the world who cares about me because I'm Chris—only because I'm Chris Chandler, Actor."

"Oh my God, Chris. I had no idea," Sofia said. "I never imagined it was like that."

"It is what it is." He shrugged. "It's what I signed up for when I decided I wanted to be an actor." He shifted awkwardly on the couch, picking at the seam of his jeans. "What I really want is sex with no attachments, no gossip site speculation, no women only in it because I'm a celebrity, no bullshit. I'm looking for someone who can keep a secret, who will be what I need when I need it, and nothing more."

Her stomach dropped. Chris knew exactly what he wanted, and unfortunately, she wasn't the woman for him. This had been a mistake. She'd call Georgia in the morning and have her send someone else out. Sofia set her drink on the table and rose to her feet.

"I don't think I'm the girl for you," she said. "I'll let Georgia know. Maybe she can find someone more suited to your needs." She snatched her purse off the table and headed for the door.

"Sofia, wait!" Chris caught her at the door, his hand wrapped around her elbow, stopping her before she could leave. "I'm sorry if I said something that offended you. I'm…I'm trying to be honest. I told you I've never done this before. Can you give me a chance, talk to me, tell me what I did wrong?"

The look on his face tugged at her heartstrings. He looked so confused, so out of his element. She couldn't walk away from him without at least giving him an explanation. She dropped her purse on the chair by the door and turned back to Chris.

"You did nothing wrong." She sighed. "Georgia should have told you that I'm not that kind of escort."

"What kind is that?" Chris asked.

"The kind that has sex with her clients."

Chris released her and took a step back. Not the reaction she wanted, but it was kind of what she'd expected.

"That's why I'm not the girl for you," Sofia added. "I'm happy to keep you company, act the part of a girlfriend, but I won't have sex with you. I'm sorry if that disappoints you. I don't want to waste your time, or mine for that matter. I'm sure Georgia can find someone at Private Lives who is right for you. I don't think that's me."

"I'm sorry," Chris said. "I didn't mean to assume." He pushed a hand through his hair, tugging it slightly. "I'll tell you what? I don't want you to feel like I have wasted your time, so why don't you stay and have dinner with me? At least you'll get a free meal out of it."

She wasn't sure that was a great idea, but Chris was so sincere, so sweet, that she couldn't say no. "That would be great." Sofia smiled. He was certainly trying; she had to give him that.

Chris called room service while she returned to the sofa. She picked up her drink and finished it in just a few swallows. That had gone better than she'd thought it would. Now she could enjoy dinner and go home without feeling guilty. Telling clients she wouldn't sleep with them was one of the harder parts of her job; it often led to hurt feelings and irritated phone calls to Georgia. Fortunately, her boss always sided with her employees, and she never forced anyone to do something they weren't comfortable doing. It was one of the reasons Sofia continued working for her.

She shifted in her seat so she could see Chris on the other side of the room, the wide expanse of his shoulders, body tapering to a toned waist, thick muscular thighs, and bulging biceps. Another tattoo was visible under the edge of his sleeve. For a moment, Sofia wondered what else he had hidden under his clothes. He really was attractive; it was a shame that she wouldn't get to spend time with him, get to know him. But she wasn't about to compromise her principles, not even for him.

"Sometimes, I am an idiot," she muttered to herself.

Chapter Three

CHRIS

He sprawled out across the sofa after Sofia left, staring at the door, replaying every moment of the evening in his head. It hadn't turned out at all like he'd expected.

Sofia had promised to call Georgia in the morning, have her find him a replacement. She'd apologized profusely before she'd left, even kissed him on the cheek, her lips soft, the scent of vanilla and lavender filling his head.

She was stunningly gorgeous: long red hair, dark blue eyes, and a body to die for. He hadn't been able to take his eyes off her all night. To his surprise, she was also easy to talk to—articulate, intelligent, and sweet. The evening had flown by, too fast for his liking. It had been one of the best dates he'd ever been on.

Sofia hadn't been what he'd expected, not that he'd known what to expect; after all, he was calling an escort service, albeit a high end one, but an escort service, nonetheless. He'd almost backed out, almost walked out of the hotel room before she'd arrived, but at the last second, he'd changed his mind. It couldn't hurt to see it through, to at least try to get through the evening.

Chris scrubbed a hand over his face and closed his eyes. The decision to call Private Lives had been an impromptu one, born out of desperation. He was lonely and miserable, his anxiety off the charts after everything that had happened, and he just wanted something easy, something meaningless with someone who didn't want anything from him. He didn't think about it, didn't give himself time to second guess himself; he just picked up the phone and dialed.

It hadn't been easy, booking an appointment with Private Lives. He thought it would take one phone call, but it was so much more than that. He'd had a brief visit with an extremely professional older woman, Georgia Pierce, who'd had him sign a slew of paperwork. Despite the doubt and the knots of tension in his stomach, he signed it. The next day, he'd received an email approving his application—though he hadn't realized it was an application when he'd filled it out—and informing him that once he'd been fully vetted, he would be contacted to set up his first date.

Four days later, after an extensive vetting process involving a numerous phone calls and a meeting with his lawyer, he'd received a call from the owner, Georgia, welcoming him to Private Lives. She'd promised to find him the perfect woman, even assured him she had someone in mind.

His nerves had skyrocketed, and he'd immediately started second-guessing himself. He felt guilty about using Private Lives. He had visions of all of this going public and destroying his career. He was tempted to call Georgia and back out, make some excuse not to meet with anyone. He could pretend it never happened and go back to his lonely, miserable life.

He kept telling himself it was a decision born out of necessity; the life he led had pushed him to do this, forced him to make this decision. That didn't change the fact that his gut twisted with guilt, shame—whatever you wanted to call it—every time his phone rang. Chris knew what he was doing was considered wrong by a lot of people, and if anyone found out, it would ruin him, destroying everything he had worked for since he was twenty years old.

But before he could back out, Georgia called him that same evening to arrange a time for him to meet with Sofia. She had assured Chris that he would love her.

She hadn't been wrong; he adored her. Aside from her good looks and her fantastic personality, she helped him forget all the stuff that was making him crazy. He hadn't thought about Lillian, work, or therapy even once. He'd gotten lost in her, the lilt of her voice, the way she smiled, and the cute way she tipped her head to one side when she was concentrating on something or listening to him talk. Her laughter was infectious, her presence overwhelming in the best way possible. For the first time in God knew how long, the voices in his head were quiet. He could only assume that was because of Sofia.

Chris was taken with her.

He must have dozed off because the next thing he knew his cell phone vibrated, startling him enough to make him jump, his foot hitting the glass table in front of the sofa. He checked his watch; it was after midnight. He picked up the phone and opened his messages.

Dude, how'd it go?

Seth. Chris had forgotten to text him after he'd met with Sofia. The only person he'd felt comfortable telling about this little endeavor was his best friend. He also knew that Seth wouldn't breathe a word to anyone. It violated the non-disclosure agreement, him telling Seth, but he told his best friend everything and this was no exception. Seth wanted an update.

Okay. I liked her, but she's not what I'm looking for. Back to the drawing board.

Chris hated how that sounded. Apparently, so did Seth because his phone rang, his best friend's number popping up on the screen.

"Hey," he answered.

"What do you mean, she's not what you're looking for?" Seth demanded.

"Isn't it like two in the morning in New York? You should be asleep."

"Don't change the subject, asshole. What's wrong with the girl?"

"Nothing is wrong with her. In fact, I really liked her. But she's not the kind of escort I'm looking for, so she's going to ask her boss to find me someone else."

"What kind of escort are you looking for, exactly?" Seth asked.

Chris sighed. "Don't yell at me, okay?"

"Okay," Seth muttered.

"She isn't the kind of escort who has sex with clients," Chris explained.

"Oh, um, okay. So, it didn't work out then?"

"I don't know. I really liked her. A lot."

"Even without the sex?"

"Even without the sex," Chris chuckled.

"What are you gonna do?"

"I said I don't know," Chris said.

"Look, it wouldn't hurt you to have someone around to talk to, hang out with, you know? Maybe that's all you need. Sex complicates things anyway. Sleep on it. You can decide tomorrow."

"Why are you always right?"

"Glad to know you finally figured it out." Seth laughed. "It only took you twenty years."

"Whatever," he mumbled. "I'll talk to you later."

"Let me know what you decide."

Before saying goodbye, Chris promised to update Seth the next day, after he'd slept on it and talked to Georgia at Private Lives. He contemplated heading home, but he had the hotel for the whole night, so he might as well take advantage of it. He kicked off his shoes and climbed into the bed, falling asleep within minutes.

"I'm so sorry it didn't work out, Mr. Chandler," Georgia said. "Rest assured, I will find the right girl for you. It might take me longer than expected, though."

"Actually, I was wondering if I could set up another date with Sofia?" He shifted his phone from one ear to the other as he turned away from the crowd of people gathered along the street to watch them film.

"Oh," Georgia said. "Um, okay. I apologize. I thought things had not gone as anticipated, and you were interested in another girl. But I can certainly arrange another time for you to meet with Sofia. Did you have a day and time in mind?"

"Maybe this weekend, Saturday or Sunday? Late evening is best. At the same hotel?"

"Of course. I'll be in touch."

Chris shoved his phone back in his pocket just as one of the many interns on set appeared at his side. He followed the young man, weaving through the cameramen, riggers, hair and makeup people, and all the other people that populated a movie set. Ten minutes later, his hair had been properly coiffed, his makeup reapplied, and he was ready to step in front of the camera. He pulled the scenes' pages from his pocket and quickly scanned them, then he exhaled a long, slow breath and stepped to his mark.

Surprisingly, he felt good. Normally, he'd be tired, grouchy, and out of sorts, but he felt the opposite: wide awake, and for once, together. He'd slept great, falling asleep almost immediately and sleeping straight through until his alarm went off. It had been weeks, maybe months, since he'd gotten a good night's sleep. And the only thing that was different was that he'd had a date with Sofia.

He hadn't been able to think of anything other than her since their date. He'd woken up determined to try again; maybe she wouldn't sleep with him, but being around her certainly made him feel better. Seth was right – not that he'd ever tell his best friend that – sex wasn't everything. Maybe he just needed someone he could talk to and hang out with, someone who didn't care that he was a celebrity. True friends were few and far between in Hollywood; if he had to pay for one, so be it.

Thanks to his good mood, time flew by, his day ending before he knew it. He begged off getting drinks with some of the crew, choosing instead to call his driver and head home. He'd been anxiously waiting for Georgia to return his call, but hours had passed, and he'd heard nothing. He wondered if Sofia had declined going out with him again. The thought made him sick to his stomach.

Chris took Ollie for a run and cooked himself some dinner before turning on the baseball game and hopefully, settling in for the night. He had the game on for less than half an hour when his phone chimed with an incoming email.

Mr. Chandler –

Thank you for your phone call earlier today. I have arranged a date between you and Sofia for this Saturday at 9 p.m. at the Westerfield Hotel in Beverly Hills. If this time works for you, no other correspondence is necessary. Should you not be able to attend, please give at least twenty-four hours' notice by responding to this email.

Thank you,
Georgia Pierce

A smile spread across Chris's face. He hadn't realized how worried he had been that Sofia would not want to see him again until he'd received the email. He quickly typed out a text message to Seth, letting his friend know that he'd decided to see Sofia again and when their next date would be, then without waiting for a response, he shut down his phone and tossed it on the table. Seth could bug him about being right later.

Ollie jumped up beside him and laid his head in Chris's lap, snoring softly within a few minutes. He rested his hand on his dog's head, scratching between his ears, his eyes drifting closed as the baseball game played in the background. He didn't stay awake long enough to see the Mets win.

Chapter Four

SOFIA

Chris's message said casual and comfortable, so she wore jeans. Apparently, it threw Billy for a loop, if the astonished look on his face was any indication, though he quickly composed himself and opened the back door of the SUV, hand outstretched to help her inside.

Sofia waited until he was behind the wheel before asking her question. "Do you know where we're going?"

"I programmed the directions into the GPS," he replied. "We should be there in about twenty minutes."

Sofia nodded and settled into the seat, watching the world fly by outside the window. This was her third date with Chris. It had surprised her when he wanted to meet the second time, and she was downright astonished there would be a third. The second date had been a lot like the first, dinner and drinks in his hotel room, followed by the two of them getting to know each other. It had been nice, almost like an actual date. At the end of the evening, he'd even given her a chaste kiss on the cheek, even after she'd reiterated that she would not sleep with him. He'd merely smiled and held the door open for her.

She convinced herself that would be the end of it—that he wouldn't call again. She had no plans to have sex with him, and she was holding firm. But late yesterday afternoon, she received an email from Georgia, asking her to meet with Chris again. She had reluctantly agreed. She wondered if he thought maybe he could convince her to sleep with him if he just kept trying. Too bad he didn't realize that there was no chance of that happening. She'd learned her lesson about intimacy in this profession the hard way.

Georgia emailed her the information about the date in the morning—clients could not have the escort's contact information; all contact was to be initiated through Private Lives—including a personal note asking her if she wanted to see Chris again. She did. Her curiosity had gotten the best of her; she had to know what he was up to. And not that she would ever admit it, but she enjoyed Chris's company. He had a wicked sense of humor, he was extremely intelligent, and of course, he was astonishingly attractive. She'd had a good time on their second date, so why not give the third one a try? At least, that's what she kept telling herself.

Sofia pushed a hand through her hair and sighed. She was dying to tell Sasha about Chris, but it was strictly forbidden under the terms of the non-disclosure agreement. While Sasha knew what she did for a living, she had no idea whom Sofia dated, and it had to stay that way. If she needed someone to talk to, she was supposed to call Georgia.

Billy turned off the main road onto a two-lane road lined with trees, following it for about ten miles before turning again onto a dirt road for another five minutes before pulling into a small clearing. He shifted into park, sat back, and looked at her in the rearview mirror.

"We're here, Ms. Sofia." He smiled.

Out the window, she could see a dark blue BMW parked off to one side. Chris was sitting on a picnic table, staring out over a small meadow. He turned when he heard the car, a smile brightening his face.

"Sofia, hi!" He waved as she stepped from the vehicle, jumped off the table, and jogged over to her. "Thank you for coming."

"You're welcome," she replied. "How are you?"

Chris shrugged. "Okay, I guess. I, uh, hope you don't mind this location. It's private. Quiet. I thought we could go for a hike and have a picnic." He pointed to a cooler on the ground and held his hand out to her.

She took it and smiled. "That sounds lovely." No one had ever made her a picnic before. It was sweet. She turned to wave and smile at Billy as he pulled away. He didn't look happy.

Chris scooped up the cooler and led her through the trees down a narrow path, ducking to avoid tree branches over her head.

"How was your week?" she asked.

"Long," he sighed. "I'm glad it's over."

"Anything you want to talk about?"

He glanced at her out of the corner of his eye, opened his mouth, shut it again, then he was spilling his guts about the week he'd had. He talked as they hiked up the path, eventually coming to a stop beneath a beautiful tree where he laid out a blanket and set out the food.

Sofia didn't know how he did it, living in the spotlight the way he did. He'd done some whirlwind press junket on Tuesday, twenty interviews in one day; he'd worked all week, sometimes fourteen-hour days; and now, he was here, doing his best to impress her. She couldn't help but appreciate the effort he was putting forth just for her, especially when he didn't have to try so hard.

"Um, Chris?"

He stopped opening the bottle of wine and looked at her. "Yeah?"

She leaned forward, her elbows on her knees. She brushed a leaf off his shirt, her heart skipping a beat at the feel of his muscles beneath the sleeve. "You know you don't have to impress me, right?"

Chris sat back on his ass, a soft grunt leaving him. "I-I-I'm not trying to impress you."

"You are." She laughed. "And I appreciate you trying, but, uh, I'm an easy date."

"Not that easy," he muttered under his breath.

"I heard that."

"I know. I wasn't trying to be quiet." He blew out a shaky breath. "I'm sorry. That was rude. My mom would smack the back of my head for that." He glanced up at her through impossibly long eyelashes. "Look, this is…this is all new to me. I'm not sure what to do or how to act. I'm doing my best."

"You know, this is kind of new to me, too," Sofia whispered. "Most of my dates are much older men who take me out to show me off. As if they could really get a woman twenty or thirty years their junior." She shrugged her shoulders, leaned back on her hands, and crossed her ankles. "I'm used to being in a crowded room, filled with socialites, businessmen, and entrepreneurs. I'm used to putting on a show. This," she gestured between them, "I'm not used to. I'm out of my element."

She wasn't lying when she said that. She could do fancy parties, fundraisers, mega-events of any kind, she could dress up and play the part of the doting girlfriend, but this one-on-one with no one else around stuff was new to her.

She hadn't dated much in high school after her father passed away; the turmoil of losing one parent to cancer and the other to alcohol sent her life into a tailspin that she couldn't fix. Boyfriends were off the table—any kind of social life was off the table—as she tried to get on a path to success, alone, without the help of her mother or father.

Her first boyfriend had been Robert, whom she'd met in college. They had a simple relationship, fulfilling, but looking back, she realized it hadn't been normal. They hadn't spent a lot of time alone, often going on group dates, or out in public. It never occurred to her that was out of the ordinary. They had a good relationship, or so she thought until Robert had cheated on her. After that, forced to start over yet again, she hadn't had the time, nor the inclination, to date. Then Private Lives had come along, and she began dating for a living. Not only was she not in the mood to date for fun, but as far as she was concerned, no one in their right mind would want to date an escort.

Chris said something, but she missed it, lost in her own thoughts.

"I'm sorry. What?"

"I said, I guess we're both kind of flying by the seat of our pants, huh?"

"Yeah, I guess so." Sofia laughed. "So, you were opening a bottle of wine?"

Chris nodded and finished opening the wine, then he pulled two glasses from the cooler, filled them halfway, and handed one to Sofia.

"Thanks," she murmured. She took a sip, smiling as the sweet rosé exploded across her taste buds. It was perfect.

Chris continued pulling food from the cooler: sandwiches, pasta salad, strawberries, grapes, even some carrots, and celery. Sofia couldn't hold back a giggle at the seemingly bottomless container.

"How much food did you bring?"

Chris shook his head and laughed. "Way too much. I wasn't sure what you liked, so I ordered a ton of stuff."

"Ordered? You didn't make it yourself?"

"Oh god, no," he snorted.

"You can't cook?" she asked.

"I can, I just haven't in…well, forever. I don't have time when I'm filming. When I'm on set, there's always someone there to get me whatever I want, whenever I want it. I don't get to cook very often. I guess I've gotten accustomed to someone else handling it."

"So, you're spoiled?" Sofia teased.

"A little, yeah," Chris chuckled.

Once the food was all set out, they dug in. They didn't talk much as they ate, but it was a comfortable silence, much to Sofia's surprise. She rarely spent time alone with clients, so she'd been worried things would be awkward between her and Chris. She'd convinced herself that their second date had been a fluke and this one would be different. She was glad she was wrong.

Sofia had two glasses of wine, a sandwich, fruit, some of the vegetables, and two helpings of the pasta salad. After they finished the main course, Chris pulled out an apple pie and some whipped cream.

"Oh, lord, I don't think I can eat anymore," she groaned, her hand on her stomach.

"You sure?" Chris laughed as he covered a piece of pie with so much whipped cream, she couldn't see the pastry beneath it. He held the plate out to her with an irresistible smile. She took it from him and put a huge bite in her mouth.

"You've got some, uh, cream right there," he said, pointing at her face.

Sofia stuck her tongue out and tried to lick off the whipped cream, but she must have missed because Chris reached over and brushed the corner of her mouth with his thumb. A strange tingle raced down her spine, and goosebumps covered her arms. She swallowed around the lump that the pie had become in her throat and mumbled, "Thank you."

Chris nodded, those deep blue eyes of his locked on hers, then he looked away, a tiny smile ghosting his lips as he started eating his pie.

Sofia set her empty plate down and stretched out on the blanket with a quiet groan. She closed her eyes, the sun warming her skin, the gentle breeze blowing her hair across her face.

"This is nice," she whispered.

She felt Chris shift beside her, then a soft touch pushing her hair off her face. She opened her eyes to see him looking down at her with an odd expression.

"You okay?" she asked.

"Yeah, I'm good."

To her surprise, he laid down beside her, his leg touching hers, his clean, masculine scent washing over her. They laid side by side, silence filling the space between them. She resisted the urge to reach over and take his hand, unsure why she even wanted to; nothing like that had ever happened to her before—unprovoked intimacy, touching her clients—she'd never wanted to do that with anyone else. Sure, she'd held a client's hand or looped her arm through theirs, even let them put their arm around her, maybe even a chaste kiss, but nothing more. She'd never wanted anything else, not until Chris. The thought scared her.

Sofia didn't know how long they were there, lying side by side, comfortable in their silence. When she could no longer feel the sun on her face, she sat up and checked her watch. It was almost six; she'd been with Chris for almost four hours. Not that it felt like it; it felt more like time had stopped, the clock no longer moving when they were together. She enjoyed it.

"I suppose we should head back to the city," Chris mumbled, eyes still closed, a faint smile on his face. "Unless you want to stay out here in the woods?"

Part of her wanted to do just that, but she knew it wasn't possible. They'd scheduled her to be with Chris for another hour, and she knew that once that hour had passed, Georgia, or one of her assistants, would call to see if she had made it home.

"I'd love to stay out here," she sighed, leaving the "with you" unsaid, "but we do have to get back. Billy will be expecting me."

"And if I don't have you back in time, do they send out the cavalry?"

"Probably." Sofia shrugged. "I've never been late before."

Chris sat up with a groan. He rested his hand in the center of her back and leaned so close she could feel his breath against her ear. "Well, I wouldn't want to be the reason you're late for the first time ever, now would I?"

Sofia shook her head, ignoring the shiver that raced through her. To avoid further conversation, she started gathering up the remnants of their picnic and shoving them into the cooler. It only took a few minutes before they had everything cleaned up. The sun had dropped beneath the horizon by the time they started back up the path, her hand in Chris's. She knew he was only doing it so she wouldn't trip and fall in the dark, but she still liked the feel of his powerful hand wrapped around hers and the way he took charge, leading her down the path back to his car.

What the hell is wrong with me? Clients didn't elicit these types of feelings in her. Ever.

Chris opened the trunk and set the cooler inside, then he opened the passenger door for Sofia, holding her hand as she settled in before jogging around the front of the BMW and dropping behind the wheel with a grunt. He started the engine and backed out of the clearing, driving carefully down the dirt road. When he hit the pavement, he accelerated, flying down the road so fast the trees seemed to be whipping past the car.

It was exhilarating.

It took them no time at all to get back to the city. Chris followed her directions to the neutral location where they were meeting Billy. Chris must have driven faster than she realized because they got to the designated pick-up spot ten minutes before Billy. Sofia sent him a text to let him know she was waiting. He responded with his estimated time of arrival and a question mark, his way of asking if she was okay. She shot back a thumbs up and shoved her phone in her purse.

"Everything cool?" Chris asked.

"Yeah, just Billy making sure I'm okay."

"Is he like your bodyguard or something?"

"Kind of." She nodded. "He's my driver, but he's also tasked with keeping an eye on me, making sure that I'm safe."

"How does he know you're not? I mean, could someone force you to...I don't know, lie or something? How would he know that you're in trouble? Are there, like, code words or something?"

Sofia narrowed her eyes and tipped her head to one side. "Why? What are you planning?" She bit the inside of her mouth to keep from laughing.

Chris chuckled and shook his head. "You're a riot. You know that, right?"

"I have my moments. Seriously though, you know those are kind of creepy questions you're asking, right?"

"I do," he laughed. "But I would never hurt you, Sof." His voice dropped an octave and his blue eyes flashed with something indescribable.

Sofia's stomach twisted oddly at the use of her nickname. She'd never told Chris to call her that, in fact, she never let her clients use her nickname. She didn't mind with Chris, though.

"You're sweet. You know that, right?" she asked, brushing a strand of hair off his forehead.

"I am, huh?"

"The sweetest."

Chris leaned into her and brushed a kiss across her lips. Her eyes slipped closed, and she responded, humming low in the back of her throat. Chris's hand slid around the back of her head, twisting in her long, red tresses, tugging her closer, his mouth slanting over hers, his tongue tracing her lower lip. She opened her mouth and let him in, the kiss soft and sweet.

Headlights splashed across the windshield, startling them. Reluctantly, Sofia pulled away, shaking her head when she realized what she'd been doing. It went against every one of her rules.

Don't get emotional. Don't get involved. Don't bring the job home with you.

"I'm sorry, Chris," she mumbled. "That shouldn't have happened." She snatched her purse off the floor and fumbled for the door handle, falling out of the car, almost hitting the ground before getting her feet under her and hurrying across the lot to the SUV, Chris calling after her.

Billy's eyes widened when he saw her and then he was out of the vehicle, rushing toward her.

"Ms. Sofia, are you okay?"

"I'm fine, Billy. Let's just…can we go? Please?"

"Of course," he said, taking her arm and leading her to the passenger side door, yanking it open to usher her inside. He slammed it closed and shot a glance at Chris, who had gotten out of his car and was watching them. Billy's look was not nice from what Sofia could see, then he was in the car starting the engine.

"Did he hurt you?" Billy demanded.

"No." She shook her head. "I'm fine. He was a complete gentleman, Billy."

"Then what's wrong if you don't mind me asking? You've got me on edge here."

"Nothing, just...feelings, I guess."

Billy gave her a weird look, but she ignored it, staring straight ahead out the car window. She wracked her brain, trying to figure out when her feelings for Chris had turned into a jumbled mess.

Chapter Five

CHRIS

C hris watched as Billy, Sofia's driver, ushered her into the SUV, glaring at him as the driver got behind the wheel. He did not understand what he had done or why Sofia rushed off. All he knew was that he would have loved that kiss to continue.

I'm sorry, Chris. That shouldn't have happened.

Except what she said didn't jibe with the way she'd kissed him. She had leaned into him with a low hum, her mouth opening when his tongue drifted across her lips, the kiss deepening. He'd tangled his fingers in her hair, and he wanted nothing more than to sit there all night and kiss her senseless.

Then she'd pulled away and run as if she were afraid to be alone with him. It sucked. He thought they had a good time on their date; he thought they connected. The kiss had just been the icing on the cake.

He watched the SUV until he couldn't see the tail-lights anymore, then he climbed into the BMW and turned toward home, his thoughts consumed with what had gone wrong. It had to be the kiss; he'd moved too fast, expected too much. Chris knew her rules, knew that sex, even intimacy of any kind was off the table, yet he'd kissed her anyway. He wanted to kick himself. He had to remember that Sofia wasn't an ordinary date.

He was almost home when his phone rang. He hit the button on the steering wheel without seeing who it was, hoping against hope that it was Sofia, and they could clear the air.

"Chris!"

"Hey, Jack," he replied. He rested his elbow on the door and pinched the bridge of his nose. His manager was difficult to take on a good day. "What's up?"

"Are you available tomorrow? Around ten or eleven? Paul and I have a project we think you might be interested in, and we want to talk to you about it."

Chris narrowed his eyes. Being tag teamed by his agent and his manager was never a good thing. Last time they'd ganged up on him, he'd ended up doing some deodorant commercial in his underwear, a pair of tight briefs, his entire package on display for everyone to see. Fortunately, it had only aired in some obscure European country he couldn't pro-nounce. If his mother had ever seen that, she would have killed him.

"What ridiculous thing are you going to ask me to do now?" he grumbled.

"It's not ridiculous, I swear. In fact, it could be a game-changer."

"What's that supposed to mean?"

"It means this could change the course of your career for the better."

"My career is fine—"

"I'm not saying it's not, Chris. But if this works out, we're talking movies, sequels, franchises... You name it, you could have it."

"Well, how can I say no?" he asked. "I'm sure I can make it. I'm in the car. Can I call you back when I get home?"

"You mean you're not home watching the Mets stomp on the Yankees?" Jack laughed. "That's a surprise."

"Nah, I was, uh, out hiking," Chris lied.

"Alone?"

"Yeah."

"You shouldn't do stuff like that alone, Chris. If something happened to you, the show would lose their mind—"

"I think I can hike a level nature trail by myself, Jack," Chris snapped. "I don't need a babysitter for everything."

"I just think when you're out in public like that you should take Alex," Jack said. "That's what you pay him to do."

Alex was Chris's driver and bodyguard. His team had insisted Chris hire him a little over a year ago when one of his fans had gotten a little too overzealous. Or stalkerish if you asked Jack's opinion. Alex went where

Chris went, but he wasn't about to ask Alex to go with him when he met with his escort. That would violate his non-disclosure agreement.

"I wasn't in public," he sighed. "I was in the woods hiking."

"Still, you shouldn't go alone."

"Fine, I won't go alone again," he muttered. At this point, he'd say just about anything to shut Jack up; his head was pounding, and he just wanted to sleep.

"So, tomorrow?" Jack asked.

"Yeah, I'll see you then." He hit a button on the steering wheel and disconnected the call.

"The lead?" Chris tipped his head to the side and scrubbed a hand over his face. "They want me for the lead? I don't have to audition for it or anything? They're just offering it to me?"

"The director is a fan." Paul, his agent, smiled. "He's seen *Hunting the Criminal*, and he thinks you're perfect for the part."

"He called us," Jack interjected. "Insisted that it was you he wanted and no one else."

"It's a two-movie deal, Chris," Paul added, tapping a piece of paper sitting on the table. "But that's only the beginning. If it takes off, if it's a hit, if it makes money, we're talking a lot more movies, a lot more money. This character, these books—people are obsessed with them. And Mark Wilson and the studio want you for the part."

"Wow," he mumbled under his breath. "I don't understand why they want me. My last two movies were trash. I figured I would be on TV forever."

Paul sighed. "Mark's not looking at those movies; he knows they were poorly written, poorly directed, and the marketing was mediocre. He's not basing your worth off a couple of shitty movies. Besides, you know damn well the critics loved you in both films."

Chris nodded, though the things Paul said weren't making him feel any better. "I don't know."

"If you agree to take this part, when it comes out, the buzz will be incredible," Jack said. "It will make you an A-lister overnight."

"I... I don't know what to say."

"Say yes, you idiot." Paul slapped him on the shoulder and pushed himself to his feet. "It's an easy decision. You say yes and the contracts will be on my desk by tomorrow morning."

"Um... Jesus. This is... holy shit." He put his head in his hands and tried to catch his breath. That piece of paper Paul kept tapping was an offer for eight million dollars, guaranteed, if he would play some character from a bunch of books that were ridiculously popular. Two movies to start, more depending on their popularity. How the hell could he say no to something like that?

Paul and Jack were staring at him, waiting for an answer. "Can I...? I need to think about it."

Jack dropped into the chair beside him and patted his arm. "What do you mean: you need to think about it? It's the opportunity of a lifetime."

"I need to think about it," he repeated. "It's a lot. The pressure from the fans alone? Jesus, I heard they're rabid, crazy. The press for this will be insane, and you know how much I hate the press. It's not just the movies I'm agreeing to; it's an enormous commitment. If you guys can't see that..."

"You're right," Paul said. "It is a lot to take on. You can take some time to think about it. But Chris—"

Chris shook his head. "There's always a 'but.'"

"They want an answer today."

"What?" He thought his head might explode. The slight pressure turned into a giant boulder sitting on his chest.

"They're fast-tracking this, and the woman they want for the love interest will only do it if it's you. They want her, Chris, and it all hinges on you."

"Who is it?" he asked.

"Ginny Etling."

"Who?" Chris asked. "Who the hell is that? I've never heard of her."

"Ginny Etling," Jack explained. "She's a reality star, hot shit right now." He flipped his phone around, showing Chris a photo of a platinum blonde, large chested, too much makeup, scantily clothed. "Now do you know who she is?"

"No." Chris arched an eyebrow. "I don't get any say in this? No screen test, nothing?"

"No. The studio is insisting it be her. When she found out they wanted you for the male lead, she was ecstatic. Popped off with something about only doing it if you were one hundred percent on board. She won't sign until you do."

"Can she act?" Chris huffed.

"Who knows?" His manager shrugged. "But she's getting the part, regardless. Mark's afraid the studio will pull the funding for the first film if they don't get their way, so he agreed."

"Jesus, this is a cluster fuck," Chris groaned. "Can you guys give me a minute? I need a few minutes alone to think about it."

Jack nodded, poking Paul in the shoulder and pointing at the door. "We'll leave you alone for a while. Let us know when you're ready."

Chris waited until the door closed behind them before pulling his phone out. He checked his email for the millionth time. He'd been obsessively checking it since last night, afraid he'd get something dismissing him from Private Lives or telling him that Sofia would no longer be available to him. There was nothing.

He breathed a sigh of relief, then he dialed the only person he trusted to be honest with him.

Seth.

Twenty minutes later, he opened the office door and nodded at his agent and manager. They came back inside and sat at the conference table, both with solemn faces.

Chris slid into the chair across from them and folded his hands in front of him. He cleared his throat before speaking, enjoying the panicked looks on their faces.

"I'll do it."

"Thank God," Paul muttered. "I'll call Mark." He dialed his phone as he moved across the room to stand by the window.

"There's something else," Jack said.

"What?" Chris didn't like the tone of Jack's voice.

"It's about you and Ginny."

Chris knew that look. Jack was about to ask him to do something he would not like.

"You're not dating anyone are you?" Jack continued, attempting, and failing, to look like he didn't care.

Sofia's face flashed in Chris's head, but he couldn't bring that up. He gnawed on his lower lip before telling Jack that no, he wasn't dating anyone, not right now. A knot of tension formed deep in his gut, twisting painfully, fueling the anxiety in his chest.

"Neither is Ginny." Jack grinned. "I think you two should go out."

"No." Chris shook his head. "Absolutely not." That was the most ludicrous thing he'd ever heard.

"The studio was hoping—"

"What? That I'd date this girl for publicity?"

"Actually, yeah," Jack said. "They're planning on announcing the film in the next couple weeks and they thought it might be kind of cool if you two were an item. It'll create buzz, maybe spark interest in the film."

"I think the film will spark interest on its own. I don't think dating my co-star is going to make a difference."

"Look, Chris, it's not that hard," Jack explained. "You and her, a few dates, out in the public eye, let them see you together, make people excited for the film. That's all they're asking. You need people excited about this movie; you need people to want to see it. This could be a big win for you, and if dating this Ginny chick helps to generate excitement, great. It's a win-win no matter what. You date, you hit it off, it's adorable that you're making a movie together. You don't hit it off, people will want to see the two of you together in a movie, kind of a 'can they make it work' thing."

"So, what, you're going to pimp me out like I'm a prostitute or something?" His mouth snapped shut, the irony of his statement dawning on him. He swallowed around the lump rising in his throat. "All to generate buzz for a movie I haven't even shot yet?"

Jack stared at him, silent. Chris knew his manager was right, at least about the movie. He needed a win in the worst way. It was true his last couple of movies flopped, and while his television show was doing well, he wanted more. He wanted to be known for more than working on TV; he wanted to be known for more than being one of the endless men named Chris working in Hollywood. He needed this movie to do well, or his movie career would tank before it even began. Generating buzz ahead of filming could help.

"All right," he sighed. "Set it up."

Chapter Six

SOFIA

"Talk to me, Sofia. Is this about Chris Chandler and what happened the other night?"

"Nothing happened," Sofia muttered.

"That's not what Billy said," Georgia scoffed. "You know if something happens, you're supposed to let me know. You're *obligated* to tell me. I shouldn't get a phone call from Billy at ten o'clock at night telling me he's worried about you. Did Chris try something, do something he shouldn't? You tell me right now, and I will yank his Private Lives contract so fast his pretty little head will spin."

"Georgie, stop," Sofia insisted. "He was a perfect gentleman and we had an enjoyable time. It's just... he, well, he kissed me."

"Oh," Georgia sighed. "What would you like me to do? Do you want me to find him another girl?"

"I don't know," Sofia sighed. "I mean, yes…no…"

"Sofia."

"I know, Georgie. I'm sorry. I'm just…confused. Can I call you back? Think about it?"

"Are you sure? I can find him someone else. It might take me a few days, but I'm sure I can find somebody. I know how you feel about getting intimate with clients, and I don't want to put you in a position that makes you uncomfortable."

Sofia was tiring of this conversation. She wasn't sure what she wanted to do. She enjoyed spending time with Chris, but kissing him had gone against every rule she had. It scared her.

"I promise I'll let you know by tomorrow. I need time to decide what I'm going to do." She shifted from foot to foot and pushed a hand through her hair. "Has he contacted the agency or anything? Asked for another date?"

"No, I don't think so. I'll let you know if he does though."

"Thanks," she said. "I'll call you tomorrow. Tell you what I've decided."

Sofia dropped her phone on the bed and returned to unpacking. She had maybe five or six boxes left to empty, and she'd promised herself she would finish them today. It was all clothes: dresses and shoes that she wore for the various events she had to attend. There was a huge walk-in closet in the extra bedroom, and she was putting them in there.

As she unpacked, her mind wandered back to when she'd first started at Private Lives. She'd been so naïve, so unsure of what she was doing—no rules, no guidelines, flying by the seat of her pants.

One of her first clients had been Malcolm Porter, a middle-aged entrepreneur worth twenty million dollars, a fact that he'd been quick to point out. Sofia had been taken with him; he'd spoiled her, taking her to the fanciest restaurants and the hottest clubs, buying her clothes and gifts, treating her like a princess. She'd forgot her job was to be his companion, to be the pretty girl on the arm of the millionaire. She forgot that she was only pretending to be his girlfriend, that she wasn't *really* his girlfriend. At some point, that line blurred so much that after a late night filled with a lot of alcohol and a lot of coaxing on Malcolm's part, she'd slept with him. Two days later, Georgia had notified her that Malcolm had moved on to another girl and he would no longer require her services. It hurt her, and she mourned the loss of something that, to her, had become real, while to Malcolm, had been nothing. Once he'd gotten what he wanted out of her, he moved on.

That was when she'd established the rules.

Don't get emotional. Don't get involved. Don't bring the job home with you.

It was for her own sanity, to keep her from becoming invested in something that wasn't real. She decided she wouldn't sleep with her clients, no matter what. For her, sex was too emotional; there were too many feelings, too many complications that came with a sexual relationship. She couldn't let that happen again.

Except those lines were already blurring with Chris, and it scared the shit out of her. She couldn't go down that road again, couldn't let herself get attached. He would break her heart, just like Robert had and just like Malcolm had.

"Sof!"

"Back here, Sasha!"

Her best friend peeked around the corner of the door. "Hey, girl, how's it going?"

"Slow." Sofia smiled. "I hate moving."

"Me, too." Sasha grinned. She dropped her bag on the floor. "Oooh, your clothes. I love going through your clothes."

"Even though most of them don't fit you?" Sofia teased.

Her best friend was her complete opposite. At five foot, seven inches in her bare feet, Sofia towered over Sasha, who topped out at only five feet. Sasha was voluptuous and curvy, while Sofia tended toward the thin side. She was olive-skinned, with black hair and dark, chocolate brown eyes, nothing like Sofia with her fiery red hair, blue eyes, and creamy white skin. Sasha's mother called them Sugar and Spice whenever they were together.

"We're not 'going through my clothes,' Sash. We're putting them away." She laughed, eyeing the dark-haired vixen out of the corner of her eye. Sasha rummaged through a box, pulling dresses out and holding them up to herself.

"God, this is gorgeous," Sasha said, holding out a deep blue cocktail dress. "Can I borrow this for the fundraiser at work?"

"Sure," Sofia replied. "It looks gorgeous with your dark hair and olive skin. I know a lady who can shorten it for you, too."

"Are you saying I'm short?"

"Yes." She giggled.

"Rude." Sasha laughed. "But you're right. I'm petite."

"That sounds much better than short." Sofia smiled. "You know what? I need a glass of wine. What do you say?"

"God, that sounds good." Sasha sighed. "You keep unpacking and I'll go get it." She stopped at the door. "Hey, how's work? You haven't called to grumble about anybody lately. Is it going that well?"

"Um, no." Sofia snorted. "In fact, things are kind of different, kind of off-kilter."

"Do you want to talk about it?"

"Wine first."

Fifteen minutes later, they were sitting in the living room, each of them with a glass of wine, a plate of cheese and crackers on the table between them.

"Alright, spill," Sasha ordered.

Aside from Georgia, the only person Sofia could talk to about her job was Sasha. She was always careful not to say names or give away who she was dating; she didn't want to violate her non-disclosure agreement. And Sasha, being the perfect friend she was, never asked for details that might give away who the clients were. If Georgia found out, Sofia would lose her job, but she needed an outlet that wasn't someone from the agency. She trusted Sasha.

"I have a new client," she said, sipping her wine.

"Okay." Sasha nodded. "I thought you weren't taking on any other clients?"

"This guy is special, a personal request from Georgia. He's an actor. And not some no-name either, Sash. He's big."

"Anybody I know?"

"Probably." Sofia sighed. "So, no names."

"Right, no names. You said things are off kilter. What's wrong?"

Sofia pushed a hand through her hair and swirled her wine in her glass. She wasn't sure how to start. It had been so long since she had allowed emotions of any kind to factor into any part of her professional life that talking about them was difficult. She hated the fact that she had to deal with them at all.

"My new client, he's great. We've gone out three times and all of them have been crazy wonderful dates. He doesn't want somebody for movie premieres, or fundraising events, or anything like that. He just wants to be with someone who isn't dating him for his celebrity status." Sofia blew out a shaky breath. "He wants someone he can have sex with, no strings attached."

"But...but you don't do that, right?" Sasha said. "Or...have you had sex with this guy?"

"No, I haven't. I figured that would be the end of it; when I said I wouldn't sleep with him, I thought he'd have Georgia find him someone else. Instead, he asked to see me two more times."

"Really? Even though you won't sleep with him. So, what? Are you guys going out on normal dates or what?"

"Sort of. We don't go out in public. One thing he's trying to avoid is the paparazzi dissecting his relationships, so he doesn't want to go anywhere or do anything where we might be seen. We've had dinner twice at a hotel and the last date, we went for a hike and a picnic."

"Wow, that's...that's different. How's that going?"

"It is different and it's kind of weird. I'm out of my element when we do stuff like that. I'm used to putting on a show, playing the pretty little girlfriend on the powerful man's arm. But he doesn't want that from me. He just wants to hang out. It's like we're, I don't know, friends." Sofia set her wine glass on the table and rose to her feet. She needed to move, to walk off some of this excess worry and energy gnawing at her nerves. "He's, well, he's amazing, Sash. It's not just that he's handsome or a famous actor; he's smart, he's funny, he makes me laugh, he's sweet, and...and he kissed me."

Sasha choked on her wine, almost spitting it on the couch. "You let him kiss you?"

"I let him kiss me." Sofia nodded. She gnawed on her lower lip, unsure if she wanted to say what she'd been thinking since her last date with Chris.

"And?" Sasha prompted.

"What do you mean, and?"

"I mean, you wouldn't be telling me any of this unless there was an 'and.'" Sasha shrugged. "I know you, Sof. There's something more going on. What is it?"

"You'll hate me if I say it," she whispered.

She knew that wasn't true, but telling Sasha what was on her mind scared her. They had been friends since college, and she was okay with Sofia's job as an escort. She didn't judge her; she didn't condemn her. In fact, she accepted it as if it were the most normal thing in the world, and she was one hundred percent supportive. But that could all change in an instant.

"You know that's not true," Sasha scoffed. "I could never hate you."

"I've been thinking about saying yes," she mumbled.

Sasha set her wine glass on the table and took a deep breath. "Wait? Did I hear you correctly? Did you say you're thinking about saying yes? Yes, as in 'yes' to the sex?"

Sofia closed her eyes and nodded. She waited for Sasha to say something, anything, except nothing but silence came from her best friend. She opened her eyes to see Sasha staring at her, arms crossed, and a stern expression on her face.

"What?" Sofia sighed.

"You've caught feelings."

"I have not," she protested. "I barely know him."

"So, you're telling me you *are* thinking about breaking your own rules, in particular, that one very specific rule, the no sex rule, because this client is so nice and amazing and sweet, even though you barely know him? That's it? Not because you in any way, shape, or form caught feelings for this guy?"

"Okay, maybe a little." She dropped to the couch beside her friend, her head in her hands.

"Sofia, that's why you can't have sex with him," Sasha said, her arm sliding around Sofia. "You don't want this to be another Malcolm situation, do you?"

"No."

"If you sleep with him, it will be. You know as well as I do that sex complicates things. Sex changes things. If this guy will go out with you despite your no sex rule, then great, stick with that. But sex, Sof, that's a whole different story. The one time you broke that rule, the lines got blurred and your heart got broken. Don't do it again."

"Why are you always the voice of reason?" Sofia laughed.

"That's my job as your best friend." Sasha grinned. "And as your best friend, I'm thinking it might be a good idea for you to tell Georgia you don't want to see him anymore."

"I don't know if I can do that, Sash," Sofia muttered.

"You mean you don't want to do that," Sasha scoffed. "Okay if you don't want to do that, at least promise me you will not sleep with him. Promise me."

"I promise."

Now if only she could keep her promise.

Seven a.m. was too early for her doorbell to be ringing. Sofia dropped the bag of coffee on the counter, yanked her hair up on top of her head in a messy bun, and stalked down the hall to the door. She pushed aside the curtain and peered out.

Georgia stood on her front stoop, two cups of coffee in her hand, her face stern and irritated, foot tapping. Sofia yanked open the door.

"Georgie? What are you doing here?"

"Can't I visit my favorite girl?"

"Not without an excuse." Sofia smiled. "But you've got coffee, which I need since it's seven o'clock on a Saturday morning." She pushed the door open all the way and stepped to the side. "Come on in."

Georgia followed Sofia back down the hall to the kitchen. She eased onto a stool at the breakfast bar and set the coffee down in front of Sofia.

"I love your new place," she said. "It's beautiful."

"Thanks." Sofia sipped the coffee, humming when the sweet nectar hit her tongue. "Mm, that tastes good." She glanced at Georgia. "You're here because I didn't call you, aren't you?"

"Maybe." Georgia shrugged. "Among other things." She tapped her fingers on the table, a habit that annoyed Sofia to no end, though she'd never mentioned it. "After what Billy said, I can't help but worry about you, Sofia. He seemed concerned about you. I thought maybe you'd talk to me face to face since you wouldn't talk to me on the phone."

"I told you—I'm fine."

"Again, Billy didn't seem to think so."

"I just…I had a moment…I thought maybe I didn't want to see Chris anymore, but I swear to you it wasn't anything he did. He has been a perfect gentleman. He's very sweet."

"Why did you think you didn't want to see him anymore?"

Sofia sighed and shook her head. "I'm not sure I'm the right girl for him. He might want you to find him someone he's more compatible with."

"He seems to think he's compatible with you," Georgia chuckled.

"Yeah?"

"Yes. In fact, he put in a call late yesterday, asking for you. Tonight."

"He did?"

"Would I lie?" She downed the rest of her coffee, her nails tap-tap-tapping on the counter. "Especially about business?"

"No, of course not." Sofia smiled.

Georgia reached across the counter and took her hand, squeezing it gently. "Are you sure everything is okay? Ever since you started seeing Chris, you've seemed off."

"I'm fine, Georgie. You know I'd tell you if I wasn't."

"I'd like to think you would," Georgia said, giving her hand another squeeze. She rose to her feet and hefted her purse up on her shoulder. "I need to get back to the office. Can I tell Chris you'll be there?"

Sofia nodded. "You'll send me the details?"

She pulled her phone from her purse and typed out a message. "I'll have my secretary send them over right now. As long as you're sure?"

"I'm sure," Sofia said.

Her resolve was weakening. Agreeing to see Chris again so soon after they'd shared a kiss proved that. She knew what she had to do, what she should do, but she didn't know if she could. She had to keep this professional. She'd promised Sasha she wouldn't sleep with him. Which meant no more kissing, no more answering personal questions, no letting Chris get her all twisted up inside. Sofia raised her hand and knocked on the hotel room door.

It opened immediately, as if he'd been standing in front of it waiting for her to arrive. He looked laid back and comfortable in jeans and a t-shirt, his feet bare, his hair falling over his forehead, a smirk on his gorgeous face. He took her hand and dragged her inside.

"It's the seventh-inning stretch," he explained. "The Mets are down by two. I don't want to miss anything." He gestured for her to sit. "You want a drink?"

"I'll have what you're having." Sofia set her purse on the table and sat down, her hands folded in her lap.

Chris grabbed two beers from the bar and popped them open before dropping to the couch beside her, his arm thrown over the back of it, his fingertips brushing her shoulder, sending an unexpected tingle down her spine. She forced herself not to respond, though she desperately wanted to lean into him. His warm, clean scent washed over her.

"You hungry?" Chris asked.

Sofia shook her head. "No, I'm fine. The beer is enough. Is this what we're doing, watching the game?"

Chris shrugged. "I didn't have any plans. I wanted to see you because I'm heading home in a few days and I thought…" He cleared his throat and squeezed his eyes closed for a brief second. "Are you sure you're not hungry?"

"Why are you always trying to feed me?" Sofia teased. "Do you think I'm too skinny or something?"

"No, you're perfect just the way you are," Chris told her, eyes downcast. "My mom taught me to be a polite host. I guess I feel like offering to feed you makes me seem like I'm not disappointing her."

"You're a perfect gentleman, Chris. No need to worry. Your mom would be proud." She glanced at the TV. "Baseball, huh?"

"Yeah, I love baseball. I played throughout high school, even thought I might play in college, but I caught the acting bug my junior year and never looked back. I'm a huge Mets fan, though. My dad used to take me to games. Still does. In fact, we're going next week when I go home."

"You're from New York?"

"I am," Chris nodded. "Took a lot of coaching to kill the accent, though every now and then it slips through. How about you? Where are you from?"

"The Midwest." She shrugged. "Nowhere as exciting as New York."

"What brought you to California?"

"Chris," Sofia sighed. "I can't answer those questions."

"Sorry," he said. "Too personal, right?" He scrubbed a hand over his face. "I forget sometimes that I'm not on an actual date. No more personal questions, I promise."

"Okay." Sofia nodded and pointed at the TV. "Tell me what's going on in the game." Hopefully, that would distract Chris from asking any more questions she couldn't answer.

Chris grinned and launched into a play-by-play of the game. Sofia thought it might bore her, but Chris was animated and funny, interjecting his own thoughts and feelings regarding what was happening. Within minutes, she was laughing so hard that tears streamed down her face.

"You're adorable when you laugh," Chris said. His fingers brushed her bare arm again, causing heat to explode in her lower belly.

"And you are the funniest person I've ever met," she countered, ignoring the way his touch excited her.

"Makes spending time with me easier, doesn't it?" Chris leaned over her, his voice dropping an octave, the sound bringing goosebumps to the surface of her skin.

"You're easy to be around," she murmured. "In fact, I like spending time with you."

Chris shook his head, one eyebrow raised. "So much that you run away when I kiss you?"

"I'm sorry about that," she said. "It…it took me by surprise."

"It's okay. It only killed my ego a little." He chuckled. "I always thought I was a good kisser until you bolted after we kissed."

She opened her mouth to tease him, maybe tell him they couldn't kiss again, shouldn't kiss again, but the words that came out were not what she expected to say.

"Maybe you should kiss me again."

Chris didn't even blink. He cupped her face in his hand, his thumb caressing her cheek. "Is that what you want? Do you want me to kiss you again?"

It was what she wanted, despite her rules, despite Sasha's warnings and Georgia's concern, despite her resolve to set things right. She wanted Chris to kiss her. She thought her heart might pound right out of her chest as she nodded, her eyes locked on Chris's brilliant blue irises.

He tugged on her chin, urging her to move toward him. She slid closer, meeting him halfway and then his perfect, full, pink lips brushed across hers, his hands brushing the skin between the waistband of her skirt and her shirt as he gathered her into his arms. He licked her bottom lip until she opened her mouth, Chris's tongue moving over her teeth and lips, his nose brushing against hers as the kiss deepened. She wrapped a hand around the back of his neck, her fingers brushing over the short hairs on his neck.

The kiss was over far too soon, Chris pulling away, his forehead resting on hers. "Not so bad, right?" he whispered.

"Not so bad."

"Are you going to run away again?"

She shifted uneasily, Chris's grip on her tightening, as if he thought she would try to run away. Her fingers drifted down his chest, tracing the taut muscles beneath his shirt. This wasn't supposed to happen; she wasn't supposed to fall for her clients.

She cleared her throat. "Maybe I should go."

"You are going to run away." He sighed. His fingers tangled in her hair, tugging as he kissed her again. "Please don't." His lips brushed against hers as he spoke, his breath warm against her skin.

"Chris—"

He released her, his hands falling to his lap, his head down, a heavy sigh escaping him. "I understand. I'm sorry, Sofia. You can go." He scrubbed a hand over his face, hunched over, his elbows resting on his knees, one hand rubbing the back of his neck. Defeated.

Her stomach twisted. This wasn't what she wanted. She didn't want to hurt Chris; she didn't want to leave him with nothing. She liked him, she enjoyed spending time with him, and yes, she was attracted to him, more than she should be. Maybe she could do it. Maybe she could have sex with him and keep it professional. She was a lot older and wiser, and Chris wasn't Malcolm. She could put feelings aside and enjoy spending time with him, enjoy physical intimacy with him, and keep the emotions out of it.

Sofia put her hand on his thigh and squeezed. "I won't run away," she whispered.

Chris turned to look at her, staring at her like she was a bug on the wall. "What are you doing, Sof?"

"I'm staying right here. With you. I'll stay as long as you want me."

Chris's mouth fell open, and his eyes narrowed. He gnawed on his lower lip, his head tipping to one side as he scrutinized her. "Are you saying what I think you're saying? Because I thought you weren't that kind of escort?"

"Maybe for you, I am that kind of escort."

"Sofia, you know I don't want to pressure you," he whispered. "I don't want you to think you have to—"

She put a finger to his lips, cutting him off. "I want to, Chris, but *only* with you. I swear I'm okay with this. I want this."

Chris nodded, a tentative smile dancing across his lips. He pulled Sofia into his arms, flush against his body. Heat exploded through her, anticipation burning through her nerves.

She wanted this.

She wanted him.

Chapter Seven

CHRIS

Chris ducked his head, his lips brushing hers, hoping his kiss would tell her what he was feeling. His heart pounded against his ribcage, his skin aflame with want and need for her. He wanted her to know he needed her, and she wasn't making a mistake. He tightened his grip on her waist and pulled her into his lap, kissing her neck beneath her ear, his lips sliding along her jaw to her mouth, his hand on the back of her head, pulling her close so he could catch her lips in his, his tongue tangling with hers. She moaned into his mouth, her nails digging into the back of his neck, her back arching as she pushed herself against him.

God, he wanted to rip the clothes from her body and take her, drown in her. He squeezed his eyes closed and forced himself to breathe, forced himself to slow down and take his time, to relish every second he had with her, even though his body was screaming for more, now.

His hands slid under her shirt, the feel of her bare skin making him ache with need. When she shuddered in his arms, it only fueled his desire.

"Am I going too fast?" he asked.

Sofia shook her head, her lower lip trembling, her cheeks tinted a lovely shade of pink, her blue eyes shimmering. "Take me to bed, Chris."

Chris stood, his arms still around her waist. He kissed her again before setting her on her feet. He took her hand and led her across the room to the bed. He sat on the edge, Sofia between his legs. She leaned over, her hands on his shoulders, and kissed the corner of his mouth.

With a low growl, he pulled her down on the bed beside him, rolling her beneath him, hitching one of her legs over his hip. He rocked forward, pressing his aching cock against her warm center.

She put her hands on his chest and exhaled. "Wait a second."

Chris rose to his knees, pushed a hand through his hair, anxiety rushing through him, wondering what he'd done to upset her.

She sat up, a soft smile on her beautiful face. She grabbed the hem of her shirt and yanked it over her head, then she shimmied out of her skirt, leaving her in nothing but her soft white panties and bra.

His breath caught in his throat at the sight of her full breasts covered by the lacy white bra. His mouth watered at the sight. He took her nipple in his mouth, sucking greedily, bringing it to a hard peak, his cock twitching with need at the sight of it pushing against the damp material of her bra.

Sofia groaned, her fingers catching in his shirt, dragging him close, her lips against his ear. "What do you say we get you out of your clothes?" she murmured, tugging open his jeans.

Chris stood up and quickly shucked off his clothes, then he took her back in his arms, his attention on her neck, kissing his way down her throat. He rubbed circles up Sofia's side until he reached her breast, his thumb brushing across the nipple, still covered by the thin lace of her bra. Sofia gasped, which only made him want to hear more. He took her breast in his mouth again, suckling the nipple, laving it with his tongue, drawing an obscene moan from her.

"Hmm," he hummed, kissing his way back to her mouth. He brushed a hand through her hair, tucking it behind her ear as he rained kisses over her face and neck. He slid his hand down her body, his fingers dancing over her core, still covered by her lace panties.

"Chris…" she breathed.

"Do you want me to stop?" he asked, his lips pressed to her ear.

"No, no, please don't."

Chris's hand skimmed along the edge of Sofia's underwear and slid past the waistband, his fingers brushing against her. Her hips rose to meet his hand, her legs falling open, her eyes closed, her skin a delectable shade of pink. His lips closed over her pulse point as he slipped a single finger into her wet entrance, tracing the silken folds, a deep rumbling groan leaving him.

Sofia pressed herself against him, her hips rocking, moaning louder as he eased another finger into her and rubbed his thumb across her clit. She trembled, clutching at his biceps, her nails digging half-moon crescents in his skin, her breathy moans making him ache with desire.

He crooked his fingers, his palm pressed against the swollen nub of nerves, his mouth covering hers, swallowing Sofia's gasps of pleasure as her back bowed off the bed, her eyes squeezed closed as she came.

Chris kissed her as she came down, his body flush against hers, his need for her overwhelming him, putting him on edge. When her soft hand closed around his hard cock, stroking him, he could barely hold himself back. He rolled to his back, taking her with him, tucked against his side, her hand still between his legs, her thumb brushing the tip of his shaft, sending a shiver down his spine.

When he couldn't wait any longer, he pushed her underwear off, adding it to the growing pile of clothes on the floor. She removed her bra as he fished a condom out of his jeans and slid it on before he nestled himself between her legs, his arousal aching painfully as he positioned himself at her entrance, his forehead resting against hers. He caught her lips in his as he eased into her, taking his time, giving her a chance to adjust to his substantial size, still kissing her until he was buried deep in her warmth. He moaned as her walls closed around him, the feeling like nothing else he had ever experienced.

Sofia wrapped her legs around the back of his thighs, pulling him into her, her arms around his waist, giving herself over to him, her body his for the taking.

Chris moved slowly, flexing his hips, deeper and deeper, her soft, silky warmth surrounding him, pushing everything else out of his head. The only thing in his universe was Sofia. He took his time, his eyes closed, his face now buried against the side of her neck, his entire being lost in the sensations over-taking him, letting himself get lost in Sofia.

He couldn't hold back any longer. The sounds she made encouraged him to move faster and harder, his hands on her hips, holding her still, slamming into her, thrusting deeper and deeper, pounding her into the mattress, his body tensing as he came with a deep groan. He held himself above her, balanced on his forearms, his lips roving over her neck and shoulders, then he collapsed to the bed beside her, rolling to his back, her hand in his.

"Wow," he breathed. "That was amazing, Sof." He kissed the back of her hand and squeezed it.

He propped himself on his elbow and looked down at her, her long red hair spread out around her, a faint smile on her face. He kissed her cheek, nuzzling her neck with his nose, making her giggle. She rolled away from him, snatched his shirt off the ground, and pulled it on before disappearing into the bathroom.

The second she was out of sight, he pushed a hand through his hair and sat up. He couldn't believe what had just happened; he hadn't expected it, not after what she'd said and the way she'd reacted to their first kiss. Chris wanted to bask in the afterglow of all of it, but the panic set in, his heart beating out of control, his hands shaking, every move he'd made replaying in his head. He kept finding himself coming up short. He blew out a shaky breath, climbed out of bed, and yanked on his pants. By the time she came out of the bathroom, he'd convinced himself that the evening had been a disaster.

Sofia picked her clothes up off the floor and put them on, glancing at Chris out of the corner of her eye every couple of seconds. He leaned against the bar, watching her every move, wondering if he should say something. Once her clothes were on, she crossed the room to stand in front of him, a worried smile on her face.

"Are you... um... are we okay?" she asked.

"I'm good." He nodded. "And we're good." He kissed the tip of her nose and smiled down at her.

"I should go." She pushed up on her toes and pressed a kiss to the corner of his mouth.

"I hope this doesn't change anything, Sof. That was... you were great."

"Thank you." She sighed. "And nothing has changed. Nothing."

Chris wasn't buying it; Sofia didn't sound convincing. He wanted her to be honest with him, not lie to make him feel better. He had enough of those people in his life. He crossed his arms over his chest and eyed her up and down.

"You're okay with going out with me again, right?"

"Of course." Sofia nodded and then she left, the door swinging closed behind her.

After the amazing date he'd had with Sofia, the last thing Chris wanted to do was go out with some reality star. But he'd told Jack to set it up, which he had rushed to do. Jack had arranged everything about this date, right down to the day and time, even picking the restaurant and making the reservations for them. Not being in control only ratcheted up Chris's anxiety, making him worried and anxious over how this evening would go. He silently cussed out his manager and agent as he drove to pick up his "date."

"It's only dinner. Two, maybe three hours," he reminded himself. He stood in the elevator of an overpriced apartment building in a posh section of L.A., watching the floors pass, his fingers itching to hit stop and escape this madness. The voices usually clamoring for attention in his head were a dull murmur at the moment, especially since he'd seen Sofia the previous night, but he knew it wouldn't be long before they were scrambling for his attention, louder and louder until he couldn't concentrate, until he couldn't think. He closed his eyes and counted to ten as he sucked in a deep breath.

He didn't want to get out when the elevator opened. He hadn't met this girl yet; he hadn't spoken to her or seen anything more than the photo provided by Jack. How was he supposed to get through a date with her? A date everyone would know about, since its sole purpose was publicity. Chris walked down the hall toward Ginny's apartment like a man walking to his death. He stopped in front of her door, wiped his hands on his jeans, and knocked.

Ginny "call me Gin—like the alcohol" Etling opened her apartment door with a flourish, one hip jutting out, her fake breasts on full display, spilling out of her lightweight, see-through dress, her bright red lips pursed, false eyelashes batting a mile a minute. She was exactly what Chris had expected: loud, squeaky, flirty, needy, and not his type. Fake everything—breasts, nails, extensions, a spray-on tan. You name it, it wasn't real. Ginny Etling was an over-the-top phony in a way that drove him crazy.

"Chris!" she squealed, throwing herself into his arms, hands clasped around his neck, rock hard breasts pushed against his chest, her cloying perfume suffocating him.

"Ginny, I presume," he said, trying not to inhale the sickening scent as he disentangled himself, his regret at ever agreeing to this jumping up another notch.

"My God, it's so great to finally meet you!" She grinned. "I am so excited about this date! You don't even know!"

Chris cringed at her over-exuberance. He could feel the exclamation point at the end of every sentence skittering across his skin like tiny, painful pinpricks.

She grabbed his hand and dragged him into her apartment, insisting on showing him around, her too-short skirt swinging around her legs as she moved, showing off her thong-clad ass. She made a point of showing him the bedroom, a sly smile on her face, clinging to his arm and winking at him as she mentioned how comfortable, how sturdy, the bed was. They hit every room in the house, concluding the tour with Ginny showing him off to her friends sitting in the living room, women she introduced to Chris as her "squad"—Tammie with an *i* and an *e* and Tanya—both of whom spent several minutes fawning over him, making him incredibly uncomfortable. He wished a hole would open in the floor and swallow him.

Ginny couldn't stop going on about how excited she was, how this was going to be the most amazing night of her life, how she could already feel a connection between them, and a bunch of other stuff he didn't catch because she talked so fast he couldn't decipher half of what she said. Not to mention, her high pitched, squeaky voice grated on his nerves; it had ever since she opened the door and squealed his name.

Chris endured ten minutes of farewells and Instagram potential photos between Ginny and her "squad" before he could get her out the door. He hoped once she was away from her friends, she might tone it down a bit, but she didn't stop, blabbering on and on all the way to the restaurant. It was like she physically couldn't stop talking. This was going to be a long night.

They started the evening at Rossoblu in downtown LA, the place to be if you wanted to be seen. Their table on the patio was out in the open, right where everyone could see them. Jack wanted the paparazzi to get their pictures. Ginny sat beside him, so close he could smell the disgusting combination of the mint gum she was popping every few seconds, her oppressive perfume, and the nauseating hairspray, all while she kept her knee pressed against his and her hand on his thigh. Every couple of minutes she would lean into him and whisper-shout something in his ear, most of which he forgot the second she said it.

Chris downed two beers within the first half an hour, trying to calm his frayed nerves, but it didn't help. If he hadn't been driving, he would have switched to the hard stuff, but instead, he ordered another beer. Ginny knocked back shot after shot of Liquid Cocaine along with margarita chasers. By the time they finished eating, her words slurred and her eyes were glassy and unfocused. She'd also gotten very handsy, constantly touching him, her hand drifting further up his thigh every few minutes, until she was only millimeters away from his cock. He grasped her fingers, squeezing them and doing his best to subtly move her hand away, but she seemed to take that as an invitation, scooting closer to him, her breasts pressed against his arm, her chin resting on his shoulder.

"Let's go back to my place." She did that whisper-shout thing again, drawing the other patrons' attention, most of them with knowing smirks on their face.

Chris signaled the waitress and paid the bill, hoping to get Ginny out of the restaurant before she embarrassed them. He took hold of her elbow and helped her to her feet, catching her when she staggered and fell against him, tottering in her three-inch heels, a drunken giggle hiccupping out of her. She wrapped her hands around his arm, her claw-like nails digging into the flesh of his bicep.

He hurried them out the front door, gesturing for the valet to get his car. Across the street, he could see the paparazzi with their high-powered cameras and telephoto lenses snapping pictures, invading his privacy. Over the years, he'd grown accustomed to it, though it still irritated him, like tonight when he felt forced to put himself in the public eye, forced to make sure they noticed him. God, how he hated this. It was obvious Jack was going to get the press he wanted. To anyone on the outside, it would look as if he and Ginny were close, intimate with each other. The thought made Chris nauseous. They would splash it all over the tabloids tomorrow.

Ten minutes after leaving the restaurant, Ginny passed out in the passenger seat, her head slumped against the window, mouth hanging open, soft snores coming from her. She didn't stir, not even when he parked the car and shut off the engine, not coming awake until he pulled open the door and she almost fell out. She groaned, a hand to her head as she extricated herself from the car, her arms right back around him, unnecessarily clinging to him as they walked into her building. He had no choice to hold on to her, hoping she didn't topple them over.

Once they were in the elevator, Ginny turned to face him, her hands on his waist, her heels making her almost as tall as him, her breasts, now falling out of the dress—he could actually see her nipples—pressed to his chest, her alcohol-laden breath blowing in his face.

"I've been waiting all night to get you alone," she giggled, then she was kissing him, her tongue forcing its way into his mouth, her hands sliding around his waist and down to his ass, tugging him closer. She squirmed, rubbing her body against his, a quiet groan falling from her lips.

Chris clenched his hands at his side, grimacing as the combined taste of stale margaritas, the lobster she'd had for dinner, and the waxy taste of her bright red lipstick washed across his tongue. He pulled away, gagging as he stepped to the side, out of her death grip.

"What's the matter, baby?" she asked. "Don't you want me?" She pouted, her smeared lipstick making her look clownish, gaudy.

He could feel his chest tightening as he struggled to breathe, could feel his anxiety kick up a notch, sweat pouring down his back, pooling in the waistband of his jeans, his hands trembling, his heart pounding. Every part of him wanted to scream, "Fuck, no, I don't want you" at the top of his lungs, but he knew he couldn't. He just couldn't. Jack would kill him if he ended this before it began.

Instead, Chris shook his head. "Ginny, we only met a few hours ago," he chided.

"Gin," she interrupted. "Call me Gin."

"You've also had a lot to drink," he continued, "so I think it's best if we say goodnight and go our separate ways."

The elevator doors slid open. Chris didn't move, just looked pointedly at his soon-to-be co-star and then at the open doors. Ginny dragged her purse up her arm, her lips tight, eyes flashing in anger. She spun on her heel and stomped down the hall to her door, wobbling thanks to the alcohol in her system and the high heels, one hand on the wall to steady herself, the slam of her door echoing back to him as the elevator doors closed. Jack was going to be pissed when he heard about this.

Back in his car, he pulled his phone free and checked the time. It was only a little after ten. He'd promised himself he wouldn't call until he got back from New York, promised himself that he could go two weeks without seeing Sofia. That had been before the date with Ms. Etling. He took all of thirty seconds to decide. Phone pressed to his ear, he pulled back into traffic. If he timed it right, he could be at the hotel before Sofia.

Chapter Eight

SOFIA

She had feelings for Chris.

Sofia had spent the last twenty-four hours telling herself she didn't. Forget that she couldn't stop thinking about him and what they'd done. Forget that she'd relived it a thousand times and it never failed to make her heart beat faster and her stomach twist with desire.

By midnight, she'd concluded that yes, she had feelings for Chris, but she wouldn't let it affect their working relationship. She would do her best to control them.

Despite her exhaustion, Sofia couldn't sleep, so she showered, then she laid on the couch to watch a movie. An hour into the movie, she decided to go to bed but the telltale chirp of an incoming text came from the coffee table.

It was too late for her normal clients. For a split second, she considered ignoring it, but she reached for it, knocking the phone to the floor, cursing when she had to drop to her hands and knees to retrieve it from under the couch. Once she had it in her hand, she opened the notification with the name of the client and where she was to meet him.

It was Chris.

Her heart raced and her mouth went dry. She'd seen him last night. She couldn't believe he wanted to see her again so soon. She replied with the standard answer.

Accepted.

It never crossed her mind to say no. She climbed to her feet and hurried through the condo to the back bedroom where she kept her work clothes. She exchanged her shorts and t-shirt for a short, flowy, blue-flowered skirt and a white tank top. She slipped on a pair of blue sandals and pulled her hair into a ponytail.

Billy arrived ten minutes later, grumbling under his breath when she told him she was going to see Chris. Thirty minutes after that, she was standing in the Westerfield Hotel lobby, checking her phone for the room number.

The room Chris chose was on one of the uppermost floors, at the end of a hallway, far from the elevators. Sofia stopped in front of the door, just like she'd done twenty-four hours ago, took a deep breath to steady her nerves, and knocked. The door flew open and Chris grabbed her hand, dragging her inside and slamming the door closed behind her.

Sofia stumbled after him, her purse and sweater falling to the floor beside the door as Chris's arms slid around her, crushing her to his chest, his lips crashing into hers. She moaned into the kiss, her fingers interlocked behind his neck, one leg sliding around the back of his, hooking her foot around his calf. His hand slid up her thigh and under her skirt, heat prickling her skin everywhere he touched. Long fingers slipped beneath the edge of her panties, pushing them down and off her legs, along with her shoes. His thick digits grazed her heated core, drawing a needy gasp from her. Chris bent at the knees, his hands on her ass, lifting her, muscles flexing as he pulled her legs around his waist. His lips never left hers, even as he effortlessly carried her to the sofa and sat on the edge.

She straddled him, her skirt up around her waist, Chris's hands on her hips, pulling her down onto him, the hard line of his cock, still trapped behind the thick denim of his jeans, pressing against her. She moaned his name and rocked forward, shuddering, her body betraying every emotion she wished she weren't feeling.

Chris pushed a hand between them and opened his jeans, shoving them down past his hips. He slid a condom on, then he picked Sofia up and eased her onto his cock, her body stretching to take his substantial length, a strangled hiss leaving her as he filled her. She braced a hand on the back of the sofa, pressing forward, taking all of him, aching for him, despite having been with him only a day ago. He yanked the tank top over her head, tossing it aside before pulling the thin lace cups of her bra down, his hand covering her breast, twisting and plucking at the nipple, balancing her on the edge of pleasure and pain. His hips shot up, burying himself deep inside her, his tight abs brushing her clit, startling her with the intensity of the sensations rushing through her body. She rolled her hips, her thighs trembling, both hands on either side of Chris's broad shoulders, holding on so tight her fingers ached. Chris held her tight, guiding her, fucking her, making her feel things she never felt before.

The coil deep in the pit of her stomach was wound so tight she was close to losing it, her head thrown back, eyes closed, heat blasting through her as Chris pushed her closer to climax. His hand slid into Sofia's hair, cupping the back of her head, his other hand on her shoulder, pulling her down as he thrust up, their bodies so connected that Sofia wasn't sure where he ended and she began.

"Open your eyes, Sofia," Chris growled. "Look at me."

She moaned in frustration, but did as he instructed, gasping as his lust blown blue eyes locked with hers, his lips spit slick, his cheeks flushed red, droplets of sweat glistening on his neck, his grip tight on her shoulder, so tight she'd notice faint bruising the next day, his cock throbbing as he held her in place, all of it perfect torture. He caught her lips in his, the kiss sending her reeling, the orgasm raging through her, her entire body trembling, Chris's arms around her the only thing keeping her grounded.

Sofia fell against him, even as he kept slamming into her, every thrust harder than the last, until a shudder ran through him, his head resting on her shoulder, his groans of pleasure vibrating against her skin.

Chris held her, his lips drifting over her skin, not really kissing her, more like he was memorizing her. It was heaven. Terrified he would let go, she didn't move, didn't breathe, her cheek resting on his chest.

After a few minutes, he laid his head against the back of the sofa, his eyes closed, his hands resting on Sofia's thighs. She cupped his face, brushing her thumb over his cheek, amazed at how beautiful he was.

"Your call surprised me," she admitted. "I just saw you yesterday."

"I needed to see you. I had a shitty night and I needed to quiet the noise in my head. I can only do that with you." He flinched, scrubbed a hand over his face, and pinched the bridge of his nose, then he grabbed her hand and kissed the palm, followed by her shoulder, her neck, her lips, before picking her up and setting her on the sofa beside him. Chris pushed himself to his feet, yanked off the condom, and dropped it in the trash, then he pulled his jeans up, though he didn't button them. He poured some whiskey in a glass and downed it in one swallow.

Sofia straightened her skirt, folded her legs beneath her, and held her hands in her lap. "Do you want me to stay?" she asked. She was almost afraid to hear the answer.

Chris poured another drink and drank it as quickly as he had the first. He licked his lips, staring at a spot somewhere over her shoulder.

"Yeah." He nodded.

Sofia fell into bed early the next morning, exhausted. She slept like the dead for five hours, only dragging herself out of bed because she was dehydrated after the night she'd spent with Chris.

It had been bizarre. Chris was eerily quiet, unlike his normally talkative self, offering no explanation why he'd called Sofia so soon after their last date or why he was so quiet. Any time she tried to bring it up, he'd kiss her or have sex with her, as if he was intent on keeping her from asking questions. When she'd left at dawn, he'd been asleep on the bed, curled on his side, his hand resting on her leg, a light scruff covering his cheeks. She'd pressed a kiss to his forehead and left.

After she satisfied her thirst, she opened her phone and scrolled through her newsfeed, skipping past irrelevant news stories, not looking for anything specific, just passing time, wondering what she could make herself to eat. Maybe Sasha would join her for breakfast.

She froze, her hand poised over the phone, the story jumping off the page, assaulting her, the photo burning a hole in the center of her brain. Her hands shook so much she had to set her phone down, but the picture still mocked her, ruining her high. It was

Chris, with an overly made up, fake blonde hanging off his arm, gazing adoringly up at him.

Sofia recognized her immediately; she didn't even have to glance at the accompanying article to know who she was. Ginny Etling, reality star, wannabe actress, and former employee of Private Lives.

The picture was of Chris leading her from one of the more popular restaurants in town, one Sofia had been to several times with clients. The photograph was taken the previous evening, hours before Chris called for her.

She skimmed the article—Chris Chandler seen out on a date with Ginny Etling, reality star and aspiring actress. The couple had been hanging off each other most of the night at Rossoblu, the evening wrapping up with Chandler entering Etling's apartment building. The article ended with the tongue in cheek question of whether the two were an item, perhaps practicing for roles as lovers in an upcoming movie.

Sofia swallowed around the lump in her throat. It shouldn't bother her. She was nothing more than hired help, a way for Chris to relieve tension with no strings attached. She had no claim to him, something she was painfully aware of, something made clear via their contracted agreement at the start of their arrangement. She couldn't let this affect her; she knew Chris wanted someone with whom he could have a sexual relationship without all the press and garbage. Sofia was that someone. Emotions were not part of the deal. Falling for Chris wasn't in the cards. She alone was responsible for the consequences of her actions when she'd had sex with Chris. Her relationship with Chris wasn't an actual relationship. She needed to remember that.

The pain blossoming inside her was real, the pulsing ache in the center of her chest one she couldn't ignore no matter how much she wanted to. If Chris had a girlfriend, her time with him would be over. Last night may well have been a goodbye. It all made sense now, why he'd kept her with him all night, why he'd seemed so attentive, so caring. He was saying goodbye. The thought made her sick to her stomach.

Worse, not only did Chris have a girlfriend, but it was someone she knew and disliked. Ginny had once worked at Private Lives, though she hadn't cut it as an escort; her personality had been too off-putting for most clients. They had relegated her to an office position, taking phone calls, filing, mundane things that no one else wanted to do. Ginny was unpopular, and no one had liked her; she was brash, loudmouthed, difficult to work with, sporting an "I'm a diva" attitude that everyone disliked. Ginny left abruptly, under unknown circumstances, her desk cleared off overnight, all traces of her wiped away, her name never spoken again. Not that any of the other girls missed her. Sofia had forgotten about her very existence until this morning.

Sofia pushed her phone away, bile rising in her throat. Her heart hurt. No one ever wanted her; no one ever needed her. Her own mother abandoned her after her father's death, her only serious boyfriend cheated on her. She had one friend, Sasha. She was accustomed to being alone. Everyone she cared about turned their back on her eventually. Every time she got attached to someone, her heart broke. That was why she kept her emotions in check, kept herself from letting anyone get too close. Instead of basking in the afterglow of sex with Chris Chandler, she needed to pick herself up and be a professional.

Don't get emotional. Don't get involved. Don't bring the job home with you.

"This is so wrong," Sofia muttered to herself. "I'm not supposed to feel like this. I'm not supposed to care." She rubbed a hand over her face, surprised at the sting of tears pricking at her eyes. This was not what she needed, not what she'd wanted to happen. Chris Chandler had wormed his way into her life, into her heart, and now she was afraid she couldn't let him go.

Chapter Nine

CHRIS

"I don't want to go back to L.A.," Chris groaned, head falling against the headrest. "Can't I just stay here?"

"Where are you gonna stay? In your mom's basement? What are you, twelve?" Seth laughed.

"Sometimes I wish I was." Chris sighed. "Then I could stay in New York."

"Yeah, but don't you want to go back to that new girlfriend of yours? According to The Gossip Monger, you two are pretty chummy."

"You believe that rag? They wouldn't know the truth if it slapped them across the face."

"I take it all is not well in La La Land. Talk to me, dude. That woman has called you no less than what, ten times in the last week? Not that you answered any of her calls. So, tell me, what is going on with you and Miss Spray-On Tan, anyway?"

"Nothing," Chris snapped. "I went on one date with her to appease Jack and the damn studio. I'm not interested in any kind of relationship with her."

"Does she know that?" Seth asked.

Chris narrowed his eyes. "Why?"

Seth glanced over at his friend, changed lanes, holding the wheel with one hand while he fished his phone out of his pocket and tossed it on Chris's lap. "Look at that. The website is open."

Chris pinched the bridge of his nose as he opened Seth's phone; The Gossip Monger website popped up.

Ginny Etling spoke exclusively with TNG about her budding relationship with one of America's most eligible bachelors. "Chris and I have really hit it off. We've gone out several times and we've enjoyed our-selves. We're taking things slow and I'm excited to see where our relationship goes."

"Are you shitting me?" he grumbled. "Gone out several times, my ass. Once. We went out once."

"What are you gonna do?" Seth asked.

"I don't know. Move to Siberia?"

"Ha, ha, hilarious." Seth smiled. "Seriously, are you going to keep seeing her?"

"I don't want to, but I'm trying to land that movie contract. It would be huge for my career. Huge. Money like I've never imagined. I'm willing to do whatever it takes. If that means going on a few dates with Ginny, so be it."

"Alright, brother, but don't come whining to me when it blows up in your face." Seth swung his pickup truck into the right lane and pulled to a stop. "No other reason you want to go back to L.A.?"

Chris scrubbed a hand over his face and tried not to smile. "I can think of a couple."

"How is Sofia?"

"You know I'm not supposed to talk about her with anyone, Seth. It violates my non-disclosure agreement."

"You violated the NDA five minutes after your first date with her, remember? So, how is she?"

"She's perfect," Chris told him. "It's the easiest relationship I've ever been in."

Seth snorted and shook his head. "It's not a relationship, Chris. You're paying her to spend time with you. She's a prostitute."

Chris snatched his backpack off the floor and pushed open the truck door. "She's not a prostitute, Seth," he grumbled. "I gotta go. I'll call you when I land."

"Chris—"

He slammed the door, grabbed his carry-on out of the back of the truck, and headed inside the airport, ignoring Seth calling after him. Sofia wasn't a prostitute. What she meant to him was indescribable; he wasn't sure Seth could understand what she did for him, how much he needed her. He'd been away for more than a week, and every day away from her had the voices in his head getting louder and louder. For the past two days, they'd been screaming at him. He hadn't slept, hadn't eaten, and he'd drank far more than he should have trying to quiet them. He tried to convince himself that it wasn't Sofia keeping the voices at bay; it was work, the positive direction his career was headed, anything but the woman he paid to date him, paid to have sex with him. Because that might make him crazy.

He breezed through security and headed for the first-class lounge where he ordered a drink and some food before hiding in the corner until his flight left. He argued with himself for almost half an hour before opening his phone and emailing Private Lives.

Chris's phone vibrated with multiple notifications as soon as he turned it on. He had an email from Private Lives informing him that Sofia would not be available until the next day, two missed calls and a voicemail from Seth, and at least ten texts from Ginny, and several text messages from Jack, insisting Chris call him right away. Back to business.

Disappointed he couldn't see Sofia right away, he listened to the voicemail from Seth and dialed Jack's number as he took the elevator downstairs to meet his car. He juggled his phone and a large bottle of water one of the flight attendants had shoved in his hand right before they'd landed, along with her phone number on a slip of paper.

"Chris! How was New York?" Jack bellowed into the phone.

"Cold," he replied, sipping from the water bottle. "What's so urgent you had to text me five times?"

"I got you tickets to the Lakers game tonight, court-side seats," Jack responded. "You and Ginny."

"Jack, I just got back. I have been off the plane for less than ten minutes, and I am not in the mood to see anyone, especially Ginny. I'm exhausted and I want one day to myself at home before I go back to work on Monday. Being around Ginny is the last thing I want to do. She grates on my nerves."

"C'mon, Chris. She's not that bad."

"Have you gone on a date with her?"

"No." Jack laughed, drawing out the word. "But she doesn't want to date me. Just give her a chance. Go to the game, drink a few beers, have some fun, hang out with the pretty, busty blonde. Maybe you'll get lucky and get laid."

Thankfully, Jack couldn't see Chris roll his eyes at the thought of sleeping with the former reality star. "I don't like her that way, Jack. She's not my type."

"You're an actor. Act like you like her."

"How much longer do I have to put on this charade?" Chris sighed.

"Until we say you don't," Jack snapped. He exhaled loudly. "Look, humor me, okay? Alex is there to pick you up. He's gonna swing by and grab Ginny, then straight to Staples Center. The game is at seven. Try not to look constipated while you're there. You're sure to get your picture taken several dozen times. Put on your best face and take advantage of the free press."

Chris rolled his eyes again. Free press. Nothing was free when it came to the press; it took an emotional toll that tore him to shreds. Jack didn't have to deal with that shit. Only he did.

"Speaking of the press, did you know Ginny talked to The Gossip Monger?"

"Yeah," Jack scoffed. "Wendy wrote her statement."

Chris choked on the water he'd been drinking, some of it dribbling down his chin. "Wendy? My publicist, Wendy?"

"We thought it best if we controlled the messages going out about the two of you. Her agent didn't like it, but we insisted. So, anything she says, any statements she makes, those come from us." Jack talked as if Chris should know this information. "Ginny didn't tell you?"

"When would she have told me?"

"I assumed she told you when you two spoke last week. She said she called you when you were back home."

"I haven't spoken to her," Chris said. "She called and I didn't answer. I don't even know how she got my number."

"I gave it to her," Jack said.

Chris could imagine the smug look on his manager's face. If they'd been standing in the same room, Chris would have decked the man.

"Jesus, Jack, what were you thinking?"

"I thought it was my job to keep your career on track, and if this is what we need to do, then damn it, we're going to do it. And you're going to quit bitching about it. Get over yourself, Chris. Suck it up and go have a good time. Call me tomorrow."

Jack ended the call, leaving Chris with an unpleasant taste in his mouth. He stepped outside, right into a crowd of men and women shouting for his attention and snapping his picture. His name came from every direction, one voice drowning out the other until his head was spinning.

"Chris!"

"Over here, Chris!"

"Tell us about you and Ginny, Chris!"

"How long have you been dating Ginny Etling?"

"Is it serious?"

"Is it true you're up for the part of Nico Bianchi?"

Chris's hands shook and his heart pounded, his hands clammy with sweat. He opened his mouth and closed it again; his brain shut down and his tongue froze.

"Mr. Chandler!" A familiar, loud, deep voice echoed over the crowd. Chris spun around to see his driver and sometimes bodyguard Alex striding toward him. Chris was a tall man, but next to Alex, he looked like a toddler. The next thing he knew, Alex was leading him back through the mass of humanity to the car, politely but firmly shoving people out of his way. He yanked open the back of the SUV and ushered Chris inside.

"You good, Mr. Chandler?" he asked once they were both safe in the car.

"Yeah." Chris nodded. "I'm good. Thanks for that. They came out of nowhere."

"Just doing my job, sir." Alex smiled. "Welcome back, by the way."

"Glad to be back," Chris mumbled.

"I understand you're going to a basketball game?"

"I guess I am."

Alex looked at his watch. "We should be at Ms. Etling's place in about forty-five minutes."

"Great. I can't wait." He poured a drink from the bottle of Scotch in the center console before resting his head against the back of the seat with a heavy sigh.

Alex looked Chris over, one eyebrow raised, but he didn't ask any more questions. It was one reason he was good at his job. He put the car in gear and pulled into traffic.

Chris stared out the window, wishing this night were over.

Photos of him and Ginny at the Lakers game were everywhere: on every gossip site, every social media fan account, and even on a few of the more reputable news sites. He hated that he looked like he was having a good time, hated that he looked as if he enjoyed Ginny's company. What none of them knew was that he had been half-drunk by the time he got to the game and completely drunk by the end of the first quarter. He barely remembered the second half, and he remembered nothing about the ride home.

Ginny had her own idea of how the evening had gone. A picture had appeared on her Instagram and her Twitter less than twenty minutes after they had picked her up—a selfie with him sitting in the background, staring out the car window. She had captioned it with something idiotic—*out with my man*—and it was trending within the hour. It had brought out every paparazzi imaginable, brought them right out of the woodwork to catch a photo of the supposedly happy couple leaving the basketball game. Every time he saw a new photo from yet another angle, he wanted to puke.

The clincher, the photo that had prompted his second phone call of the morning, this one to Jack, was another one on Ginny's social media: an enormous bouquet of red roses with the simple caption "From Chris." He knew he'd been drunk, but not so drunk that he would have sent her flowers. He hadn't been able to get his phone out of his pocket fast enough.

It had been a terse conversation, one in which Jack tried to appease him, promising to talk Ginny about her social media use, in particular, her blatant lies regarding her relationship with Chris. She was pushing too hard, too fast, and he wanted it to end.

Chris's first phone call of the morning had been to Private Lives to arrange a meeting with Sofia. The voices in his head were screaming at him, and despite the alcohol in his system, he hadn't slept well. He needed to burn off the energy, shut up the voices in his head, forget how crazy his life had become, if only for a little while. He needed Sofia.

He was at the hotel early, pacing the room, glancing at the clock on the wall every few seconds. Every second that passed increased his anxiety, his entire body thrumming with an inexplicable need.

He almost jumped out of his skin when he heard the knock on the door.

Chris strode across the room and yanked it open. Sofia smiled at him and stepped inside. She dropped her purse on the chair and slipped off her sweater.

"How was New York?" she asked.

"Lonely."

"I didn't think I'd hear from you again," Sofia said.

He stopped mid-stride, confused. "Why?"

"You have a new girlfriend." She shrugged.

"I don't want to talk about her." He pushed a hand through his hair and stared at the floor.

"But if you have her, why would you need me?"

"I'll always need you, Sofia," he growled, lunging for her. She surprised him by meeting him halfway, falling into his arms, their lips crashing together.

They yanked at each other's clothes, stumbling across the room, falling onto the bed in a heap. Clothes flew around the room, landing on the floor, the dresser, even the windowsill and the lamp. Chris was all over her, his lips on her neck, licking and biting, moving down her body to her breasts, pulling her nipple into his mouth, sucking greedily.

Sofia's hands ran down his back, over his stomach, and between his legs, closing around his cock, her thumb smearing pre-cum across the tip and down his length. She grabbed his wrist with her free hand and pulled it between her legs.

"Touch me," she whispered. "I need you to touch me, Chris."

His fingers grazed the lips of her pussy, seeking and finding her clit, his fingers brushing over it, a low growl leaving him when her hips jerked in response, and she groaned into his mouth. Jesus, that sound made his cock achingly hard.

Sofia broke off the kiss and slid down his body until she was between his legs, his cock in her hand, her lips brushing the tip, her breath blowing over him. She wrapped her lips around his shaft, hollowed her cheeks, and sucked, one hand on his sensitive sac, fondling him as she pulled him deep into the wet heat of her mouth. She slid up the length, grazing him with her teeth as she adjusted her position, rising to her knees so she hovered over him, the new angle allowing her to take him even deeper until he hit the back of her throat. It constricted around him, and he almost lost it.

Chris couldn't hold back a groan, his fingers twisting in her hair as she repeated the movement several times, each time taking more of his cock into her mouth, opening her throat to accept his tight, even thrusts.

"Fuck, Sof," he gasped, his hips rising to meet her mouth, her hands splayed over his thighs, squeezing and releasing, her head bobbing as she worked him over. He was close, his breath tearing in and out of his throat, his heart about to pound out of his chest, his balls drawn up tight, his stomach jumping in anticipation.

She released him right before he came, moving to straddle him. She slid a condom down his length before lowering herself onto his cock, rocking forward, leaning over him to catch his lips in hers. Chris planted his feet on the bed, his hands on her waist, holding her tight against him as he buried himself inside of her. She moaned, the sound sexy and perfect. He wanted to be the only one to pull those sounds from her, the only one to make her moan, the only one to make her cry out his name like a filthy curse.

Chris pulled her down on his chest, rolling her to her back, his cock still inside of her, his hips moving, her legs wrapped around his waist as he pounded into her. Sofia clawed at his back, her voice rising in a crescendo of yeses as he pushed her toward orgasm until she screamed his name as she came, her perfect skin flushed, sweat on her forehead, her entire body convulsing around him.

He let out a long, stuttering groan as her walls tightened around him, her nails digging into his shoulders, his own orgasm pushing the voices out of his head. Sofia was everything—her body, her scent, her taste on his tongue, those glorious sounds she made echoing in his ears. He collapsed on top of her, his lips on hers, consumed by her. The only thing that mattered was Sofia and how she made him feel.

Chapter Ten

SOFIA

Sofia slipped into the bathroom and flipped the lock. She sagged against the counter, holding herself upright by sheer force of will. After tonight was over, she planned to tell Georgia she didn't want to see this client anymore.

Patrick Garth, spoiled trust fund brat, was a new client, another one of those she had agreed to take on for Georgia's sake. He was in his late thirties, recently divorced, and eager to rub a new relationship in his ex-wife's face. Enter Sofia. This was their fourth date in the last two weeks. Every date had been some big event, and tonight was no exception. The place was packed with celebrities, Hollywood elite, producers, directors, and multi-millionaires, all there to spend an exorbitant amount of money under the guise of raising money for the museum. There were so many people her head was spinning.

Not that she had mingled much. Patrick kept her on a tight leash, his arm around her waist or a hand locked on her upper arm. In fact, he was a little too hands-on for Sofia's liking. He'd been reluctant to even let her go to the restroom, making a show of pulling her close and smearing a kiss across her lips, his whiskey-thick breath washing over her as he tried to shove his tongue in her mouth. She politely wrenched away from him, the back of her hand pressed to her mouth, and hurried to the restroom.

Sofia splashed some water on the back of her neck, then she scrubbed her lips and reapplied her lipstick. Once she felt somewhat composed, she straightened her tight black dress, trying to pull it down a few inches to cover her thighs. She never would have chosen the revealing dress for any date, let alone one with Patrick. He'd had it sent over for her to wear, and he seemed to think her wearing it was as an invitation to put his hands all over her, despite her whispered protests and reminders that it was not part of their agreement. She examined her hair and make-up one more time before taking a deep breath and strolling out the door and down the hallway, determined to finish out the evening with a smile on her face.

The hallway was quiet and empty, the evening's festivities contained to the large banquet hall at the other end of the convention center. Sofia didn't want to go back in there, didn't want to deal with any more of Patrick's self-possessed, self-involved, possessive nature. She stopped halfway down the hall, leaned against the wall, closed her eyes, and sent up a brief prayer for patience. All she wanted to do was kick off her heels and get out of this ridiculous dress. She checked her watch and groaned. Two more hours. She wasn't sure she could last that long.

"You feel a little sleepy?" A familiar, velvety smooth voice murmured close to her ear. "What's the matter? Your date not entertaining enough?"

Sofia jumped, but she couldn't help the smile that crept over her face. She opened her eyes to see a pair of gorgeous blue eyes staring into hers.

"Chris," she breathed.

He glanced down the hallway, back toward the double swinging doors leading to the banquet hall. When he didn't see anyone, he took Sofia's arm and led her down a short passage and into a small, dimly lit room. He pressed her against the wall by the door, his fingers tangled in her hair, tugging her head back so he could brush a kiss over her lips.

"What are you doing here?" Sofia asked when they broke apart.

"Putting on a dog and pony show," he chuckled. "I'm one of the celebrity ambassadors for the museum. They required my presence." He shifted back a step and eyed her up and down. "I've been watching you, Sof. I like your dress."

Chris's hands were heavy and warm on her waist. They moved to the hem of her skirt, inching it up until it rested just below the curve of her ass. "You look absolutely edible." He ducked his head and kissed her neck, his tongue sliding over her pulse point, nipping at the spot just under her jaw, sending chills down Sofia's spine and heat pooling in her stomach. Chris used his knee to push her legs apart, his thigh now pressed against the warm heat emanating from between her legs.

She could have stayed in his arms all night. Not only to get away from Patrick, but it had been over a week since they'd last been together. She ached for him. Instead, Sofia put her hands in the middle of his chest and reluctantly pushed him away. Chris took a step back with a groan, his hands still on her hips.

"Chris, I can't. I'm working." She sighed. "I'm sorry."

"I know," he muttered. "I don't like the guy you're with. He's a tool."

Sofia pressed her fingers to her lips, trying to hold back a giggle. "He is. But that doesn't change the fact that I'm working. I'm sorry." She brushed a hand through his hair. "Are you here alone?"

Chris pulled her into his arms, his nose buried in her hair. "No." He kissed her temple but didn't offer any additional information. "I need to get back, too. I'd rather stay in here with you. I'll see you later." Another kiss, then he was gone.

Jealousy shot through her veins like a thick poison, making her cold all over. Chris had to be here with Ginny. She wasn't sure she could handle seeing him with that woman. For a second, she considered escaping out a side door and calling Billy, but she knew she couldn't. Her sense of duty demanded she finish the date with Patrick. She took a few minutes to center herself before heading back to the banquet room.

Her eyes were drawn to Chris as soon as she stepped into the room. She couldn't believe she hadn't known he was there. Of course, she'd been spending most of her time fending off Patrick's advances. Now she couldn't look away. Chris looked gorgeous, not that it surprised her, he always looked good, but he looked insanely attractive in the suit he was wearing, like Prince Charming.

Out of the corner of her eye, she glimpsed Ginny descending on Chris, clinging to his arm and whispering in his ear, her substantial breasts pressed against his arm. Sofia didn't miss the momentary look of disgust that crossed his face before he composed himself, a not-so-genuine smile plastered to his lips.

"There you are," Patrick grumbled. He wrapped his hand around her upper arm and yanked her tight against his side. "You were gone forever." He leaned closer, scrutinizing her. "Are you okay?"

"I'm not feeling well," Sofia mumbled. "Sorry."

"Well, you're going to suck it up," Patrick demanded. "You're mine until midnight."

Sofia bit her lip and nodded, glancing at Chris out of the corner of her eye. Seeing him with Ginny, the two of them together, in person, made her nauseous. They had never discussed Chris's relationship with Ginny—Chris never wanted to discuss it—but being in the same room as the two of them felt like a slap to the face. She reminded herself that she wasn't his girlfriend; she was the woman he paid to have sex with him.

"I could use a drink," she said.

"That sounds like a great idea." Patrick nodded. "Maybe it will loosen you up."

Or maybe it would help her forget the image of Chris and Ginny together, the platinum blonde staring adoringly up at Hollywood's most eligible bachelor.

———————————

By eleven-thirty, she'd had enough. She couldn't handle watching Ginny hang all over Chris, making a spectacle of herself and him, touching him everywhere, possessively, like she owned him or something. It had gotten to her so much that she'd resorted to keeping her back turned to them for the rest of the night. Relief flooded her when she saw Chris sneaking out a side door, alone.

She was done with Patrick. He forgot that Sofia was not his girlfriend; he kept putting his hands all over her—an arm around her waist, his hand on her thigh, holding her flush against his body. He refused to let her out of his sight again, keeping her close the rest of the night.

It wasn't until he was bent over the table, scribbling a check to the museum, that Sofia could pull out her phone and send a quick text message to Billy.

Come get me. Now.

Billy stepped through the door less than five minutes later, his presence putting a scowl on Patrick's face. Billy didn't approach them, merely stood at the entrance, arms crossed, watching.

"What is he doing here?"

"It's almost midnight. He's here to escort me out." She eased a step away, knowing Patrick wouldn't touch her with Billy nearby.

"I wanted to take you home," Patrick said, his fingers twitching against his thigh, eyes narrowed.

"You know it doesn't work like that, Patrick. I'm not going home with you and you are not taking me to my place."

"We could renegotiate…"

"No, we can't. In fact, I think it might be best if Georgia found a new girl for you. I'm not sure you and I are compatible. Now, if you'll excuse me?" Sofia turned and headed for the cloakroom, Billy falling in step behind her.

She hoped to make a quick exit, but the girl manning the coatroom had stepped away, a small "Back in five minutes" sign left on the counter to indicate her imminent return. Sofia set her bag down and propped a hip against the counter to wait, Billy a few feet away, leaning against the wall.

"Fancy running into you here," a familiar, obnoxious, squeaky voice said.

Sofia's shoulders sagged. So much for avoiding Ginny. It surprised her that the reality star bothered to speak to her; it wasn't like they'd ever been friends. They'd barely spoken when Ginny worked at Private Lives and never after she left.

"Ginny," Sofia sighed, turning around. "How are you?"

"Well, aren't you just the fakest person ever?" Ginny snorted.

Sofia had to bite her lip at that, especially coming from the spray-tanned, botoxed, fake blonde woman standing in front of her. She wasn't sure why she'd expected decorum, she'd forgotten that Ginny had none, and apparently, she had learned nothing in the last year since she'd left Private Lives.

"Did you want me to make a spectacle of myself like you do? Because it will not happen. Now, if you'll excuse me…"

Ginny put her arm out, stopping Sofia's attempt to go around her. "I see you still think you're too good for me, that you're somehow better than me? Well, who's laughing now? Did you see who I'm with, who I'm dating?"

"I don't care who you're dating," Sofia lied.

A loud guffaw came from the blonde, the sound piercing Sofia's ears. "Whatever. At least I'm not a prostitute."

Ginny hadn't changed at all. Same hideous personality, same horrid attitude. For the life of her, she couldn't understand why Chris dated her. Sofia leaned closer, her voice dropping to a whisper.

"Are you really going to act like an ass, here, in front of all these people you're trying so hard to impress? You know someone will see you and whoever that someone is, they will tell the press, or worse, they'll film it and leak it, and you'll come off looking ridiculous. I know what you're trying to do, Ginny, how you're desperately trying to prove to everyone how wonderful you are, how perfect you are, how you deserve whatever fame it is you've achieved. You sure the hell will not get it if anyone sees the real you. And you know it."

"You're a bitch, Sofia," Ginny hissed. "You always have been."

"At least I'm real," she snapped. "At least I'm not trying to be something I'm not." Sofia snatched her bag off the counter and spun around, head held high. Forget her coat. She'd buy a new one. "Come on, Billy. Let's go."

Sofia's phone was in her hand, Georgia's number pulled up before Billy closed the car door behind her.

"Sofia?" Georgia answered. "Are you okay?"

"I think you should find Patrick Garth another girl. He and I aren't...compatible."

"Are you sure?" Georgia asked. "He's a good client."

"He's also a jerk who can't keep his hands to himself," Sofia said. "I'm positive, Georgia. Find him someone else."

"I think Mr. Garth and I might have to have a chat about his contract before I do that. Speaking of contracts, that's the third client you've dropped in the last couple of months. What's going on? Are you going to quit on me?"

"Patrick was a favor to you, Georgie. It's not working out. I'm not quitting. I'm just...cleaning house. If I have fewer clients, I have more time for the ones I already have."

"You mean you'll have more time for Chris," Georgia said. "Oddly enough, he just sent a message. He was wondering if you were available?"

"Tonight? It's after midnight."

"I just got the email. He said he understands if you're not—"

"No, no. I'm available."

"I'll let him know," Georgia said. "I'll text you the details. Hey, are you sure you're okay? Was there anything else that happened? Anything you want to talk about?"

Sofia gritted her teeth. "No, I'm fine. Let Mr. Chandler know I'll be there within the hour."

She couldn't understand why Chris continued to see her; he and Ginny were all over every gossip magazine and website imaginable. Pictures of them constantly assaulted Sofia: out and about in the Los Angeles area, attending some fundraiser or gala, out to dinner, a basketball game, a movie premiere, a never-ending stream of press coverage that seemed directly aimed at her. Every new picture was like a punch to the gut.

They never talked about her. Chris never mentioned her, never said he had a girlfriend. But they had established a pattern, a pattern that Sofia was quick to pick up on. Chris always called her after going out with Ginny; no matter the time, the day, whatever, Chris would contact the service, and she would be ready. It was always crazy and intense, the sex mind-blowingly perfect, ranging from rough and quick to slow and sensual; she never knew what to expect. Sofia's worries about Chris being done with her were unfounded; they saw each other more than they ever had before.

An hour later, Billy pulled to a stop in front of the Westerfield and helped Sofia from the car. She checked her phone, surprised to see that Chris wasn't in their usual room, instead leaving instructions for her to talk to the concierge.

Sofia did as instructed, following the concierge's directions to the back of the hotel. She found Chris in a deserted, dark bar, sitting at the piano, tapping at the keys with his index finger, playing some nameless tune.

She weaved through the tables toward Chris and the piano, stopping behind him.

"I didn't know you played," she said, just loud enough for him to hear her.

Chris's hands fell to his lap as he turned to look at her over his shoulder. He still wore the tux from the fundraiser earlier in the evening, the bowtie undone, and the top button of his dress shirt, the jacket tossed over a nearby chair.

"I don't." He shrugged.

"Where's your date?" she asked, regretting it when Chris flinched, his eyes dropping to the floor.

"I ditched her," he explained. "Made some excuse about not feeling well."

"What is it with you two?"

"You know I don't like to talk about her," Chris said. "That topic is off the table."

"I know." Sofia sighed. "I'm sorry, but I can't help but be curious about her. Everywhere I look, I see photos of the two of you together. All the gossip sites claim you're a couple, that you're together. But when I ask you about her, you shut me down and refuse to talk about her. And you keep seeing me. Don't think I haven't noticed that you always call me right after you see her. Every time, Chris."

Chris shrugged, a frown on his face. "I said I don't want to talk about her." He shoved himself to his feet, stalked across the room, and sat at a low table next to a waist high stage lined with instruments. He picked up a drink from the edge of the stage and downed it in two swallows.

"I'm sorry," Sofia sighed. She slipped off her heels, snagged them with two fingers and set them on a chair, along with her purse, then she slowly walked toward Chris.

He watched her as she closed the distance between them; she didn't like the dark circles under his eyes, or the way his brow furrowed, or how the smile that flitted across his face didn't reach his eyes.

"I'm glad you called," she told him, one hip resting against the stage.

He didn't respond, just reached over, put his hands on Sofia's hips and pulled her in front of him. He dragged in a deep breath, ran his hands up her sides, his touch careful, gentle, his brilliant blue eyes flicking up to meet hers before he leaned over and rested his forehead on her stomach, squeezing her hips in his huge hands.

Sofia put her hand on the back of his head, the tips of her fingers brushing over the short hairs on his neck. He sighed and looked up at her as he ran his hands over the material covering her thighs and back, then he rose to his feet, ducked his head, and caught her lips in his, kissing her with a deep hunger.

A shiver of desire raced through her, goosebumps on her skin, warring with the heat coming from the man who had her trapped in the circle of his arms, kissing her breathless. She moaned in the back of her throat when he pulled away, but it died away when he scooped her up and set her on the stage.

Chris cupped her cheek, pushed her hair off her face, and kissed her again, his hands sliding down her sides to pull her toward him as he pushed open her knees and stepped between her legs. He pushed his hands under the hem of her short black dress, his hands on her thighs, a moan leaving him when he touched her bare skin, his lips sliding along her jaw and down her neck.

Sofia leaned back, balancing on her arms, Chris's hands caressing and touching her everywhere, tracing her spine, drifting across her breasts and down her stomach. He lifted her, pushing her farther onto the stage as he slid the silky material of her dress up her body and over her hips, bunching it at her waist. He eased her black panties down her legs, his lips trailing after them.

The first touch of his lips made her gasp, the feel of his breath blowing across her heated core made her body ache for more. The way he held her, the way he possessed her, made every nerve tingle with need. Sofia planted her feet on the edge of the stage, her knees falling open as Chris's tongue slid through her slick folds, a low hum rumbling through him.

He pushed forward, his tongue sliding deeper into her, his mouth closing over her, his fingers digging into her hips as he pulled her closer. Sofia scrambled for purchase on the smooth wooden stage, finally giving up and locking her hand around the back of Chris's head, clutching it so tight her knuckles ached.

Chris was ravenous, insatiable, eating her out like a starving man, his head moving from side to side, his tongue buried deep in her pussy, his nose pressed to her clit, small grunts of satisfaction coming from him as he devoured her.

God, the things this man did to her, the way he made her feel! It was indescribable, unbelievable. She lost track of how many times she orgasmed, one rolling into the other until it seemed like she was having one long, unending climax. She turned her head and pressed her arm against her mouth, desperate to hold back the filthy screams of decadent pleasure building in her throat.

Sofia couldn't move when he released her, completely spent. Chris yanked open his dress pants and pulled himself free. He slid a condom down his length, then he pulled her legs around his waist and entered her, a deep guttural moan leaving him as he buried himself inside of her.

Chris braced his hand on the edge of the stage, his hips moving in slow, tight circles, his mouth on Sofia's, licking at her lips, demanding entrance. She wrapped her arms around his neck and held on, letting the sensations take her, pure, unadulterated, intense pleasure winding its way through her veins, consuming her, overwhelming her.

He pushed her right up to the precipice, her body still wound tight from the earlier orgasms, his hard length brushing her sweet spot with every thrust. It wasn't long before her back arched and her body tensed, another wave of intense sensations washing over her.

Chris was right behind her, growling as he came, the sound rumbling through his chest, his hands tightening on her hips as his stuttered out of control. He buried his face in the crook of her neck, nuzzling her, holding her close, his breath tearing in and out of him, his own orgasm rushing through him.

He released her, pressed a kiss to her forehead, and took a step back. He pulled down the edge of her dress, covering her, then he tucked himself back into his pants before helping her off the edge of the stage. He took her hand, intertwining his fingers with hers, and with a gentle tug, led her from the bar.

Chapter Eleven

CHRIS

"Chris, she gets paid to act like she likes you, man," Seth reminded him. "You need to remember that."

"I know, but what if—"

"No buts or what-ifs, Chris. Sofia is an escort. Nothing about her is real. She's putting on a show, giving you what you want."

"You don't know what it's like when I'm with her. It feels like we could be a couple."

"But you're not," Seth said.

"Jesus, you're a killjoy," Chris huffed, switching his phone from one ear to the other.

"No, I'm your friend, and I'm watching out for you. I don't want you to get hurt. If you keep thinking Sofia has feelings for you, that she gives a shit about you for anything other than your money, you will get hurt. It's not real, brother. It's all an act."

"It feels real," he sighed.

"That means she's doing her job," Seth said. "Look, I gotta go find Alex. You okay?"

"No worse than when I called you."

"I'll see you in an hour, then you can yell at me face to face. Until then, try to chill."

"Easier said than done," Chris complained.

They said their goodbyes and he hung up, tossing his phone on the couch. There was no way he was going to chill. He couldn't get Sofia off his mind. He knew he was falling for her; all the signs were there: the inability to think about anything but her, the need to be with her constantly, everything about her consuming his every waking moment. He wanted her. Wanting her, needing her, it was getting worse. Week after week, the desire for her was turning into a monster he could no longer control. When he first started seeing her, he figured once or twice a month would be enough; he wouldn't need anything more. That was before they had sex, before he discovered that she calmed him like nothing else ever had before.

He knew he was in trouble when the urge to punch the trust fund brat feeling up Sofia had come over him. Patrick Garth was annoying on his best day; they'd had several run-ins, their circles occasionally crossing, and Chris had never liked him. He liked him even less knowing he was one of Sofia's clients. Every time he'd seen Patrick touch Sofia, he'd had to stop himself from crossing the room and rescuing her, like some kind of knight in shining armor.

This wasn't supposed to happen; he wasn't supposed to fall in love, not now, not when everything in his life was so complicated. He couldn't love someone who couldn't love him back. Like Seth said, she was doing her job. Being in love was nothing more than a pipe dream.

He pushed himself to his feet, patting Ollie on the top of his head as he passed him. He didn't have time to feel sorry for himself and the state of his love life. He had contracts to sign.

"Thank you for this." Chris hugged his best friend. "You know I can't sign a contract without you."

"I have been in L.A. for every major contract you've signed—*Hunting the Criminal*, that cartoon you did, your last movie, all of them. I wasn't about to miss this one. I'm your good luck charm."

"Yeah, well, I don't deserve you as a friend."

"I know you don't," Seth chuckled. "Besides, if I hadn't come, who would you go out and celebrate with after it's signed?"

Ginny stepped through the door, a huge grin on her face. "He could go out with me." She wrapped her arms around Chris's waist and rested her head on his arm. "The press would expect him to celebrate with his girlfriend slash co-star. How are you feeling, baby? Better?"

Chris extricated himself from Ginny's grip and moved out of her reach, easing into a chair on the other side of the table. "I'm fine. Thank you for asking," he said. "And you're not my girlfriend, Ginny."

"For all intents and purposes, I am your girlfriend," Ginny snarled, dropping into the seat across from him. "Everyone thinks we're an item."

"It's all for show," Chris snapped. "You know that as well as I do." He pushed a hand through his hair. "After I sign a major contract, I always celebrate with Seth. I'm not about to change that."

"I could tag along." She shrugged.

"That would be excellent press," Jack interjected, popping into the room, an enormous smile on his face. "Sorry, I overheard you guys. Ginny's right. She could tag along with you guys. The press would be phenomenal once we leak that you've signed the contracts. What do you think, Chris?"

"No."

Ginny and Jack both looked as if they had something to say about that response, but thankfully, Paul chose that moment to come in, followed by a petite brunette in a power suit. The brunette introduced herself as Magdalene, Ginny's agent. Once the introductions were over, she and Paul set the contracts on the table in front of them.

Chris's lawyer had already gone over his with a fine-tooth comb, standard procedure any time he agreed to do anything. He learned the hard way, back in his early twenties, that trusting your agent to have your best interests in mind wasn't a good idea. He knew what he was signing before they even put it in front of him.

He took the pen Paul offered him and signed where needed, tossed the pen on the table when he finished, sat back, and crossed his arms over his chest. Now that it was done, he and Seth could celebrate, and he knew just the place to go.

"What the hell is this bullshit?" Ginny shrieked.

"Jesus Christ," Seth said, sticking a finger in his ear and wincing. "That hurt."

"Right?" Chris snorted, rolling his eyes at Ginny's dramatics.

"Ginny, love, what's wrong?" Magdalene asked, her voice dripping with concern.

"This is for one movie," Ginny grumbled. "One. I thought I was the love interest in all the movies. What the hell is that all about? And what the fuck is this right here?" She tapped the paper in front of her and glared at Chris.

Magdalene leaned over Ginny's shoulder, looking where she pointed. She picked it up and read it, then she stood up and shot a dirty look at Chris. "What is this?"

"Why the hell is everyone looking at me?" he snapped.

Ginny's agent tossed the contract on the table in front of Chris. He pulled it close enough to read, skimming it until he found what was making everyone so upset.

If at any time during pre-production or filming, should the studio, the director, Mark Wilson and/or Ms. Etling's co-star,

> *Chris Chandler, decide that Ms. Etling is not fulfilling her role as the love interest, or if they feel that Mr. Chandler and Ms. Etling are not compatible or believable as love interests, then Ms. Etling's contract with Indigo Pictures will be terminated, and she will be paid the sum of $150,000.*

Chris put his hand over his mouth to hide a smile. He and Mark had discussed the possibility of Ginny not working out as his love interest, especially given the fact that most of the time Chris could barely tolerate being in the same room as her. Their fake relationship was getting harder to maintain, and when he found himself with no one to turn to who would discuss it with him, he'd gone to the movie's director. Neither of them was on board with the decision to cast her; in fact, Mark had been quite vocal about it. Chris had thought they couldn't do anything about it, but he was wrong.

"I had nothing to do with this," he said, pushing the contract back across the table. "What kind of power do you think I wield?"

"I'm not signing that," Ginny squeaked.

"Gin, it's okay." Magdalene patted her shoulder. "We'll get this straightened out. There has to be some mistake."

"Excuse me," Jack interrupted. "If you don't sign today, then the offer could be pulled."

Magdalene pulled her phone out, still glaring at Chris as she dialed, then she pressed her hand to her ear and hurried to the other side of the room, her voice raised in frustration.

"Chris." Ginny leaned over the table, her eyes flashing in anger. "You need to fix this."

Chris pushed himself to his feet and waved his hand over the papers on the table. "None of this is my doing," he said. "It's not my fault you didn't have the contract looked over sooner. It's a hard lesson to learn. Trust me. I know."

"You must have said something to someone," Ginny accused. "I know you did."

"You don't know shit," Chris growled. "Now, if you will excuse me, I'm going out with my best friend to celebrate. Seth, let's go."

He didn't bother to look back as he stalked from the room and down the hall, not stopping until he stood in front of the elevator.

"Alright, what the hell was that about?" Seth asked.

Chris stabbed repeatedly at the elevator button. "They put a clause in her contract that if we aren't compatible or if we're not believable as a couple, they can release her with a tiny paycheck."

"That's what she's freaking out about?" Seth laughed.

"Yeah," Chris chuckled. "God, I'm gonna send Mark a fifth of his favorite scotch."

"Did you know about it?"

"Nope but thank God he did it. And trust me, I am not complaining. Come on. Let's go to Harry's. I need a drink."

———————

Twenty minutes later, they were at Chris's favorite bar. Alex parked around back, promising to stay put in case Chris needed him. He and Seth headed inside, the two of them cutting through a small but tidy kitchen and a crowded storeroom before emerging inside a large room, one side dominated by a long, mahogany bar. There were tables scattered around and booths beneath the windows. One end of the bar held five pool tables, while the other sported a small stage, a jukebox, and a dancefloor. It was neat and clean, its only downfall the country music being piped in through the overhead speakers, something that Chris teased Harry about. It was quiet inside, deserted. Two waitresses sat in the corner, neither of which paid attention to them when they entered. Chris's friend Harry was behind the bar, greeting them with a wave as they came in.

"Well, if it isn't the infamous Chris Chandler." Harry smiled. "How are you, kid?"

Chris reached across the bar and shook Harry's hand. "Not too bad," he said. "Harry, you remember my buddy Seth."

Harry shook Seth's hand. "Nice to see you again, Seth." He turned his attention back to Chris. "So, since you're here, I'm guessing something big happened? New contract?"

"New contract." Chris nodded. "I promised my good luck charm here I'd get him a drink. Let's start with two beers."

"You got it." Harry nodded.

Chris and Seth sat at the bar, chatting with Harry, discussing Chris's new contract. He felt like maybe things were coming together. If things went his way, he wouldn't have to deal with Ginny any more after today.

Four beers and several shots later, he was feeling pleasantly buzzed and thoroughly enjoying himself. It was nice to be out in public without worrying about the press, which was the reason he had chosen Harry's. Harry had a strict "No Press" policy, one he adhered to no matter what. If he even thought someone might be a reporter, if he caught a whiff of someone asking questions they shouldn't be, he sent them packing. He also had some of the best security Chris had ever seen. It was one of the few places besides home where he could relax.

"You're all smiles," Seth said, setting a plate of nachos and another pitcher of beer on the table.

"Yeah, things feel like they're coming together," he nodded. "The movie contract—"

"The possibility that Ginny might bail on the movie," Seth laughed.

"There is that," Chris chuckled. "Now, if I could just get my love life straightened out."

Seth leaned forward and dropped his voice to a conspiratorial whisper. "You mean Sofia."

"Yes, I mean Sofia. If she and I could just get on the same page, things would be perfect."

"Why don't you tell her how you feel?" Seth asked.

"You say that like it's no big deal. You know why I don't tell her, dude. It wouldn't go well."

"You don't know that. Do you know what you should do? You should talk to Ingrid about it. Maybe she could give you some perspective. Or at least a fresh perspective. Maybe you'll listen to your therapist."

Chris waved him off. "Like I need somebody else telling me that what we have isn't real, that it's just a job to her."

"So, you want someone who'll lie to you?" Seth grunted. "That's stupid."

"Shut up and pour me another beer. I'm gonna call Paul and see if he knows what happened with Ginny and her contract."

Chris left Seth at the table, crossing to the other side of the bar. He leaned against one of the pool tables and pulled his phone from his pocket. Paul answered immediately.

"You disappeared awfully fast," Paul grumbled. "Thanks for leaving me to deal with your upset girlfriend."

"She's *not* my girlfriend," Chris snapped. "How many times do I have to tell you that?"

"For all intents and purposes, she is," Paul echoed Ginny's words. "And she's pissed. Did you have anything to do with that clause in her contract?"

"No," Chris snorted. "You think I have that kind of pull with the studio?"

Paul chuckled. "That's what I tried to tell Ginny. But she wasn't buying it. She's convinced you are the reason that clause is in her contract. Said you're not invested in the relationship."

Chris closed his eyes and pinched the bridge of his nose. An image of Sofia popped into his head. How could he date someone like Ginny when he had Sofia in his life? There was no comparison.

"Look, Paul," Chris sighed. "She knows I only tolerate her on my best days. Shit, I can't believe the press hasn't figured it out yet. I am not happy when I am with her. She's fake from head to toe, including her personality. I didn't insist on any kind of clause in the contract, but I'm sure the hell not going to argue about it. If the studio doesn't think we're convincing as a couple, that's on them. If Ginny doesn't like it, then she can negotiate with the studio."

"That's what she's doing," Paul said.

"And?"

"And nothing," Paul laughed. "The big draw for the studio is you. Ginny is a flash-in-the-pan as far as they're concerned. The only reason they wanted her for the movie was because she's hot shit right now. I think they're regretting that decision. It sounds like either she signs as is, or they find someone else. Period."

"Thank God."

"Go celebrate with Seth. I'll let you know how things go."

Chris disconnected the call, relief flooding him, bringing a smile to his face. For once, it was good news. Maybe now he could get rid of the albatross around his neck.

"Chris!" Seth raised the pitcher of beer over his head and pointed at it.

He waved at his best friend and smiled. Things were good. Now he just had to figure out how to deal with his growing feelings for Sofia, and all would be right with his world.

Easier said than done.

Chapter Twelve

SOFIA

One day bled into another and before Sofia knew it, she'd been seeing Chris for six months. The frequency of their dates had increased so much she considered dropping other clients to accommodate Chris's insatiable need for her. The closer it got to filming his new movie, the more she saw of him. Private Lives was good at juggling her schedule, sometimes scheduling her two dates a day, one with Chris and one with one of her other regulars. He became her most important client, a priority for her and for Private Lives.

Sofia adjusted her skirt and pushed her dark red hair out of her face. She'd worn blue, the color of Chris's eyes, the color of hers, his favorite color, *her* favorite color, a conscious choice, subtle, never discussed, never acknowledged, but one that Chris seemed to appreciate. She tapped on the door, looking over her shoulder and down the silent hallway, wondering if anyone had seen her. Force of habit. It wasn't long before the door opened, and she slipped inside.

"Hi," she whispered, smiling up at the man towering over her. Even at five feet, seven inches—more in her heels—Chris towered over her.

"Hi," Chris replied, pushing the door closed and leaning against it, his steel-blue eyes locked on hers.

Sofia let her lightweight jacket slide down her arms, dropping it, her purse, and the package she was carrying onto the chair as she sauntered past it. She poured herself a drink from the well-stocked bar, appearing calm and casual on the outside, but on the inside, she was a bundle of nerves. It was always like that when she met with Chris, without exception, even after all this time. She had to do everything in her power not to let him see her true feelings. She took a sip from the drink and stared right back at Chris.

"What's in the box?" He nodded at the package on the chair.

"A gift." Sophia shrugged.

Chris raised an eyebrow, a faint smile on his face. "Oh, really? You brought me a gift?"

"It's a thank you. Open it," she laughed.

He snatched the box off the chair, tore the colored paper off, and opened it. Sofia wanted to get him something special, something personal he would appreciate. It took her forever to decide on the bottle of Macallan Rare Case Scotch, and even after she bought it, she'd been unsure about giving it to him, even though she knew it was his favorite.

Chris shook his head, his eyes wide. "I can't accept this."

"I know it's...well, a personal gift, but I wanted to get you something...something that would express how I feel," Sofia whispered, her sapphire eyes locked on the floor, her fingers twitching against her leg. "You've been so...so kind and sweet. I wanted you to know how much I appreciate it. Please, it's not a big deal."

Chris set the bottle on the bar and slid his arm around Sofia's waist. He tugged her close, his nose brushing against hers, fingers tangled in her fiery red hair as he pushed it away from her face, a low hum leaving him.

"Thank you," he breathed.

"You like it?"

He nodded, brushing her cheek with the back of his hand. "I love it, Sof. Thank you."

He hugged her tight, her breasts pressed against his chest, then he plucked the glass from her hand and dropped it on the bar, the glass clanging against the metal top. He slid his hand up her arm, his fingers twisting in the thin strap of her dress, pulling it down her shoulder, his lips following it.

She tipped her head to the side, sighing as Chris's lips moved along her shoulder and up her neck, the beard he'd recently grown scratching her skin, burning, his desire marking her skin.

"You're fucking amazing, sweetheart," Chris murmured. "I don't know what I'd do without you."

Sofia ignored the lump in her throat and the tears stinging her eyes. She couldn't let her feelings for

Chris get the best of her. Not now. He needed this, needed her.

Her dress fell to the floor, Chris's hands on her waist, squeezing hard enough to bruise. He nipped at her lower lip, the sting making her eyes water and her heart pound. His mouth slanted over hers, the kiss consuming her.

He laid Sofia across the enormous bed, his hands all over her, his lips roaming over her bare skin. He suckled her breast, his tongue flicking at the nipple as he moved down her body, kissing her bare stomach, her hips, even her inner thighs, until his head was between her legs. He slid his hands beneath her, lifting her to meet his mouth, a groan leaving him as her taste flooded his mouth.

"Chris—" she gasped.

He ignored her, pulled her leg over his shoulder, braced his foot against the floor, and pushed forward, his tongue sliding deep into her, his forearm resting on her stomach, holding her down. One finger teased at her entrance, slipping in beside his tongue, twisting and crooking, grazing against her sweet spot, pushing her to the edge, her thighs trembling, beads of sweat breaking out across her body, everything on fire.

Chris was a diligent man, repeatedly pushing Sofia to the edge then backing off, working her over until she begged him to let her come. Just as she she was about to orgasm, he pulled away, rose to his feet, and stripped off his clothes, a condom in his hand. He opened it, the wrapper fluttering to the floor as he slid it down his throbbing length. He pulled her legs around his waist and eased into her, his lips on hers, kissing her until she couldn't breathe, her taste still on his tongue. He pumped his hips, every thrust taking him deeper, so deep Sofia could feel it in the pit of her stomach, feel it in every nerve, her body wound tight, a scream building in her throat. The length of his body was flush against hers, and she could feel *everything*, every stuttering breath, every tick of a muscle, all of it. Chris groaned, his forehead pressed to hers, the sound vibrating through her body. He grabbed her hands, pulling them over her head, securing them in one of his, holding them tight as he slammed into her. His exuberance pushed the air from her lungs, chased by a grunt, a grunt that Chris echoed, low and primal.

His long fingers dug into her soft skin, his blunt nails scraping over freshly bloomed goosebumps as he moved to cup her ass. Without warning, he tilted Sofia's hips so that with every thrust, the wide head of his cock dragged over her sweet spot.

Stars burst in her vision as she came, blinding her, as if she were witnessing a galaxy being born. Plush lips tickled her earlobe as he praised her, worshipped her body. Every obscene moan that fell from his perfect mouth was like throwing gasoline on the already raging inferno she could feel burning inside of her. The air was trapped in her throat, smothering the scream of his name; she thrashed on the bed, the blankets falling to the floor, the headboard slapping against the wall the harder Chris pounded into her.

He came with a snarl, his teeth bared and exposed, scraping her pulse point. Sofia collapsed to the bed, spent, Chris sprawled over her, his cock softening between her legs. He hugged her close, his lips drifting over her neck and chest, his fingers drawing circles on her sweat-slicked skin. She closed her eyes, enjoying the feel of lying in Chris's arms. She traced the curves of his muscles, wishing she could stay there forever.

His phone vibrated on the table across the room. Chris tensed, those muscles now hard and taut under Sofia's hands. He pushed himself off the bed and hurried to the bathroom, snatching his phone on the way by, the door slamming closed behind him. Sofia propped herself up on her elbows with a sigh, her wildly tousled hair falling over her face. Something was different; she couldn't put her finger on it, but after six months of seeing each other, Chris had inexplicably built a protective shell around himself, and she couldn't break through it.

By the time he came out of the bathroom, clad in a plain gray t-shirt and a pair of sweatpants, Sofia had dressed, put her jacket on, and brushed her hair. She clutched the black business card with gold lettering in her hand, the edges digging into her palm.

"Everything okay?" she asked.

He nodded, though he didn't meet her eyes. He scrubbed a hand over his face, crossed the room, and pulled a bottle of beer from the small refrigerator.

"Will I see you tomorrow?"

"I don't know yet. Filming starts this week." He shrugged, his eyes on the floor. He opened his mouth and closed it again before speaking. "I'll call." His blue eyes flashed with an emotion she couldn't decipher.

Sofia took a deep breath and stepped up next to him, only mere inches between them. She tried to ignore his crossed arms and off-putting posture as she held out the card.

He grabbed it, holding it gingerly between two fingers, sparing only a cursory glance at the front.

"I know how to get a hold of you, Sofia," he muttered, his blue eyes flashing.

She cleared her throat, her nerves making it hard to swallow, to talk. "The number on the back," she said, staring at her feet. "It's my cell phone number, in case you ever want to skip the escort service, and call me directly." She peeked at him from beneath her lashes.

Chris flipped the card over, one eyebrow raised, examining the number on the back far longer than necessary. Sofia was on the verge of snatching it out of his hand when he shoved it in his pocket, put his hand in the middle of her back, and guided her to the door. He opened it for her and pressed a kiss to her cheek, her cue to leave.

Her heart in her throat, Sofia gave him her best smile, patted his cheek, and stepped out of the room, the door swinging shut behind her with a loud and audible click.

"Damn it," she sighed, eyes falling closed, head lolling back and hitting the door.

Chapter Thirteen

CHRIS

"She did what?"

"She gave me her number," Chris repeated, waving the business card in front of the camera. He propped his phone against his computer so he could see his best friend, who was back in New York, while he plowed through the dozens of emails in his inbox.

"I'm confused. Don't you already have Sofia's number?" Seth asked. "How else would you get a hold of her?"

"I contact the service, either by phone or email," Chris explained. He flipped the card around and showed Seth the handwritten number on the back. "This is her cell phone number. Her private cell phone number. It's a direct line to her. No going through the middleman."

"Wait, can she do that?"

"No," Chris said. "All contact goes through Private Lives. I'm not allowed to have her phone number or her address."

"So, here's the real question. Is she trying to get you off the books so she can pocket all of the money, or…?"

"Or does this mean what I hope it means," Chris finished.

"What are you going to do?" Seth inquired.

Seth tried to act nonchalant, like he wasn't insanely curious how Chris would deal with this recent development, but he failed. Chris shrugged his shoulders and raked his hand through his hair.

"I don't know," he replied. "I haven't thought about it."

"You're a liar," Seth laughed. "You've thought about nothing else since the first time she slept with you and you know it."

"You're an ass," Chris grumbled.

"I'm just keeping it real," Seth said. "Speaking of which, did you ever talk to your therapist about any of this? I vaguely remember a half-drunk conversation that had something to do with you discussing your feelings for Sofia with Ingrid."

He rolled his eyes. What he hadn't told Seth was that he hadn't seen his therapist since he'd met Sofia. He discovered rather quickly that being with Sofia was more effective than seeing an expensive therapist once or twice a week. Sofia was all the therapy and medication Chris needed. He'd kept that to himself; he wasn't about to tell Seth that fucking the beautiful escort was the best therapy he could ever hope to find.

"Chris?" Seth prompted.

"I'll think about it, okay? That's all I can promise."

"That's all I ask."

He reached for his phone. "I gotta go." He sighed, punching the end button before his friend could protest.

As much as he needed someone to talk to, he also needed time to wrap his head around this strange development. And even though Seth was the only person in the world that knew about Sofia—though he was sure Alex suspected—Chris didn't feel like talking about it with his best friend. He knew Seth only had his best interests in mind, he always had, going all the way back to grade school. They'd had each other's backs through thick and thin; none of that had changed. Chris didn't think it ever would. He needed time to figure things out on his own.

His cell phone rang, pulling him from his musings.

"Yeah?" he answered.

"Mr. Chandler?"

"Alex? What's up?"

"I'm out front, sir. You're due at the studio in an hour."

"Shit, I forgot. Give me five minutes."

"Of course," Alex responded.

Chris was so caught up in his own head, wondering about Sofia, that he'd forgotten he was due on set for the first day of filming. He wasn't sure how he could forget something like that, but he had. He rushed through the house, grabbing things he might need, including his bag and Ollie's leash. Chris whistled for his dog, who came running, sliding to a stop beside him. Once he secured Ollie's leash, they hurried outside. Alex met them at the car, stopping to pet Ollie before opening the door and ushering them inside.

Thankfully, he arrived on set with time to spare. Mark Wilson, the director, greeted him with a smile, showed him to his trailer, and introduced him to the young man who would be his assistant during filming, Theodore.

"I'll see you in a half an hour," Mark said as he stepped out of the trailer, waving over his shoulder.

"Theodore, this is Oliver, Ollie for short," Chris said, letting the dog off his leash. "One of your responsibilities as my assistant will be to keep an eye on him. I always bring him to set unless I'm out of the country. He's well-trained and easy to get along with."

Ollie sat on the floor in front of Theodore, staring up at the young man, his tail wagging. Theodore knelt in front of him and scratched behind his ears, murmuring about what a good boy he was.

"See, you guys are already good friends," Chris laughed.

"He's great, Mr. Chandler. I love dogs."

"Call me Chris. And it's a damn good thing you like dogs; otherwise, this wouldn't work. So, tell me about my day."

"Yes, sir." The young man leapt to his feet. He pulled his phone from his pocket and began going through Chris's schedule.

Once they'd gone through his schedule and discussed a few basics, day-to-day things that Chris would expect of his new assistant, he headed to the makeup trailer. As soon as they stepped outside, one of the AD's stopped them and told him sit tight. When Chris asked why, the only answer he got was that there had been an "unexpected development" delaying the start of the day.

Curious, Chris headed toward the building where they would be shooting, after telling Theodore to stay put with Ollie. He slipped in a side door and walked past several stacks of boxes, sticking to the shadows, following the sound of raised voices. He stopped at the end of a long hallway. In the distance, he could see the director, Mark, and Magdalene, Ginny's agent.

"So, this is how we're starting out?" Mark said tersely.

"She's on her way. She's thirty, maybe forty-five minutes out," Magdalene replied.

"She's late. On the first day of filming. She better have a damn good excuse for costing us a hundred thousand dollars."

"I'm sure there's a good reason, Mark."

"You better talk to her, Mags. I'm not doing this with her. I was assured there wouldn't be any of her shit while on my set."

"There won't be. Don't worry. I'll talk to her. I promise."

Magdalene turned and hurried away with her cell phone pressed to her ear. Chris waited until she was out the door before he emerged from the shadows.

"Mark!"

"Jesus Christ," the director sputtered. "What the hell?" He swung around, laughing under his breath when he saw Chris. "Good lord, what are you doing lurking back there?"

"Sorry," Chris mumbled. "What is going on? What are we waiting for?"

Mark sighed and scrubbed a hand over his face. He shot a glance over his shoulder before turning back to Chris.

"We're waiting for Ginny. She's...well, she's running late."

"Shocker," Chris smirked. "You know, she's a pain in the ass."

"I know." Mark nodded. "I've heard the rumors—difficult to work with, bitchy, a diva, demanding—you name a pain in the ass move, she does it. Trust me—she wasn't my first choice. Shit, she wasn't my hundredth choice. Which you already know. I don't control the dough though, so I gotta do what I gotta do. I was lucky to get that clause in about your compatibility."

"I was wondering how you did that."

"I begged. They wouldn't put anything in about her being difficult, or chronically late, or anything else I fucking wanted. I only got that because the author made a big deal about how important it was that whoever they cast as Nico's love interest better be believable. Fortunately, she's thrilled with you and not so thrilled with Ginny. It was a concession to keep her happy." Mark checked his watch. "I swear to God, I'm praying she loses us a shit ton of money so the studio steps in and fires her. It's a fucking nightmare, and we haven't even started shooting yet." He clapped Chris on the shoulder. "Go to makeup. I'm gonna go rearrange the schedule so we can get something done." He spun around and walked off, muttering under his breath.

Chris shook his head and made his way back to his trailer. Things were off to a splendid start.

By the time they started filming for the day, Chris was in a shitty mood after sitting around for over three hours waiting for Ginny to arrive, then waiting for her to get into hair and makeup, and finally, waiting for her to "get in her character's headspace."

Filming started off slow and never picked up. Ginny didn't know her lines; in fact, Chris wasn't even sure she'd looked at the damn script. Their first scene together took twenty-seven takes and even then, it didn't feel right. Mark called it a day before they could start the twenty-eighth take. His anxiety at an all-time high, Chris stalked off set and headed for his trailer.

"Chris! Chris, come back here!"

He glanced over his shoulder to see Ginny following him. He ignored her, sprinting up the steps and into his trailer. Ginny caught the door before it could close, yanking it open and following him inside.

"What the fuck was that?" she snapped.

Chris glared at her and turned to Theodore, who was sitting at the table, Oliver by his feet. "Theo, will you excuse us?"

The young man nodded and hurried from the trailer, eyes down.

Chris waited until the door had closed behind his new assistant before he dropped to the couch, his hands clenched, tucked under his arms so Ginny wouldn't see them shaking. "What the fuck was what?"

"That was shit, Chris," she snapped. "Zero fucking chemistry."

"You're not wrong." He shrugged. "You're surprised? There wasn't shit for chemistry when we did the table read, or when we rehearsed it last week. The chemistry between us is nil. I know it. Mark knows. The only people oblivious to it are you and the fucking studio."

"So, whatever the problem is, we need to fix it."

"I'm not sure we can fix this." It was hard to have chemistry with a woman he despised.

"Bullshit. I'm not losing this job because you're a shitty actor who can't pretend to have chemistry with someone."

Chris kept his mouth shut, knowing if he opened it, nothing good would come out. He shrugged again, mouth closed so tight his jaw ached, arms crossed over his chest. He would not get dragged into this argument.

"That's it? You have nothing else to say?" Ginny rolled her eyes. "Guess you're a worse actor than I thought."

"You're one to talk, Gin," he scoffed, rising to his feet. "You're not even a real actress." The words fell from his mouth before he could even think to stop them.

The slap was hard, rocking his head to the side, his eyes watering.

With his fists clenched at his sides, Chris pulled in a deep breath, composing himself before he spoke. "I was good enough to make the press think I liked you."

She screamed in frustration, her face twisted in anger, and spun around, stumbling in her high heels, leaving the door open as she stomped down the stairs. Chris blew out a breath he hadn't realized he was holding and fell to the couch. He pulled his phone from his pocket and texted Alex to bring his car around.

An hour and a half later, he and Ollie were home. The dog plopped down in his dog bed and fell asleep, but Chris couldn't relax. The argument with Ginny kept playing on a loop in his head, every replay ratcheting his nerves up another notch. His skin was crawling and the voices in his head were screaming at him. He tried to sit down, tried to relax, but he found himself up and pacing around the room ten seconds later. He emptied his pockets, tossing everything on the coffee table in front of him. His wallet hit the floor, and everything spilled out, the black Private Lives business card he'd tucked inside staring up at him. He picked it up and turned it over, Sofia's private number staring up at him.

He didn't hesitate, didn't think twice about what he was doing. He just snatched his phone off the table and dialed. It broke protocol, calling her private number; it went against the carefully established rules, but he needed her, needed her before the voices in his head drowned out everything else. She wouldn't have given it to him if she didn't want him to call.

"Hello?"

The sound of her voice put him at ease, and he felt like he could breathe for the first time all day.

"Sof? It's Chris."

"Hey, hi!"

"Can I...can I see you?" He knew he was begging, but he didn't care. "Whatever I need to do to see you. Right now. I'll do it. I just...I need you."

"Are you okay?"

"No, Sof. No, I'm not."

"You can come to my place. I'll text you my address."

Five minutes later, he was in the car, Sofia's address programmed into the GPS. He had the gas pedal to the floor, his hands tight on the wheel, the car hugging the curves as he sped through the hills to his destination. The voices in his head were getting louder, barely held in check, his fingers twitching, his heart pounding, his anxiety off the charts.

Chris slowed the car, following the GPS right to her door. He parked in the driveway of a small condo, taking in his surroundings as he made his way to her front door. It was a quiet neighborhood, about twenty minutes out of downtown Los Angeles, the perfect place to escape. He reached the door, took a deep breath, and knocked three times.

The door opened. "Hi," Sofia breathed.

His heart hammered in his chest as he drank her in. She was wearing a pair of boy shorts and a tank top that hugged her curves, her face scrubbed clean of makeup, her long red hair pulled back in a loose ponytail. She looked beautiful. Chris pulled her into his arms, not even giving her a chance to shut the door before his lips were on hers, the kiss instantly calming him. She brushed her fingers through his hair, a soft smile on her face.

"You okay?" she whispered.

"No." Chris shook his head. He kissed her again, savoring the feel of her in his arms, the taste of her on his lips. He broke off the kiss with a heavy sigh. "I'm sorry about this." He was sorry for showing up at her door, desperate and needy.

"Don't be sorry," she murmured. "Come here." She took his hand and led him through the house to a stylishly decorated living room dominated by a large leather sofa. One light burned in the corner, a sketchbook sat beside a can of multicolored pencils, and a steaming mug of something spicy was on the coffee table. She pointed at the couch, silently ordering him to sit. He didn't argue.

Sofia sat next to him, snuggled up against his side, and pulled a lightweight blanket over her legs. He turned toward her, his hand on her waist, tugging her closer, not wanting an inch of space between them. The voices were screaming again, making him wince, making his eyes screw shut. He rested his forehead on her shoulder, dragging in one deep breath after another, afraid he would lose it.

"You didn't call the service." It wasn't a question.

"I couldn't wait," Chris explained. "I needed to see you." He squeezed his eyes shut and tried to ignore the rapid thump of his heart in his chest. "Are you angry?"

"What?" She sounded shocked. "No, I'm not angry. I'm glad you're here."

The words tumbled out of him, so fast he could stop them, even if he'd wanted to. "I can't think, Sof. My head, the voices, when the stress gets to be too much, when I'm feeling anxious, those voices scream at me. They scream at the top of their lungs. Nothing makes them stop, nothing. Until I met you. When I'm with you, the voices are quiet. I can think when I'm with you. You make it better."

He exhaled and turned his head enough to press a kiss to the side of her neck, her pulse beating beneath his lips. He pushed her onto her back, one hand sliding up her side, his fingers dancing over her ribs, caressing the underside of her breast, his mouth closing on the juncture between her shoulder and neck, his teeth scraping the skin, marking her.

Sofia moaned, arching into his touch, her fingers twisting in his t-shirt, one leg hooking around his calf, pulling him closer. He nestled himself between her legs, one hand under her ass, tipping her hips up to meet his, rocking forward, his cock already hard and aching for her, her body responding to his every touch. Chris caressed her breasts over the top of the tank top, his thumb circling her nipple, bringing it to a hard peak, drawing a needy groan from her. He peeled her clothes from her body, savoring every second she was in his arms, every sound she made, every touch, a greedy sigh leaving him when he sank into her, her warmth surrounding him.

Chris took his time, drawing it out, keeping her on the edge for so long, he lost track of time, his entire being consumed with Sofia and the way she felt in his arms, the way she moved, the way she smelled, the sounds she made as he touched her. God, he wanted her, wanted to own her, devour her, take her and show her she belonged to him.

It was so wrong, but it was also so right. It was all jumbled up in his head, making him want to scream. He knew he should let her go, but he wanted her, needed her more than he'd ever thought possible. But he was just a client, nothing more. He could never have her, not the way he wanted. None of this was real, not to her anyway. She was playing a part. This would have to be enough.

Chapter Fourteen

SOFIA

Sofia didn't know what time Chris left; they fell asleep on her couch, wrapped around each other, his face buried against the side of her neck, his breathing steady. He woke her up when he struggled to sit up, perched on the edge of the couch by her feet and pulled his shirt and shoes back on. He kissed her goodbye, clinging to her, breaking away with a groan, his features pinched. She walked him to the door, their hands loosely clasped. He brushed her hair away from her face, kissed the center of her forehead, murmured a thank you, and left.

It was the first time she'd been with Chris and not felt like an escort. It felt *real*.

She returned to the living room, threw herself on the couch, and pulled the blanket around her shoulders, the smell of Chris's cologne surrounding her.

Sofia closed her eyes and took a deep, shuddering breath, snuggling deeper into the warmth of the blanket. She wanted nothing more than to lie there and relive the last few hours with Chris. They'd never slept together, real honest-to-God *sleep*, the two of them snuggled together under one blanket. Chris never seemed comfortable enough, calm enough, to allow himself to sleep with her. But something had changed all of that, something he didn't want to talk about. He'd only wanted her, wanted to kiss her, touch her, feel her in his arms. She'd happily given him what he wanted, and she asked for nothing in return.

Her heart thundered in her chest, her palms sweating and her thoughts racing a mile a minute. She couldn't read too much into Chris's visit; she refused to believe it meant anything, or that his unexpected visit meant he cared about her. Believing any of that could only mean a broken heart.

Maybe it was time to end this, walk away from Chris before it was too late, and she was too far gone. Her gut wrenched at the thought, bile rising in the back of her throat, telling her it was too late; she was already too far gone. She didn't think she *could* walk away.

She squeezed her eyes closed, trying to get the picture of Chris sleeping beside her out of her head.

"Don't get involved. Don't get emotional. Don't bring the job home," she whispered.

Don't fall in love.

It was too late.

She never meant to fall for one of her clients, for things to go this far. It wasn't like she hadn't told herself repeatedly over the last two months she *wasn't* falling for Chris. Falling in love scared her to death. For three years, she'd lived by her self-imposed rules, refusing to allow herself to get emotionally involved with a client. But it had happened; she fell in love.

Exactly what she hadn't wanted to do.

"Get up."

Sofia raised her head, the bright light sending pinpricks of pain into the center of her brain. Overwhelmed by her feelings for Chris and feeling sorry for herself, she'd hid in her dark room all day with the blinds drawn, examining her life choices and trying to figure out how she'd let things go so far, how she had let herself get so attached to a client, how she'd been so stupid.

Sasha had shown up after Sofia ignored her phone calls, using her key to unlock the front door. She flipped on the light in Sofia's bedroom, mumbled a few choice expletives under her breath, dragged the blankets off Sofia, and insisted she get out of bed.

"I don't want to," Sofia grumbled, glaring at her best friend.

"Sof, you're a mess," Sasha said. "I've never seen you like this. What is going on?"

"I don't want to talk about it," Sofia insisted. "I want to hide in the dark."

"Get your ass out of bed. You get in the shower, and I'll make you something to eat."

"I don't want to eat—"

"Yes, you do," Sasha cut her off. "Now move it."

There was no use arguing with Sasha; Sofia wouldn't win. Sofia dragged herself out of bed and took a quick shower before making her way downstairs. As soon as she hit the bottom of the stairs, she smelled bacon and heard the telltale sound of a knife on the cutting board. In the kitchen, she found Sasha at the stove making omelets and a full cup of coffee sitting on the counter. She eased onto the barstool and took a sip from the warm mug. She closed her eyes and rubbed the center of her forehead.

"Talk," Sasha ordered.

"I can't," Sofia sighed. "It's about a client."

"A client has you hiding under the blankets on your bed? What happened?"

"Sasha, you know I can't discuss it." Sofia scrubbed a hand over her face.

Sasha dropped the spatula in the pan, runny egg splashing all over the stove and counter, and spun around. She leaned over the counter; her fiery Russian temper ignited.

"That's bullshit, Sof, and you know it," she spat, slapping the counter. "I am your friend, and I am worried about you. Talk to me."

Tears sprang to Sofia's eyes and her heart double-clutched in her chest. Holding all of this in, trying to stay professional, it weighed on her in ways she hadn't thought possible.

"Have you heard of Chris Chandler?"

Sasha shrugged. "Who hasn't? He's gorgeous, funny, famous, loves the New York Mets, has that cute dog named Ollie, and...Oh my god, Sof, is he your client?"

Sofia nodded.

"What did he do to you?" Sasha growled like an angry kitten. If Sofia hadn't been drowning in her own sorrows, she would have laughed.

"He didn't *do* anything, Sash." She sighed. She propped her head in her hands and exhaled. She looked at Sasha through the strands of red hair hanging in her eyes. "This stays between us, right? You cannot breathe a word of this to anyone. Ever."

Sasha drew an X on her chest. "I promise."

Sofia launched into a quick rundown of her first meeting with Chris, her initial refusal to sleep with him, their dates, and her decision to break her own rules and have sex with a client. As she talked, she saw the realization dawning in her best friend's eyes. When she finished, she folded her hands in her lap, squeezing them tight, and waited.

"You're in love with him," Sasha stated.

She opened her mouth to speak, but a heart-broken sob burst out of her. She put her head down on the counter and let it out. All the emotions she'd been holding in check for the last six months poured out of her. Sasha slid into the seat beside her, put her arms around her, and let her get it all out.

When it was over and she was down to snuffling and wiping her face with the back of her hand, she couldn't look Sasha in the eye.

"I am unbelievably in love with him," she whispered. "I've never felt like this before, never. I don't know what to do."

"Have you talked to Georgia?" Sasha asked.

"And tell her what?" Sofia laughed. "That one of her biggest money makers has fallen in love with a client? That I want to quit my job and run off into the sunset with someone I get paid to sleep with? As good as Georgie's been to me, I don't think she'll take kindly to that news."

"What about Chris?"

"What about him? I'm an escort, Sash. Chris pays me to be his companion. And one thing he likes about our relationship—if you can even call it that—is that it's out of the spotlight. No one in his life knows I exist. I don't think he's going to want to make it official. That would be an interesting read, don't you think? I can see it now: *Chris Chandler Marries Former Hooker.* Yeah, that'll go over well."

"What are you going to do?" Sasha murmured.

"I don't know," Sofia sighed.

"Maybe you should stop seeing him," her friend suggested.

Just thinking about breaking up with Chris made her head hurt and fresh tears sting her eyes. She shook her head, her damp hair falling across her face. She exhaled and shrugged, the tears sliding down her cheeks.

"I can't," she whispered. "Chris needs me."

Sasha shook her head and pushed herself to her feet. She picked up the spatula and flipped the omelet in the pan, ignoring the mess she'd made. She glanced at Sofia out of the corner of her eye, her face pinched.

"Loving someone who doesn't return that love hurts, babe. Trust me, I know. You better get ready to hurt. Nothing good will come of this. I can promise you that."

Chapter Fifteen

CHRIS

"Hold on!"

Chris finished typing the message to Sofia then he shoved his phone in his pocket. He was due on set in an hour, so it was probably Theo or one of the production assistants pounding on his trailer door. He scratched Ollie's head and pushed himself to his feet, stretching to ease his aching muscles.

"Chris? Can we talk?"

He froze, cringing at the whiny squeak of Ginny's voice. He'd avoided her all day, only speaking to her when he was on set and if it was a necessity. It was a rough day, and it was only going to get worse, especially with the pivotal love scene coming up. Thinking about it made Chris's stomach churn.

Chris took a deep breath and pushed a hand through his hair before yanking open his trailer door.

Ginny stood on the step, her hair and makeup impeccable, a pink and purple striped robe covering her from neck to knee. She gave him a tight smile.

"Hi," she whispered.

"What do you want, Ginny?"

"Can I talk to you for a minute?"

"I'm not sure there's anything to talk about," he said.

"Please?" Ginny begged.

Chris held the door open and gestured for her to come inside. He shut it behind her and hastened to the other side of the room, out of her reach. The thought of her touching him made his skin crawl.

Ginny took a tentative step forward, a dejected look on her face. "I wanted to apologize to you. I never should have slapped you. I...I was frustrated and angry, and I took it out on you. Can't we just put it behind us and make up?"

"Make up? What's that supposed to mean?"

"Why don't we go out? Give the press some shots of us getting along? Maybe a romantic dinner, a walk on the beach snuggled together, something like that. Our fans are begging for it. Let's give them what they want. Show them we're still a couple."

"We're not a couple. You know that, right? You know that this entire *relationship* is a giant farce, don't you?" Chris used finger quotes when he said relationship, hoping to emphasize the fact that it wasn't real.

"I don't know." Ginny shrugged. "I thought we were having a good time. I thought maybe, if we spent enough time together, maybe it would eventually be real. You're telling me you don't have any feelings for me at all?"

"I have no feelings for you, Ginny. This has been one giant joke from the beginning. Jack pressured me into it, and trust me, I regret every minute. It's over."

To his surprise, Ginny's eyes filled with tears, her mouth falling open in shock. She took a step back and dropped into the chair behind her.

"God, you're an asshole, you know that?" She sniffled. "I came here, ready to put all that other stuff behind us and instead you're...you're..."

"I'm breaking up with you, for lack of a better term," he said firmly. "This is over. I'm tired of pretending I like you when I can't even tolerate being in the same room as you."

Theo came through the door right then, the smile on his face fading when he saw Ginny.

"I-I'm sorry. Mr. Chandler, I came to tell you you're wanted on set, and I was going to walk Ollie. Do you, uh, do you want me to tell Mr. Wilson you're busy?"

"Absolutely not," Chris said, snatching Ollie's leash off the table and whistling for his dog. "Let's go." He attached the leash to Ollie's collar and opened the door. "Ginny?" He nodded at her, indicating she come with them.

She pushed herself to her feet with an irritated huff and stomped down the stairs, refusing to look at either him or Theo as she hurried away from them toward her trailer.

"Um, is she okay, Mr. Chandler?" Theo asked. "She seems kind of angry."

"Oh, she's furious. So furious, in fact, that I will probably regret it later." He sighed, shook his head, and handed off the leash to his assistant. "Take Ollie for a walk, kid. I need to talk to Mark."

Chris paced back and forth, clenching and unclenching his hands, checking his watch every few minutes. He'd called the service two hours ago, and Sofia still hadn't arrived. He passed the window, stopping long enough to glance outside, but the trees and bushes completely obscured the sidewalk leading up to the bungalow, burying the small building in shadows.

When his pacing brought him full circle for the fifth or sixth time, he forced himself to stop, grabbed the bottle of beer from the table, and took a long drink. He exhaled, closed his eyes, and rubbed a hand over his bearded face, trying to calm his racing thoughts.

He'd been on edge ever since the "breakup" with Ginny three days earlier. Not that it was really a breakup; it was more like the end of the charade. Ginny had been hell to work with ever since, moping around set and crying at the drop of a hat. She'd called Jack and ratted Chris out, forcing him to endure a twenty-minute ass chewing from his manager. Ginny hadn't let up, even making several posts on her social media hinting that her heart was broken, and Chris was responsible. He did his best to ignore her, but the pressure weighed on him.

After two full days of misery and dealing with Ginny, he escaped the set. He felt like a prisoner, trapped and tortured. His first phone call had been to the hotel to reserve the bungalow, and the second call had been to Private Lives. He'd blown off Alex and driven himself to the hotel. It was damn near an eternity before he received a text back from the escort service, confirming his appointment with Sofia.

Chris didn't know why his need to see Sofia was so all-consuming. It wasn't the sex; they'd done that plenty of times. It was something deeper. Something was changing. He desperately wanted to give in to it, to say fuck it and let it take over, while another part of him fought those feelings, trying to push them down and away, out of sight, out of mind. He couldn't let it take over—he couldn't.

The knock on the door sent him stalking across the room and flinging it open. Sofia's fiery, copper red hair blew back in the breeze the door created, her sapphire eyes widening as her plush pink lips formed an 'O' of surprise. Chris grabbed her wrist and yanked her inside, pinning her to the wall in time with the door slamming closed.

"Fuck," he growled. "I thought you'd never get here."

His mouth swallowed anything she might have said, his tongue dancing against hers. He ran his hands over her, finding her body pliant and surrendering under his touch. Chris popped the button open on her shorts and eased down the zipper, then he pushed them down, dropping to his knees in front of her, dragging the shorts off and tossing them aside. He pushed her shirt up, his lips drifting over her stomach as he dipped a finger in the front of her lace panties, pulling them down.

The first taste of her on his tongue made him moan, his fingers digging into her ass as he cupped it, pulling her closer. God, he needed her, needed to taste her, touch her, experience her. Days away from her felt more like weeks. Any time away from her was too much time. They'd been apart too long. The voices in his head were already quieting, her presence enough to calm his frazzled nerves. Sofia was all he needed.

Chris's mouth covered her, his tongue circling her sensitive nub, every fiber of his being working to get her off. He lost himself, utterly consumed with giving her as much pleasure as he could, getting her to scream his name, the sound like a symphony of bells clearing the noise away. His hunger for her was insatiable, his desire to ruin her for all other men overwhelming him, making him crazy. She belonged to him and him alone.

"Chris," she gasped, a shudder shaking her from head to toe as an orgasm rocketed through her. Her nails dug into his wrist, and her head hit the wall when she threw it back.

He worked her through it, holding her as she came undone, grunts of pleasure coming from him, his palm pressed against the erection attempting to burst from his jeans. She collapsed in his arms, the two of them falling to the floor, his arms around her, holding her tight. She was panting, one arm thrown over her eyes, a faint smile on her face.

"Wow," she murmured. "That was quite the greeting."

Chris chuckled and pressed a kiss to her cheek. Sofia rolled to her side, her head resting on her arm, her hand on his cheek.

"You still have the beard," she said, her nails scratching the short hairs.

"My character has a beard," he replied. "You don't like it?"

Sofia kissed him, cutting him off as she threw a leg over him, straddling him, her hands on his chest, pushing him to his back. He cupped her head in his hands, deepening the kiss, savoring the moment. But when she moved to unbutton his pants, he grabbed her wrists, stopping her.

"What?" she asked. "What's wrong?"

"Nothing." Chris shrugged. "I just...I'm good." He couldn't bring himself to tell her that this time it wasn't about the sex; it wasn't about him getting laid. It was about shutting down the voices screaming in his head, something only she seemed to be able to do.

Sofia tilted her head to the side, an adorable confused look on her face. It only made him want her more. He sat up, his arms sliding around her, his lips finding hers. He held her, kissing her, letting the quiet wash over him. When he was with her, it was about them, not Hollywood, not his money, not his status— single or taken. He didn't need the sex; he didn't need to fuck her. All he needed was her.

"Your car's here?" Chris asked, rolling to his side and propping himself on his elbow so he could look at her. She was a feast for his eyes, beautiful in any state, even with her messy hair, makeup smudged beneath her eyes, kiss-swollen lips, and sapphire blue eyes blown wide with lust.

Sofia nodded as she typed something on her phone, then tossed it back to the table and rose to her feet. She ran her fingers through her hair, the strands mussed and tangled from her time spent with him. She grabbed her clothes from the floor on the way to the bathroom and closed the door quietly behind her.

Chris snagged his jeans from the floor and yanked them on, muttering under his breath to himself. He and Sofia had spent the last three hours in bed, and it had been unbelievable. He'd done things to her that made her scream his name, made her come undone over and over until she'd passed out in his arms. He'd kept her snuggled against his side for the last hour, half asleep. They hadn't talked, and he had demanded nothing in return. The only thing he'd wanted was to keep her close to him. She'd seemed happy to oblige.

"Shit," he mumbled. "Shit, shit, shit." The one thing he hadn't wanted to happen was happening. He was falling for Sofia, and if he was being honest with himself, he didn't care. In fact, he kind of liked the idea.

He took a step toward the bathroom door, maybe to tell her, maybe to chase her away—he wasn't sure which—but his phone chose that moment to ring.

Chris yanked it from his pocket, grumbling under his breath when he saw who it was. He ignored it, like he'd been doing for days, hitting the dismiss button and dropping it to the table, but it started again almost immediately, an annoying, incessant "answer me now" ring. He snatched it off the table.

"Hello." Chris knew he sounded short, curt, irritated, but he didn't care.

It was Ginny. It was always Ginny. He couldn't get away from her, even after telling her it was over. He did his best to keep his voice even and neutral as he listened to her prattle on, begging him to reconsider, begging him to give her a chance to prove that she could be the girlfriend she needed. Her voice grated on his nerves, making him wince as her volume increased, her words slurring. He suspected she was drunk.

"I'm so sorry," she whined. "Can't we try again? Please? We could go to that fundraiser together, the one coming up next week. We were supposed to go anyway. We could start fresh, try again without our managers or the press involved. Just the two of us. Please, love, I'm begging you."

God, he hated it when she called him love. It sounded so fake coming out of her mouth. Everything that came out of her mouth sounded fake.

"No, Ginny," he replied, emotionless. "We've talked about this. I'm done. I'm not playing the game anymore." He cleared his throat and glanced at the closed bathroom door, an idea forming.

Ginny said something else, a note of irritation creeping into her voice, but he had already pulled the phone away from his ear and hit the end button before the words were out of her mouth. Chris clutched his phone in his hand, the idea now becoming a plan as he paced in front of the bathroom door, raking a hand through his dark blonde hair, waiting for Sofia to emerge.

She jumped when she found Chris standing right outside the door, her blue eyes flashing with curiosity. She squinted, looking him over carefully.

"You okay?" she asked.

"Yeah. Uh, hey, before you go," he mumbled, "can I, um, ask you something?" He took her hand, pulling her close, brushing a kiss across her lips.

Sofia smiled up at him. "What is it?"

"I've got this thing, a charity thing, that I have to attend next week, and I was wondering if you wanted to go with me? It's a big formal event in Beverly Hills for one of my favorite charities. I have to go, and I thought you might like to be my date. Is it even okay for me to ask you, or should I call the service? Fuck, I don't know. Is this stupid? I'm not sure you'll want to go. Hell, you're probably busy. And, I mean, it could be lame, or I don't know, really stupid, shit, or fun, who fucking knows, but anyway, I need a date and I figured I'd ask you." Chris rubbed a hand over his face, sighing. "I'm literally verbal vomiting here, Sofia. Sorry." He released her and stepped back, shaking his head.

"No apology necessary." Sofia reached out and put a hand on his arm. "I'd...I'd love to go with you."

"Yeah?" He grinned.

Sofia nodded. "Yes, definitely yes." She cleared her throat, and, for some reason, she wouldn't meet his eyes. "But, um, what about Ginny?"

"Ginny?"

"Your girlfriend?" Sofia said helpfully.

"She's not my girlfriend," he snapped. As soon as the words were out of his mouth, he regretted the tone he'd used with her.

"What about all of those dates? The pictures of the two of you plastered all over the internet? It looks like you're dating," Sofia argued.

"Do I look happy in any of those photos?" Chris asked, shaking his head, trying to clear it of the demons shouting in it. He grabbed Sofia's hand and squeezed it tightly. "Look, Gin is *not* my girlfriend. She's a…colleague, I guess. Nothing more. And she doesn't get to decide who I date. No one decides who I date—not anymore. I want to take you, Sofia."

The smile returned, her eyes bright and shining. "And I want to go with you, Chris."

Chris's chest loosened, air filling his lungs, flowing in and out. He nodded and scratched the back of his neck. "I wasn't sure you'd say yes."

Sofia shook her head and looked away. "How could I say no?"

For a split second, Chris thought he saw a sheen of tears in her eyes. Probably just his imagination or a weird trick of the light.

"I'll call you," he said. "Not the service. You. I've got your number, remember?"

She grinned, a blush coloring her cheeks a delicate shade of pink. She pushed up on her toes and kissed him, a long, lingering kiss. Chris grabbed her, holding her flush against his body, wishing she didn't have to go, wishing he could take her back to bed, wishing he could kiss her forever.

Too soon, she stepped away from him, gathered her stuff, and disappeared out the door. He didn't take a breath until the door had closed behind her.

"You asked her out?" Seth gasped. "Like, on a date? In public?"

"Yes," Chris scoffed. "No. Well, kind of. I mean, maybe." He sighed and shook his head. "I don't know. It's for that charity event next week."

He'd called his best friend, needing someone to talk to, someone to tell him he wasn't making a mistake, that he hadn't lost his mind. Someone to tell him that his feelings for Sofia were normal.

"Chris?" his best friend prompted. "What is it?"

"This...this thing between me and Sofia, whatever it is, it's a business arrangement, no strings, no complications, no attachments. It wasn't supposed to be like this."

"Like what?"

Chris covered his face with both hands, rubbing his eyes. "Like I...like I can't live without her," he said. "I'm not supposed to feel like I need her, like I can't

think straight unless I'm with her. This wasn't supposed to happen."

"Did you think it wouldn't? You've been sleeping
with her for six months. She's all you talk about, dude.
You live and breathe her. Shit, do you know how long
I've known you were falling in love with her? Longer
than you."

"It's that obvious?" Chris mumbled.

"Jesus, yes," Seth chuckled. "Have you told her?"

"No." Chris shook his head. "And I'm not going to.
She doesn't feel the same way. Being with me is her
job, Seth. You said so yourself. She doesn't care about
me, not like that anyway. I can't tell her. I'll just have to
learn to deal with my feelings for her."

"And if you can't?"

"I don't know," he sighed. "I guess I'll cross that
bridge when I come to it."

Chapter Sixteen

SOFIA

Sofia told herself that her upcoming date with Chris was just another date with a client, nothing to get excited about. Except it *wasn't* just another date; it was Chris and that changed everything. Because everything between them had changed.

She had only talked to Chris once since their rendezvous at the hotel, a brief conversation to arrange their date. Sofia knew that something had shifted between them; something had changed the night he'd come to her house and that night at the hotel. She didn't know what pushed him into her arms, what he needed from her; she was afraid to examine it too closely, afraid of what she might discover. She held the memories of those nights close, replaying them in her head, turning to them whenever she needed comfort.

She'd felt the difference the night he'd met her at the hotel, the subtle change in their relationship, the shift between them. It was something in the way he touched her, looked at her, made love to her. Sofia hadn't wanted the night to end, hadn't wanted to leave. It was obvious Chris hadn't wanted her to leave either.

Everything hinged on what happened at the fundraiser.

The day of the fundraiser, she was a mess: on edge, unable to focus, flighty, and her stomach fluttered constantly. Sofia spent the better part of the day deciding what to wear, combing through her closet, unhappy with everything she pulled out. She was about to give up when the peacock blue dress fell into her hands as if begging to be worn. She'd shoved it in the back of the closet behind two other dresses she hadn't worn in ages. She had forgotten about it, bought on a whim and never worn. Fortunately, she had a pair of matching strappy heels and some simple jewelry to go with it. Sofia left her hair down and went easy on the makeup, opting for a more natural look. She had never spent so much time and effort getting ready for a date with a client.

Ready far too early, she sat in the chair by the window, watching, waiting, anticipating Chris's arrival, her hands shaking, and her stomach in knots. She was off the chair and out the door as soon as she spied the limo pulling to a stop in front of her condo, her purse and wrap clutched in her hand. She locked the door behind her, turning in time to see Chris emerging from the back of the limousine, straightening the cuffs of his suit jacket as he stepped free of the long black car.

Chris took Sofia's breath away. He was wearing a double-breasted blue suit with a crisp white shirt, blue pocket square, and a matching tie. He strode up the sidewalk toward her, one corner of his mouth tipped up in a decided smirk, blue eyes sparkling, his fingers nimbly buttoning the jacket.

"I was coming to get you," he chuckled. "You didn't have to meet me outside."

"I...I'm sorry," Sofia giggled. "This...this is new to me."

He reached her side and pressed a kiss to her cheek. "Me, too," he murmured. "You look beautiful."

"Thank you," she breathed, heat rising in her cheeks.

Chris took her arm and led her to the car. He stopped at the open door. "Sofia, this is my driver and bodyguard, Alex. Alex, this is Sofia Larson."

"Ms. Larson." Alex smiled, shaking her hand. "Nice to meet you."

Chris gestured for her to climb in first. Sofia slid across the spacious leather seat, Chris right behind her, the door slamming closed behind him. Alex raised the partition as he slipped behind the wheel, affording them a modicum of privacy.

As soon as the car moved, Chris's arms slipped around her waist, his nose sliding up her neck, along her jaw, his breath hot against her skin. He caught the lobe of her ear between his teeth, biting it gently. Sofia sighed and let herself relax into his arms. He moaned low in the back of his throat, one hand slipping beneath her dress, caressing her inner thighs.

Sofia's legs fell open, inviting him to do more, aching for him to do more, and for a moment, she thought he might, but he groaned and released her, his head falling back against the dark leather seat.

"What is it?" she asked, wondering if she'd done something wrong.

He shook his head. "I forgot myself for a minute. I'm sorry."

"Don't be," she told him. She took his hand, intertwined her fingers with his, and cupped his cheek with her free hand, her thumb tracing his cheekbone. "I love kissing you." She pressed a kiss to the corner of his mouth, then another, her tongue darting out and drifting over his lower lips. Chris sighed, his mouth falling open, his fingers tangling in the hair at the back of Sofia's head, holding her to him as the kiss deepened.

"Is that okay?" he asked when she broke off the kiss.

"Always," she replied.

Chris seemed so cool, so calm and confident, Sofia couldn't take her eyes off him. He moved down the line of reporters, bloggers, and photographers with ease, chatting, laughing, and joking with everyone lined up to catch a few minutes with him or snap his picture. The smile never left his face, not for a second. She was in awe of him.

She stood under a huge awning at the end of the reception line, a reception line she had refused to be a part of, insisting it was best if she stayed out of the spotlight. Chris hadn't argued with her, merely kissed her cheek and promised he'd try to be as quick as possible.

It took more than half an hour for Chris to make his way through the line, stopping and posing every five or six feet, answering a few questions before moving on. By the time he reached the end of the line, his fingers were twitching against his leg, and he was shifting from foot to foot, his eyes darting in Sofia's direction as if assuring himself that she was still there. As soon as he stepped off the end of the red carpet, he hurried to her side and grabbed her hand, squeezing it, tugging her close against him.

"You good?" he asked.

"I am," Sofia nodded. "What about you? Are you okay?"

Chris shook his head. "I hate all of that crap: the red carpet, the posing, and the reporters. God, I hate the reporters more than anything. They're hyenas." He held out his hand, palm down, a minor tremor noticeable. "See? I'm a nervous wreck."

"I never would have known." Sofia took his shaking hand and clasped it. "You seem like you're in your element out there. Must be your amazing acting skills."

Chris laughed, head thrown back, the sound rich in her ear. "Well, thank you, but it doesn't feel like I'm in my element. I get nervous in front of all those people."

He brushed a kiss against her temple. "I have to tell you, though, it was better with you here. Easier."

Taken aback, Sofia's mouth snapped shut, unsure of what to say. She didn't have time to say anything, though, because a large group of people swooped in, surrounding them, all of them vying for Chris's attention. He kept her hand clasped in his, even as he spoke to the multitudes that seemed to come at them from every direction. Sofia kept close to Chris, but she stayed quiet, smiling and nodding in all the right places, deflecting questions directed at her. It was easy; she'd had a lot of practice. Despite all of that, she was enjoying herself immensely, more so than she ever had on any of her "dates" for work. Being at Chris's side like this was something she could get used to.

There seemed to be a constant stream of people wanting a minute with Chris, all of them wanting to talk to him, all of them wanting a few minutes of his attention. Sofia knew that he was one of the country's most popular actors, but she hadn't realized how many people wanted his attention, wanted him. It was overwhelming. She understood why he felt such crippling anxiety all the time.

Things quieted down a bit once they were inside, the stream of people ebbing to a trickle. He kept his arm around Sofia's waist or clasped around her upper arm. It differed completely from the last time she'd gone out with Patrick Garth. That had felt like a prison sentence compared to being with Chris. He was sweet, attentive, and so easy to be around. She couldn't keep the smile off her face.

The only time he left her side was to make his speech, stepping behind the podium on the stage with an uneasy smile, his eyes on her. She smiled at him, which seemed to put him at ease. He winked at her, cleared his throat, and started speaking.

"Excuse me, young lady?" one of the older women sitting at their table murmured, reaching over and patting Sofia on the arm. If Sofia remembered correctly, her name was Joan and she was one of the board members of the charitable organization putting on the fundraiser. "You're not that Ginny girl, are you?"

"No ma'am," she sighed, bristling at the mention of the reality star's name. "My name is Sofia."

"Funny, I thought Chris dated that actress, Ginny What's-Her-Name."

Sofia had no answer for her, so she shrugged and forced a smile onto her face. She didn't think it was her place to discuss Chris's relationship with Ginny, so she kept her mouth shut. She leaned across the table and whispered, "You would have to ask Chris about that."

"Oh, I will," the woman smirked.

Sofia knew she would, in fact, she would most likely give him the third degree about both her and Ginny. She didn't envy Chris that conversation. Sofia turned her attention back to Chris and his speech, still in awe over how poised and confident he seemed.

Once he returned to the table, his arm thrown over the back of Sofia's chair, his fingers brushing her shoulder, Joan cleared her throat and began the third degree, starting with the obvious question.

"Chris, darling, I thought you were dating that actress, um…Ginny?"

"No, not anymore," Chris said. "That's over." He didn't elaborate.

"So, how do you know this young lady?" Joan asked, tipping her head toward Sofia.

"We're old friends." He smiled.

"It seems like you're very good friends." She nodded.

Chris squeezed Sofia's shoulder and laughed. "Yes ma'am, we're definitely friends."

A man who introduced himself as a friend of Chris's publicist interrupted them. He dropped into the empty chair beside Chris, clapping him on the back as if they were old friends. He launched into a lengthy description of a script he'd read, helpfully adding that he thought it might interest Chris.

Sofia excused herself while Chris listened to the gentleman and answered his questions, hurrying down the deserted hallway leading out of the venue and making her way to the ladies' room. She took a minute to splash cool water on the back of her neck, her temperature on the rise. She'd gone on hundreds of dates over the last three years, but never one where she'd spent most of the night all hot and bothered. Just being in Chris's presence was enough to drive her crazy: crazy with want and need for him. Every time he'd pulled her close, his masculine scent filling her head, she'd felt dizzy with desire, heat flooding her. She couldn't wait to get out of there and get Chris alone.

When she stepped out of the bathroom door, Chris was walking down the hall, jacket unbuttoned, his hands shoved in his pants pockets, his ever-present smirk on his face. His eyes lit up when he saw her, his pace quickening. He glanced over his shoulder, the smile turning devilish, one eyebrow cocked, then he wrapped an arm around her and dragged her into one of the dark empty rooms lining the hallway.

Chris pushed her against the wall, his hands on her waist, her purse and wrap falling to the floor. He ducked his head and caught her lips in his, his tongue diving into her mouth. Sofia fisted her hands in his suit jacket, tugging him closer as the kiss deepened, the scotch on his lips and tongue flooding her mouth.

"This feels familiar, doesn't it?" he whispered in her ear when they separated. "Didn't I have you in a similar position not too long ago?"

Sofia giggled, his warm breath tickling her sensitive skin. "Why, yes, I believe you did. Except I couldn't leave with you then, and tonight, I can."

"Mm, that's right. Tonight, you're all mine."

"All yours." She nodded.

Chris hummed low in the back of his throat, his hands heavy on her waist. He caught her lips in his again and grabbed the edge of her skirt, his fingers skimming her naked thighs as he yanked it up. He pushed his hand between her legs, an obscene groan leaving him when he touched her bare skin, her panties and bra left at home on her bed. His mouth was on her, sucking greedily on that spot where her shoulder met her neck, his thumb circling her sensitive nub, two fingers easing into her, teasing her. He knew how to touch her to make her body sing, how to make her ache with need for him. Her back arched, her breasts pushing against his chest, her hips bucking under his hand, the most salacious moans falling from her lips. Chris pressed his mouth to her ear.

"Do you want me, Sofia?" he growled. "Say the word, and I'll take you right up against this wall. Because I'm having a hard time keeping my hands off you."

"Yes," she gasped, "Jesus, Chris, yes."

"Say it," he demanded, his voice low and thick with lust.

"I want you," she moaned. "Please, Chris, I need you. Right here, right now." Every inch of her skin burned, her need for the man holding her in his arms overwhelming her, driving her to the edge. She would do anything, say anything, for him. He owned her, body and soul.

Chris pulled a condom from his pocket and yanked open his pants, releasing Sofia just long enough to slide it down his length. He pushed her dress up above her hips, lifting her and pulling her legs around his waist, lowering her onto his throbbing shaft, taking his time, teasing her with the head of his cock pushing into her wet entrance, the sensation making her crazy with desire. He entered her, teasing her, drawing out the inevitable. He paused once he was fully seated, filling her completely, his face buried against the side of her neck, his breath hot on her skin. She twisted her fingers in his hair, moaning, begging him to move. He pulled out, dragging his cock across her sweet spot, pausing again before slamming into her, burying himself to the hilt once more.

Sofia held his head between her hands, kissing him with a desperate need, whimpering at the sensations consuming her. When he moved, his hips thrusting up into her, his cock hitting her sweet spot, she almost came undone. He moved, slow strokes that left her wanting more, her walls tightening around him as she moved closer to her release.

"Fuck," he exhaled, his fingers digging into her ass as he moved, tight, controlled movements that were driving her insane, breaking her down until she begged him for more.

"Oh my God," she moaned. "Harder, Chris, please don't hold back."

He followed her command without question, slamming into her, his hips moving at an ungodly pace, her back and head hitting the wall as he thrust into her. Sofia came hard, his name a curse on her lips, her forehead on his shoulder, wave after wave of intense pleasure rolling through her, driving her over the edge again and again until she was so overwhelmed, she thought she might pass out.

Chris was right behind her, shuddering as he came, his hands so tight on her hips she would find bruises the next day, his cock pulsing inside her. He groaned her name, the sound like a symphony to her ears. He held her against the wall for a few minutes after it was over, kissing her.

She could have stayed there, in his arms for the rest of her life, just the two of them—no one else. Her mouth opened, the urge to spill everything too much to bear, but she shut it, biting her tongue. She giggled, her emotions bubbling to the surface in the craziest of ways. Chris set her on her feet, laughing with her, one eyebrow raised in curiosity.

"What's so funny?" he asked, tugging her skirt back into place.

"Nothing." She shrugged, running her fingers through his hair and across the scruff dusting his cheekbones. "I just thought you'd save that for the limo ride home."

"Oh, sweetheart," he drawled. "I'm not done with you. Not by a long shot. I've got plans for the limo ride home. Trust me." He took her hand, dragging her closer, kissing her hard. Her gut twisted with need.

She groaned into his mouth. "Then let's go," she breathed.

Chris grinned wickedly, scooped her purse and wrap up off the floor, and shoved them into her hands before spinning around and stalking through the partially open door, her hand in his. Goosebumps broke out across her skin and she tingled with desire, anticipating what Chris had planned.

Neither of them noticed the man standing at the end of the hall, his cell phone clutched in his hand.

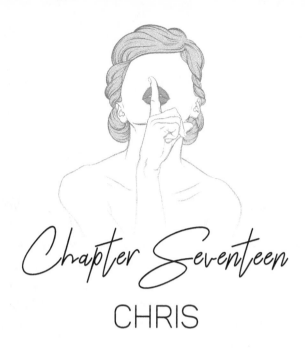

Chapter Seventeen

CHRIS

Sofia was incredible, exceeding even his wildest expectations. Not only did she look beautiful, but she was calm under the scrutiny that came with being in public with a celebrity. She brushed off questions about her relationship with Chris while still coming across as gracious and unruffled. She waited patiently off to the side while the press took picture after picture, refusing to join him, whispering in his ear it was better if she stayed out of the spotlight. Stay out of it she did, turning her back to the press line, hiding in the shadows. Everyone he spoke to went on and on about how beautiful she was, how perfect she seemed, questioning him endlessly about her.

The hardest questions came from the press: where was Ginny, were they still together, did he love her, personal probing questions he refused to answer. He cut them off, polite, yet firm, refusing to reveal anything. The press was used to his "I'm not going there" answers to their questions about his relationship status. They kept asking, even knowing they wouldn't get an answer.

It had relieved him when he could get away, free from the press for the rest of the evening. The voices in his head were clamoring for his attention, on and off most of the night, only silenced when he was near Sofia, the touch of her hand on his arm calming him in an instant, silencing the voices. He burned with need for her all night, barely able to keep his hands off her. That was why he'd pulled her into that empty room, unable to resist the temptation any longer.

Eager to get her alone, Chris hurried her down the hallway and outside, signaling his driver with a raised hand. It only took a few minutes for him to pull the car around, park, and jump from the car, pulling the back door open.

"Home, Mr. Chandler?" the driver asked.

"I don't think so, Alex," Chris replied. "How would you feel about driving us around?"

A smile danced across Alex's lips. "I'd love to, Mr. Chandler. As long as you want."

Chris smiled his thanks and turned to help Sofia into the car, his hand in the center of her back. He slid in beside her, staying close, not wanting her too far away from him. He held back, though it was difficult. Despite having just fucked her senseless only a short time ago, he wanted her again, wanted her so much he could taste it. Once the car moved, he relaxed.

Sofia tossed her things onto the other seat and turned to Chris. She didn't speak, instead, she reached for him, her fingers brushing through the short hairs on the back of his head, pulling him down to kiss her. He sighed, his hand falling to her waist, squeezing. She took his other hand, pulling it between her legs, moaning into his mouth when his fingers made contact.

"Sof," he groaned.

"Shh," she purred, moving closer to him, her skirt now hitched up to the middle of her thighs, his hand sliding farther up her leg, his knuckles brushing against her warm core.

He was going to snap, lose control, throw her down on the seat and take her, fuck her until she screamed. But even as those thoughts drifted through his head, Sofia slipped off the seat and knelt between his legs. They locked eyes, blue on blue, no words exchanged, but there was total and complete understanding. He shrugged out of his suit jacket as she opened his pants and eased them down, freeing his already hardening shaft and stroking him. His head fell against the back of the seat, his eyes closing, a heaving gasp coming from him when her tongue circled the wide head of his cock, her tongue dipping into the slit. His fingers tangled in her hair, the long red strands wrapping around his digits, a shuddering moan leaving him as his cock slid past her lips. She wrapped her hand around the base, sucking gently, rubbing it against the roof of her mouth.

"Fuck," Chris groaned, the curse stretched out, his hips rising off the seat, pushing himself deeper into her mouth.

Sofia hollowed her cheeks and cupped his sensitive sac, fondling him as she pulled him deeper into the wet heat of her mouth. She moved back up the length, grazing him with her teeth, the movement repeated several times; each time, she took more of him into her mouth, opening her throat to accept his tight, even thrusts.

God, he wanted to touch her, get his hands on her, but he was lost in what she was doing, lost in the pleasure she was eliciting from him, every neuron firing, blissful sensations exploding through his entire body. Sofia adjusted her position, raising herself on her knees so she hovered over him, the new angle allowing her to swallow him down, her palms flat on his thighs as she worked him over. He couldn't hold back much longer.

"Jesus, babe, I'm gonna come," he moaned.

Sofia tightened her grip around the base of his cock, squeezing, her mouth sliding off of him, her lust blown blue eyes locking on his. "Then do it," she ordered, stroking his length, once, twice, before she took him back into her mouth, sliding him past her swollen, saliva-slick lips. With rapid, circular motions, she explored the entire length of his shaft with her tongue, with her mouth—a mouth Chris wanted to kiss, lips he wanted to bite, a tongue he wanted to feel covering every inch of his body.

A low rumble echoed through his chest, his cock pulsing, his balls drawing up tight, even as she intensified her movements, deep throating him, swallowing him down, the pressure of her constricting throat only increasing his pleasure.

A tremble rolled through him, and he let go with an obscene groan, his cock jerking as he came. Sofia swallowed every drop, moaning, her nose pressed against his dark curls, taking everything he gave her, milking him dry.

She released him, his softening cock sliding from her mouth. Chris grabbed her, dragging her up his body so she straddled him, his hands clutching her head, his lips crashing into hers. His thumbs brushed her cheeks, and he thought they felt damp as if she'd been crying. He rolled her to her back, covering her body with his, crushing her to his chest.

"What is it?" he whispered. "What's wrong?"

"Nothing," Sofia murmured, shaking her head, a tight, forced smile on her face.

Before he could question her further, she pulled him into another kiss—slow, languid, intense—and her arms and legs wrapped around him. He could stay in her arms all night; he never wanted it to end, but he had to know what was wrong, why there were tears on her cheeks, so he pulled away, sitting up, pulling her with him.

"Talk," he demanded.

Sofia shook her head, gnawing on her lower lip. "It's not important. Just forget it." She swiped at the tell-tale tears still leaking from her eyes, a heavy sigh leaving her, her hair falling over her face. She took his hand in hers, intertwining their fingers. "Let's talk about something else. Anything else."

Chris brushed her hair away from her face and took her chin between his thumb and forefinger, tipping her head back, forcing her to look at him. He kissed her, his lips brushing against hers. "Why are you crying? Is it something I did?"

She laughed, a bitter laugh, a laugh that made him cringe. Her blue eyes were wide, tearful, unreadable. It scared him.

"You can tell me, Sofia," he pleaded.

"I'm afraid if I tell you, you won't want to see me anymore."

Chris stared at her, her words like a punch to the gut. What could be so bad that he wouldn't want to see her anymore? He already endured being in love with this woman while she saw him as only a client; how much worse could it get? He held his breath, waiting, knowing somehow that whatever she said would change things between them forever.

He exhaled slowly. "Please, Sofia. Tell me."

"Things are different," Sofia whispered. Her voice was so low he had to strain to hear her, despite being inches away.

"What do you mean, different?"

"M-my feelings for you are different," she stammered. "I'm, well, I—" She blew out a breath, her head shaking from side to side, swirls of red hair floating around her face. "I...I'm falling in love with you," she blurted.

Shocked, Chris released her, falling back against the seat, his heart thumping. He opened his mouth and closed it again, words evading him. That was not what he'd expected, not what he thought she'd say at all. Every probable scenario had been running through his head, but never, never the one where she told him she loved with him.

"Chris, say something," Sofia begged, her voice tight, strangled, and scared.

With a low grunt, he launched himself across the seat, grabbing her and pulling her against him, his hands everywhere, yanking at her clothes, wanting, *needing* her naked beneath him. In a flurry of movement, of incoherent words, of intense, pent up emotion, he removed both his clothes and hers, nestling himself between her legs, his lips never leaving hers. He somehow slid a condom down his rock hard shaft without breaking off the kiss, his need for her insatiable, pushing everything else out of his head. No voices, no anxiety, no stress, only Sofia and his feelings for her. He ran a hand up her thigh, hooking his forearm beneath her knee, opening her for him, entering her with a hard thrust.

Sofia's fingers scrambled for purchase, scratching down his back, settling on his ass, digging in, pulling him in deep. Chris twisted his fingers in her hair, tipping her head back, assaulting her neck, sucking, biting, marking her. Her breath was hot against his ear, her gasps of pleasure filling his head, her body trembling beneath him. He braced a hand above her head, using the door as leverage so he could pound into her, his control slipping, his need to take her, to claim her, overshadowing everything else.

She came, his name sin on her lips, her walls clenching around him, the sensation too much to bear, pulling his own orgasm from him. He pressed her into the seat, his hips still moving, the pleasure rolling through him, consuming him, demanding all of his attention. He caught her lips in his, her mouth opening to take him, the kiss a declaration of everything he hadn't been able to say out loud.

When it was over, Chris kept her in his arms, his forehead pressed to hers, his hands lovingly caressing her soft, supple body, their breath mingling, their chests rising and falling as one, bodies intertwined. He kissed Sofia's jaw, her cheek, catching her earlobe between his teeth, biting it softly.

"I love you, too," he whispered.

Chris didn't wake until after eleven the next morning. It had been a late night, a crazy night, an immensely satisfying night. He'd dropped Sofia off a little after two a.m., then Alex had taken him home. He and Sofia had exchanged text messages until three in the morning when he'd ordered her to get some sleep. Not that he'd been able to sleep himself; he was too busy replaying every moment they'd spent together in the limo, especially the moment in which Sofia admitted her feelings and told him she was falling in love with him. It felt too good to be true.

Around four, he had shut his phone down, set it on the kitchen counter, and called Oliver to follow him to the bedroom. Once he'd peeled off his clothes, carefully laying his suit on the chair, he'd fallen into bed, sleep hitting him hard and fast.

He might have slept longer if Oliver hadn't started wagging his tail, creeping closer and closer until his head was resting on Chris's arm. As soon as Chris stirred, the dog pounced, licking his face, growling playfully. Chris reluctantly got up and opened the sliding glass door leading outside, laughing as Oliver darted out, a blur of black and white brushing against his legs, nearly knocking him over. Chris used the bathroom, brushed his teeth, and made his way to the kitchen, in desperate need of coffee. He had it percolating before he grabbed his phone off the corner, his first thought to call Sofia. He wanted to hear her voice.

As soon as the phone powered on, his notifications exploded. He had multiple voicemails and a slew of text messages, far more than normal, none of which made sense, all of them demanding his attention. His manager, his publicist, his agent, Seth, even his mom had tried to reach him, each message more cryptic than the last. The last one from Paul scared the shit out of him.

Call me. Now. We might still have time to salvage your career.

"What the fuck?" he muttered, grabbing his laptop and opening it. He typed in the first gossip site that came to mind, the first one he thought of when he wanted to hate someone for invading his personal life, the one that always got the story he didn't want them to have: The Gossip Monger. If something had happened, they would plaster it all over that goddamn site.

Chris closed his eyes as the page loaded, praying it wasn't as bad as he suspected.

CHRIS CHANDLER ATTENDS CHARITY EVENT WITH HIGH-END ESCORT

*Chris Chandler, best known for his role as the clean-cut, goody-two-shoes detective, Ambrose Whitwood, in one of the world's most popular procedural cop shows, **Hunting the Criminal**, was spotted in Hollywood last night at a $1,000 a plate charity event with a woman that a source has revealed to TGM is a high-end escort working for a company called Private Lives.*

Chandler has recently been seen out and about with reality star Ginny Etling, his co-star in an upcoming film, but sources tell us that Mr. Chandler arrived at last night's event with the nameless woman on his arm, a woman who insisted on staying out of the spotlight, avoiding the usually coveted photo op in the press lines. She and Chandler disappeared early in the evening, though TGM has obtained footage, filmed on-site, of the two locked in what can only be described as a more than compromising position.

Mr. Chandler's publicist was unavailable for comment.

Chris clicked on the attached video, his thundering heart in his throat. It was grainy, dark, but he could just make out the two of them locked in a more than compromising position.

Someone had gotten a video of them having sex. Someone had found out that Sofia was an escort and leaked it to the press.

This was bad. Unbelievably bad.

"What were you thinking?" Paul yelled. "Jesus Christ, Chris, you may have destroyed your career just so you could get fucked."

Chris was surrounded by his management team—Paul, Jack, and Wendy—all of them seated at Chris's dining room table. They'd arrived an hour ago, descending on his house as if they were one entity, and the ass chewing started immediately. This was after dealing with a phone call from his mother—the epitome of fun—and one from Seth. He called Sofia, but it had gone to voicemail after ringing several times. He hadn't been able to find the time to try again.

"This wasn't about me getting fucked," he said, sighing in irritation. He rubbed a hand over his face. "I was sick of my personal life being in the spotlight, tired of every goddamn gossip site imaginable being up my ass. I wanted something uncomplicated with no strings."

Wendy burst out laughing. "Seriously, Chris?" she scoffed, shaking her head. "You thought hiring a hooker was the way to do that?"

"Back off, Wendy," he snapped, shooting her a dirty look. "And she's *not* a hooker."

"What are you going to do about Ginny?" Jack piped up.

"What am I going to do about Ginny?" Chris repeated. "Who fucking cares?"

"She's your girlfriend, Chris," Jack said.

Chris slammed his hand on the table. "She is *not* my girlfriend. She is the woman you idiots forced me to date for publicity's sake."

"The world thinks she's your girlfriend," Wendy corrected. "People will lose their minds, thinking you cheated on her with a hooker."

"God damn it, Wendy," he growled, pointing at his publicist. "Don't call her a hooker again."

"Fine, with an *escort*. Whatever," his publicist sighed, her eyes rolling back in her head. "But they will think it, and I'll tell you what—Ginny's vindictive enough to let it ride, to play the jilted lover in the press, to milk this for every bit of sympathetic publicity she can get. She will fucking ruin you."

"I don't think you understand how bad this is, Chris," Jack said, rising to his feet, pacing back and forth in front of Chris's fireplace. "This is catastrophic. Phenomenally catastrophic. You will lose endorsements, movie roles, all of it. You'll be lucky if you keep your job on *Hunting the Criminal*. You might lose the new movie. Shit, you'll be lucky if you ever work again."

Chris put his head in his hands. Not only had a knot of anxiety formed in his throat, one he couldn't seem to swallow, but his gut ached, churning like he might throw up. He dragged in a shaky breath. Everything he'd worked for was in jeopardy. He couldn't lose it; he couldn't. He needed to fix this and fast.

"Tell me what to do."

Chapter Eighteen

SOFIA

Sofia's phone rang early, far earlier than she appreciated, seeing as how she hadn't gone to sleep until after three in the morning. She opened one eye to look at the clock. It was a little after eleven. She pulled the pillow over her head, groaning. She dozed off and on for another hour, but her phone was persistent, ringing repeatedly.

"Good God," she groaned. "I'm up, for Christ's sake."

She stretched, working out the kinks, her body aching all over, a good ache, a satisfied ache. Sofia smiled to herself as the memories of the previous night rushed back, occupying her tired brain. Hours in the limo, circling the city, the unbelievable pleasure she'd drawn from their time together. But more than anything, she couldn't stop thinking about Chris's whispered declaration.

He loved her.

Her phone went off again, so she snatched it off the bedside table.

"Hello?" she huffed.

"Have you been online today?" Sasha asked.

"Well, good morning to you, too," Sofia snapped.

"Sof, I'm serious," her friend responded with a heavy sigh. "I sent you a link. Go look at it. Now."

Sofia pulled her phone away from her ear, grumbling under her breath. Knowing Sasha, this was some ridiculous social media crap about Chris; ever since she'd confessed her feelings to Sasha, her friend insisted on "keeping it real" by constantly updating her about Chris's life via social media. Not that it ever worked; Sofia knew the real Chris, the Chris no one else got to see. Chris's social media presence and internet fame wasn't real, though it was a constant reminder that she wasn't a part of his life. Not really.

She opened her text messages and clicked the link that Sasha had sent. The Gossip Monger opened in the browser on her phone. She scrolled down the page, freezing when the first headline appeared.

CHRIS CHANDLER ATTENDS CHARITY EVENT WITH HIGH-END ESCORT

"What the hell?" she muttered, quickly scanning the article.

"Sof? Sofia?"

"I'm here," she breathed, returning the phone to her ear.

"Did you see it?" Sasha asked.

"I saw it," Sofia whispered.

"What are you going to do?"

"I... I-I gotta go, Sash," she murmured. "I'll talk to you later." She disconnected the call.

Sofia sat staring at the wall for a few seconds, unable to comprehend what she'd just read, wondering if it were all a terrible dream, a dream she would wake up from any second. Her phone rang, startling her, a number she didn't recognize, and then it was as if something exploded inside her; she shoved the blankets to the floor, tripping and stumbling as she tried to untangle herself, a choked sob rumbling out of her, her phone falling to the floor, and then she was running, sprinting across the room, bursting through the bathroom door so hard it ricocheted off the wall and hit her in the shoulder. She fell to her knees in front of the toilet, vomiting, heaving, her body trying to expel the sudden pain.

She fell against the wall beside the toilet, her cheek resting on the cold tile, sobs tearing out of her, her head pounding, her heart racing.

"Oh God, what have I done?" she mumbled.

"Drink this." Sasha shoved a warm cup into Sofia's hands and dropped to the couch beside her. She grabbed the remote and, even though Sofia shot her a dirty look, hit mute. She'd been watching the entertainment channel, watching the constant updates about the mysterious unnamed escort and Chris Chandler. Constant updates about her and Chris.

Sasha had shown up an hour ago and found Sofia lying on the couch, television on, sobbing, a pillow cradled in her arms and pressed against her mouth, stifling her cries. Her best friend had helped her to her feet and forced her into a hot shower, ordering her to clean up and get dressed. Once she was out of the shower, she'd thrown on some sweats and a t-shirt, her hair pulled up in a messy bun on top of her head, stopping for a few minutes to stare at the marks covering her neck and torso, marks left by Chris last night. Looking at them had only brought back the tears, so she'd turned from the mirror and made her way back to the living room.

Sofia took a tentative sip from the cup, wincing as the taste of alcohol hit her tongue. "What's in this?" she coughed.

"A little bit of coffee and a lot of bourbon." Sasha shrugged. "You need it." She fussed with the blanket covering Sofia, the blanket that still smelled like Chris, pulling it over her feet and straightening the wrinkles.

"You hear from the office?" Sasha asked.

"Yeah." Sofia sighed. "They're confident it wasn't anybody there that leaked it to the press. Georgia thinks it might have been one of my clients."

Georgia had been the other person calling Sofia's phone all morning, her and Sasha. Once she'd stopped throwing up and crying, Sofia had found her phone under her bed, noting the missed call from

Chris, but unable to call him back because, at that moment, Georgia had called her.

The company was under a lot of scrutiny, thanks to her, and Georgia was pissed, though not at Sofia. Everyone in the company knew that a lot of the girls had sex with their clients, but it was intentionally kept quiet and off the books. No discussion, ever. This coming out, if it were one of her clients, would violate his nondisclosure agreement and cost whoever it was thousands of dollars.

Georgia's only goal beyond protecting Private Lives was to find out who had gone to the press. Find them and make them pay. Literally.

"Who do you think it was?" Sasha asked. "Ginny, maybe?"

"It couldn't have been Ginny." Sofia shook her head. "She wasn't there last night. At least, I didn't see her. Whoever did this was at the charity event."

"Then, who?" her friend said.

I don't know." Sofia shrugged. "One of the other girls, maybe? A client? Who knows? Maybe one of them was there last night, saw me with Chris, and for some unknown reason, it pissed them off enough to leak it to the press. They saw us having sex, and they had the gall to take video to prove it. But who hates me—us—enough to do this? This could destroy Chris's career, ruin him."

"It's not just Chris. You know that, right?" Sasha sighed. "It's you, too, Sof."

Sofia shook her head. "I can come out the other side of this okay. They don't even have my name; they don't know who I am. I'm still that nameless woman. This hurts Chris."

"Did you talk to him yet?" Sasha asked.

"He's not returning my calls," Sofia said. "Or my texts. He left me one message this morning around eleven and that was it. Nothing since."

"He'll call," Sasha promised. "He has to."

Sofia wanted to believe her, she did, but it was getting harder to do with every minute that passed. She stared straight ahead, watching the silent soap opera of Chris's life playing out on the television in front of her.

She kept the television on all day, watching for updates to the story, wondering if more information would come to light. For hours, the only thing the news shows, and gossip sites had been showing was that goddamn, grainy video on a loop. It was terrible, a cell phone video taken from a distance, zoomed in, Sofia's face unrecognizable, Chris only identifiable because of his unique physique. Over and over they'd played it until she thought she might throw up. Sasha had tried to change it as soon as she'd arrived, but Sofia wouldn't let her. She needed to know.

She decided to turn it off, give herself a break, when the words "*statement from Chris Chandler's publicist*" flashed on the bottom of the screen. Sofia grabbed the remote and turned up the volume, cringing at the excited squeak in the reporter's voice.

Chris Chandler's publicist, Wendy Trenton, released this statement regarding Mr. Chandler's supposed dalliance with an escort:

"Mr. Chandler attended last evening's charity event, but he was not accompanied by an escort as previously reported, but rather a young lady, a friend, that he has known for quite some time. The fact that someone recorded them during an intimate moment and then shared that video, accompanied by blatant lies, is quite unfortunate."

The camera cut away from the reporter to once again show the video of Sofia and Chris. Without a word, Sasha picked up the remote and shut off the television. Sofia was glad; she'd had enough.

She picked up her phone and typed out another message to Chris, her finger hovering over the send button for a minute before hitting it.

I'm so sorry, Chris. Please, please call me.

Black paint stained her hair and her forehead, along with the white canvas of the landscape she'd painted. She dropped the brush and palette on the table, picked up the full glass of wine and downed it in three swallows.

Sofia couldn't concentrate. Tired of watching the news and waiting for Chris to call, she went into her studio and tried to paint. The beautiful sunset painting she'd been working on sat on the easel, the colors soft and muted. She snatched her palette off the table, squirted dark blue, black, and brown on it and grabbed her brush. Within minutes, it was a mass of mixed tones, looking more like a storm than the subtle sunset she intended it to be.

She glanced at her phone on the table. Still no word from Chris. No phone call, no text, nothing. In fact, her phone had been quiet. Only one call from Georgia and several texts from Sasha checking on her. Almost twenty-four hours and not one word.

Not that she hadn't thought about calling him, but something deep inside of her kept her from doing it. Fear, anger, anxiety, something she couldn't put her finger on. Even though they'd expressed their love for each other, Sofia didn't feel like she could call him. Maybe she was afraid that it would be over, that Chris didn't love her, that the pressure of being caught would change his mind about his feelings for her. There was no way she could handle it if she called him and found out it was over before it started.

As if she'd willed it to happen, the phone rang. Sofia snatched it off the table, fumbling with it before hitting the button and pressing it to her ear.

"Hello?"

"Sof?"

"Hey, Sasha," she sighed.

"Are you watching the news?"

"No, I turned it off. Why?"

"You better turn it on. Now."

Her stomach twisted and her hands shook. She pushed herself to her feet and ambled back through the house to the living room. She picked up the remote, pointed it at the television, and froze, unable to to turn it on.

"Did something happen, Sash?"

Her friend's loud sigh was enough to tell her all she needed to know.

"What is it? What happened?"

Sasha cleared her throat. "Someone leaked your name to the press, Sof. They know who you are."

Chapter Nineteen

CHRIS

Wendy's statement to the press held fast for twenty-four hours, then an "unidentified source" leaked Sofia's name to the press, along with a picture that appeared to be two or three years old. Before Chris knew what was happening, the source, claiming to be a former employee of Private Lives, not only verified that yes, Sofia was an escort, producing paperwork to prove that it was true, but also provided dates, times, and places from the previous six weeks that the two of them had been together. More photos of the two of them at the charity event surfaced, including a picture of them climbing into the limo at the end of the night, his hand possessively in the middle of Sofia's back.

For the third time in a week, Chris met with his management team, all of them desperate to put out the fires before they spread any further. He was tired of being on the front page of the gossip magazines and fending off reporters every time he left the house. After a failed trip to pick up dog food for Oliver, he'd called Seth and begged him to come out to California, begged his best friend to come to stay with him until the worst of this mess had blown over. Seth agreed, getting on the next plane out of New York.

Chris only half-listened to the meeting going on around him; he figured out rather quickly his input meant zilch. His publicist, manager, and agent would decide what was "best for Chris" without actually asking Chris what he wanted. Seth stood in the kitchen, watching him, one eyebrow raised, shaking his head every now and then, disapproval rolling off him in waves. Seth had always been vocal about his dislike of the people working for Chris, and he had a hard time keeping that dislike off his face.

Wendy was in the middle of reading through the draft of her most recent press release, another carefully spun web of lies, Jack and Paul putting their two cents worth in every now and then, when Chris interrupted, rising from his seat, his nerves so raw and on edge he couldn't keep himself still any longer.

"What if I told the truth?" he asked, pacing back and forth in front of the fireplace, his fingers tap, tap, tapping the sides of his legs.

All the sound sucked out of the room; nobody moved, nobody spoke, except for Seth, who let out a low whistle. He'd encouraged Chris to come clean since he'd arrived—tell the truth, the actual truth, not just that Sofia was an escort he'd hired to have sex with him, but that she had become important to him, that he had, in fact, fallen in love with her. Seth had walked around mumbling about the truth setting Chris free since he'd arrived.

"Are you joking?" Jack asked.

Chris shot a dirty look at his manager. "No, Jack, I'm not joking," he spat. "You guys lied once already, and it fucking blew up in my face. Maybe if I tell the truth, explain why I did what I did, tell them how I feel about Sofia—"

"How you feel about her?" Jack scoffed. "How you feel about a whore? She's a goddamn hooker, Chris. Why would you throw away your career for a hooker? You shouldn't feel anything for her but contempt."

Chris took a step toward his manager, his vision going red the moment he heard the word whore, fists clenched at his side. He would shut Jack's fucking mouth if it were the last goddamn thing he did. Except Seth stepped between them, his hand on his best friend's chest.

"Whoa, whoa, whoa," Seth muttered. "Take a breath, dude."

"I swear to God, if anybody calls her a whore or a hooker again, I'm gonna bust their ass."

"We're just being honest, Chris," Wendy mumbled. "If we're honest—"

"You're not being honest," Chris growled, directing his glare her direction. "You're dragging Sofia through the mud all for the sake of my career, making up garbage to save face, protecting a woman I can't stand while degrading the woman I love. I will not stand here and listen to another minute of this shit."

"Are you fucking serious? You love her?" Jack guffawed. "You're in love with a whore?"

Seth grabbed Chris's arm, just before he swung at his manager. "Get out, Jack," Seth hissed. "Get out before Chris kicks your ass."

"What?"

"I think you should leave," Seth repeated. "In fact, I think everyone should go. Now."

Chris stood by as everyone gathered their things, Seth right beside him. Once the room was empty, Chris dropped to the couch, his feet on the coffee table, his head back, pinching the bridge of his nose. Oliver climbed up beside him, whining, his head in his master's lap.

"I should fire all of them," he muttered.

"No, you shouldn't. Don't do anything stupid. You need to calm down before you have any more meetings with your management team. I mean it, Chris. Don't do anything stupid."

"Okay, okay," Chris sighed.

Seth perched on the arm of the couch. "Have you called Sofia?" he asked.

"No," Chris replied, rubbing Ollie's head. He didn't open his eyes.

"Are you going to call her?"

"No," Chris repeated.

"Why not?" Seth sighed. "You know this can't be easy for her. You're just going to ignore the fact that she has called and texted countless times? That she wants to talk to you?"

"Talking to me will only make it worse," Chris said. "What am I even supposed to say? Sorry that I ruined your life? Sorry that being a celebrity ruined a good thing? Sorry that I fell in love with you? Fuck that. She's probably calling to tell me to fuck off. I don't want to hear it."

Silence descended on the room, the only sound Oliver's wagging tail brushing against the leather couch. Chris hadn't slept since all of this had happened, maybe two or three hours a night, most of that spent tossing and turning. His anxiety was at its peak, worse than it had ever been, the voices in his head *screaming* at him, his nerves so fried he wasn't sure he'd ever be able to relax again. God knew he wanted to sleep because all of this went away, all of it seemed like a distant nightmare. For a while, it didn't exist.

"You know she's alone, right?" Seth said. "I guarantee that everyone in her life has turned their back on her. Everyone. Including you."

Chris opened one eye and looked at his best friend. Seth didn't look at him; he stared at something outside the large glass window.

"I doubt any of her friends are talking to her, the escort service probably fired her, and imagine what her family is going through. You may have hired her, Chris, but to the rest of the world, she is exactly what Jack said she is—a whore, a hooker who deserves nothing but contempt. The only person she can talk to, the only person who might understand what she is going through, the man who told her a week ago that he loved her, well, that man has ignored her calls and texts."

"I don't know what to do, Seth," Chris whispered.

"Talk to her, Chris," his lifelong friend murmured. "You need to talk to her."

"What if she hates me? Or wants nothing to do with me anymore? Maybe she won't even talk to me. I can't deal with that."

"You don't know if you don't try," Seth replied. "Call her, Chris. Call her and tell her you love her. Otherwise, it will be over between the two of you."

"Look, Chris," Jack said, "I understand that I pissed you off and I apologize. But you must understand, I'm just looking out for your best interests. That's all I care about: making sure you come out of this in one piece and with your career intact."

Chris rubbed a hand over his face. He'd already fielded similar phone calls from Paul and Wendy, both spouting the same line, the same apology. Chris suspected they'd gotten together and discussed it prior to calling him. And while he wanted to believe they had his best interests in mind, he knew it was about lining their pockets; he was their money maker, one of the highest-paid actors any of them represented.

"I appreciate that, Jack," Chris replied. He didn't say what he wanted to say, which was *you're fired* because Seth's don't-do-anything-stupid lecture still rang in his ears. Firing his management team seemed to qualify as stupid. So, he'd wait. For now.

"I have one request," Jack added. "A favor." He cleared his throat. "Stay away from Sofia, Chris. Don't call her, and above all else, don't see her. This needs to blow over. If the press finds out you are contacting her, they'll have a field day with it. Just lay low until some other celebrity does something stupid."

"Thanks, Jack," Chris mumbled. "Thanks a lot." He disconnected the call, though he heard Jack shouting apologies before he hung up.

He tossed his phone on the bedside table, threw himself backward onto the bed, and closed his eyes, but all he could see was Sofia—her long red hair, sapphire blue eyes, her soft, creamy white skin, her perfect curves that fit his hands so well. There was an ache deep in his gut; he needed her, needed her desperately.

His phone was in his hand, Sofia's cell phone number pulled up and his finger hovering over the send button. Before he could call her, there was a knock on his bedroom door.

"Yeah?" he yelled.

Seth opened the door and stuck his head in. "You have a visitor."

Chris's first thought was that it was Sofia, that she'd come to see him, but that was a pipe dream, a fantasy that might never come true. The look on Seth's face, a mixture of disgust and irritation told him it wasn't her; it couldn't be her. Seth shot a look over his shoulder before turning back to Chris. He stepped inside the room and shut the door.

"It's Ginny," he grunted, rolling his eyes.

"Fuck," Chris grumbled, pushing himself off the bed, his phone forgotten. "What the hell is she doing here?"

"I don't know, man," Seth shrugged. "But she is pissed. And annoying. I tried to get her to go, to convince her you weren't seeing anyone. But she won't leave until she talks to you."

Chris sighed. He was not in the mood for Ginny's self-righteous indignation, her unjustified indignation. She had turned their "relationship" into something it wasn't, something it would never be. He'd always treated it for what it was—a publicity stunt. Even after he'd called an end to their pseudo-relationship, she'd continued the charade, playing the brokenhearted girlfriend because her agent liked the idea.

Chris dragged himself out of bed, used the bathroom, washed his face, and brushed his teeth. He tried to ignore his red-rimmed eyes, the black circles beneath them, and the unruly nature of his beard. He truly didn't give a shit.

Ginny wandered around the living room, examining everything on the shelves, touching everything, picking things up and setting them down—his People's Choice Award, the SAG he'd won the first year of *Hunting the Criminal*, the photo of him with Samuel L. Jackson, a picture of him and his mom, him and his sisters. Her mouth was set in a hard line, her eyes squinted half-closed. Chris never found her attractive; she was too fake, too blonde, too made up. In short, she tried too hard for him, but somehow, whatever she was feeling, whatever she was thinking at that moment only made her more unattractive.

Seth patted Chris on the shoulder and stepped outside, calling Oliver to join him. The dog, who'd been lying in his dog bed staring at the stranger wandering his master's home, didn't hesitate to follow, giving Ginny a wide berth. Oddly enough, only one of Ginny's squad—Tammie with an *i-e* had accompanied her. She sat on the patio at the large glass-topped table under the gazebo, her phone out, exactly like every other time Chris had seen her. Seth glanced his way and pointed toward the sliding glass door, which he'd left cracked a couple of inches. Chris knew Seth would come to his rescue if he needed it. He cleared his throat to get Ginny's attention.

As she turned, her face changed, no longer pinched and angry, but sad and maybe perplexed. "Chris! Oh, baby!" She flew across the room and threw her arms around his neck, pressing her waxy red lips to his cheek, the fake platinum ringlets in her hair catching in his beard. "I came as soon as I could."

He grabbed her arms and peeled her off him, pushing her away and taking several steps back, putting some distance between them. Ginny looked dejected, almost heartbroken. An act.

"Really?" Chris snorted. "All of this went down almost a week ago, and you're just showing up now? What's the matter? Your name not trending anymore?"

She ignored him, plastering a wounded expression on her face. She straightened her shoulders and stood a little taller. "Don't you have something to say to me?" she asked, the indignation he'd been expecting quite noticeable. She certainly didn't disappoint.

"What are you doing here, Ginny?" He sighed, pushing a hand through his hair, hoping Ginny wouldn't notice it shaking.

"I think you owe me an apology," she snapped. "Not only did you cheat on me, but you cheated on me with a whore." Her obnoxious red lips pushed out in a decided pout, her eyelashes batting.

Chris clenched his fists and bit his tongue. If one more person called Sofia a whore, he was going to fucking lose it. He took a deep breath and blew it out through his nose. "I don't owe you anything, Ginny. And I didn't cheat on you. That would require us being in a relationship. Which we're not."

"We've been dating—"

"We aren't dating. We've gone out together, in public, a few times, because my manager wanted me to go out with you, as a publicity stunt to promote the movie," he interrupted. "And that's it. Don't pretend it was anything more. We both know it wasn't. You also seem to have forgotten that I ended it. I told you I didn't want to play the game anymore."

Ginny's entire demeanor changed, her lip pulling up in a snarl, her arms crossed over her substantial breasts, one hip jutting out, her chin raised as she attempted to stare him down. "It could have been more," she insisted, her teeth grinding in anger as she stared at him. "I can make it seem like more to the press. Believe me, Chris, you don't want to cross me. I can, and will, make things exceedingly difficult for you. And your whore, too."

"Get out of my house," he growled. "Now."

"Fine," she spat. "If that's the way you want it." She snatched her purse off the chair, called for her friend, and stormed out, tossing one last dirty look over her shoulder at Chris.

Chapter Twenty

SOFIA

Once her name leaked to the press, Sofia's world imploded. Private Lives closed out their contract with her, stating the need to protect everyone involved, including Sofia. What they meant was they didn't want to deal with their own fallout as well as hers. They'd given her a hefty severance check, but it didn't change the fact that she felt abandoned by the company that had promised to protect her. What hurt more than anything had been losing Georgia. The woman had been the closest thing to a mother Sofia had had in years, and she'd shut down all contact with her. Not even a phone call, an email, or a text.

All her friends, other girls from Private Lives, the few casual acquaintances she had, stopped talking to her, ignoring her pleas for help, for someone, anyone, to stand at her side and help her through this nightmare. They abandoned her.

By far the worst was her mother. Even though they'd been estranged for years, rarely speaking, as soon as the news broke, she called Sofia. She listened to her mother rant on and on about how much of what was happening had hurt *her* for twenty minutes before she tried to turn the conversation back to herself, unable to listen to her mother victimize herself anymore.

"That's right, darling," her mother scoffed. "Ignore how your choices affect the people in your life like you always do. Thank God your father is dead. To know his daughter is nothing more than a common whore would kill him."

Sofia hung up without another word. After that, she ignored any call from her mother.

And the press, well, the press was relentless. They dug up her address and set up camp outside her condo. There were two or three news vans and a lot of nondescript cars. She waded through a crowd of people screaming questions and snapping pictures after her last trip to the offices of Private Lives, stumbling and almost falling before getting to her front door and inside. They were still out there, hours later, and they appeared to be in no hurry to leave. She was a prisoner in her own home.

Sofia's thoughts kept turning to who could have done this, who hated her enough to expose her to the press, to tell the entire world she was an escort, that she dated men for money. She had no enemies, no one she knew hated her enough to destroy her life. The thought occurred to her that it might have been Ginny who talked to the press, jealous after the discovery of her relationship with Chris. But Ginny had signed the same non-disclosure agreement that everyone had to sign once Private Lives employed them. Breaking that agreement could be a financial disaster for her. Sofia couldn't imagine another person, let alone another woman, wanting to hurt someone in the way they had hurt her.

Yet, with everything she was going through, the only thing that mattered to her was Chris and how it affected him, his life, his career, his anxiety. The negative press must kill him; he'd always been the good guy, the goody-two-shoes, the perfect boy next door. Not anymore. They had branded him as trouble, the guy who'd hired a whore. Every single mistake he'd ever made was being brought to light—a DUI in his early twenties, the movie he'd backed out of at the last minute with no explanation. You name it, the press found it. They relentlessly questioned Chris's former girlfriends and all of his acquaintances. Speculation ran rampant.

Sofia watched every minute, torturing herself, blaming herself for all of it. Chris's life was in shambles and it was her fault.

"You should get out of town," Sasha suggested, waving vaguely in some random direction with the wine glass in her hand, dragging Sofia's attention away from the television.

Scoffing, Sofia took a long pull of her drink. "How do you suggest I do that? I can't leave my house, let alone leave town."

"I'm sure there's a way," her friend mused, brows pulled together as she fell deep into thought.

Exhausted, unsure how many hours of sleep she had lost in the last several days, her mind racing a million miles per hour, Sofia stretched out on the couch, covered with a blanket, trying to rest. There were so many voices in her head she thought she might go insane, but none of those voices were louder than her mother's, drilling into her repeatedly that Sofia was a whore, that she was nothing but a disappointment to everyone.

Was this what Chris felt: the endless chatter, the self-doubt, the constant flow of negativity? It was debilitating. Sofia didn't know how he operated with a constant stream of cynical thoughts clogging up his head. God knew she was having a hard time functioning.

"I got it!" Sasha proclaimed, pulling Sofia from her thoughts so fast it took a moment for her to remember what they had been talking about. "My uncle has this place up in the hills, a few hours out of town. Insanely private."

"Sounds a little extreme." Did she need a break from the chaos? Absolutely. Did she want to leave Chris, to be that far away from him? Hell no.

Sasha set her glass on the table and grabbed Sofia's hands. "I know you don't want to leave, but all of this is too much for you to handle up close. I think you need to take a step back. You need this, Sof. And you don't have to stay away indefinitely, just long enough for this whole thing to blow over."

"Then what happens?" Sofia choked out. "I get a job as a barista or something, then Chris and I will get back together and live happily ever after? I hate to burst your bubble, Sash, but it will not happen. I fucked up. There is no fixing this."

"None of this is your fault," Sasha insisted. "Whoever took that video and leaked your name, they're the ones that fucked up; they're the ones that ruined everything. Not you. I'm sure Chris knows that."

Sofia was shaking her head against the tears. "I just want this to be over."

"Enough whining," Sasha scolded as she stood, pulling Sofia along with her. "Pack your things. We're getting you out of here."

The cameras flashed, doing their best to mimic a strobe light as she emerged from the condo. It was ridiculous. She felt ridiculous, having to wear sunglasses when the sun had set over three hours ago. But when it came down to wearing sunglasses or going blind, the answer was simple. Insults framed as questions were hurled at her as she pulled the wide-brimmed hat on her head down with one hand and secured the large duffel to her shoulder with the other.

Are you going to see Chris?
Has he been in contact?

How long have you been seeing each other?
What other celebrities have you had sex with?
When was the last time you were tested for an STD?

A taxi screeched to a stop just as she stepped to the curb. One reporter wormed his way between the cab and her hand reaching for the door, inches from her face. "Sources report that Chris will never act again. Care to comment?"

Not that anyone could see, but she rolled her eyes and yanked hard on the handle, the door hitting him in the back, all but throwing the reporter to the side. She threw her bag into the cab, dropped in, and gave the driver directions, adding that there would be a sizable tip should he step on it.

Tires screamed on the tarred road as the taxi pulled away and reporters dove into their cars, screaming into their cell phones that Sofia Larson was on the move.

———————————

Sofia let the curtain covering the kitchen window fall back into place. The red wig wasn't the best one she had, in fact, it was old, a little bit moth-eaten, and very dusty, part of an old Halloween costume, but Sasha hadn't hesitated to drop it on her head along with the obnoxiously large hat that Sofia had stuffed in the back of the closet the previous summer. They covered Sasha from head to toe, a hoodie, jeans, socks, and tennis shoes, careful to make sure not an inch of her olive skin was showing. She let the hair fall across her face, stuffed some folded towels in the duffel bag until it was full to bursting, threw on a pair of the biggest, most oversized glasses they could find, and declared herself a Sofia lookalike. Close enough anyway.

Twenty minutes later, the black SUV pulled into her driveway and Billy stepped out. Sofia snatched her bag off the couch and ran out the door, slamming it behind her, then she sprinted across the lawn. Billy gave her a quick hug before ushering her into the vehicle. They were pulling onto the freeway less than five minutes later.

"I really appreciate this, Billy," Sofia panted, out of breath from dashing to the car. "I know that you're supposed to stay away from me—"

"Nonsense," Billy grunted. "You shouldn't have to deal with this alone. I'm happy to help. You sit back and relax. I'll have you out of town in no time."

Sofia leaned her head back and watched the city recede out the window. It was at least two, maybe three hours to Sasha's uncle's cabin. Too much time to be alone with her thoughts, too much time to think about Chris, to worry about Chris. She swallowed back the lump in her throat. God, she missed him.

Chapter Twenty-One

CHRIS

Her phone went straight to voicemail, all night long. The voices in his head shrieked at him, so loud, so shrill he couldn't sleep. He tried all the tricks his therapist had taught him—deep breathing, focusing on the positive, picturing something calm and safe— but none of them worked. He itched to have her in his arms. He needed her more than he'd ever needed her before. Just after two a.m., he threw the blankets covering him to the floor and sat on the edge of his bed, his head in his hands.

Chris made his way to the well-stocked bar in the corner of the living room. He found the bottle of expensive scotch tucked in the back corner behind the glasses. He opened it and poured it into a glass,

watching the amber liquid swirl in a circle, mesmer-
izing him as he remembered the day she had given
it to him.

"Hey, you okay?"

Startled, his hand clamped down on the glass in
his hand, squeezing it so hard the edge of the crystal
tumbler dug into his palm.

"Christ, Seth, stop sneaking around," he snapped,
turning on his best friend.

"I'm not sneaking around," Seth chuckled. "I'm worried about you, man. I'm just making sure you're okay."

"I'm fine," Chris growled.

"You're a liar," Seth argued. "I haven't seen you
like this in years." He leaned against the doorjamb,
his arms crossed. "You call her yet?"

"She's not answering." He shrugged. "Straight to
voicemail."

"Thank God you called her." Seth looked at his
watch. "I bet she's asleep."

"I need to see her." Chris sighed. "I want to apologize to her for...for everything. I ruined her life. The
least I can do is apologize in person."

"So, go see her."

"Jack told me to stay away from her. 'Don't call her.
Don't go see her, Chris. Just stay away.' He said it's for
the best." Chris downed the alcohol in the glass, grimacing at the sharp bite hitting the back of his throat.

"What are you gonna do? Listen to Jack? He's an
asshole. You need to do what's best for you."

Seth was always the no-nonsense friend, Chris's
biggest supporter, and the only person outside his

family to be honest with him. He knew how Chris felt about Sofia, and he wasn't about to let him hide from his feelings. His friend was right.

"Let's go," Chris said. "You drive."

Thirty minutes later, they were in his car, backing out of the garage, the reporters sitting outside his house, half asleep just moments before, clamoring for their equipment, cameras flashing, questions being shouted. He ignored them, his head down, sunglasses on, staring at the floor of the car as Seth backed out, hitting the gas the second the car was clear of the reporters surrounding it, the engine surging, taking him to Sofia.

Seth followed his directions, pulling into Sofia's drive less than twenty minutes after they left Chris's. It was oddly quiet, no cars, no reporters camped out front. There were no lights burning inside, not in the middle of the night.

"Where are all the reporters?" Chris mumbled. He'd seen the news; he knew what she'd been dealing with for the last two days.

"Who knows?" Seth replied, leaning over the steering wheel and peering at Sofia's front door. "You think she's in there?"

"I don't know." Chris shrugged. "But I'm gonna find out." He shot a glance up one side of the street, then down the other side, hesitating for less than a second before throwing the door open and striding across the lawn to the door. He raised his fist and pounded as hard as he could, calling her name.

She had to be in there, had to. He couldn't take another minute, another second, without her. The voices screamed in his head, all of them, clamoring for his attention, his entire body wound so tight he couldn't stay still—feet tapping, fingers twitching. He was like a live electrical wire. The only thing that would calm him down, that would quiet those god-damn voices, was Sofia. His need for her was a hunger he couldn't satisfy. If he had to tear down this door to get to her, he would.

If Seth hadn't followed him, grabbed him, tried to stop him, Chris might have done just that, banging on the door until his knuckles were raw and bloodied. He tried to wrench his arm free, but his friend held tight, swung him around, and slammed him against the door, so hard Chris's head snapped back and hit it, the coppery taste of blood flooding his mouth as he bit down on his tongue.

"Knock it off," Seth growled. "She's not here, Chris, so just knock it off."

Chris sagged against the door, a sob thick in his throat, strangling him. He felt like he was drowning, suffocating beneath the weight of the anxiety that was eating him alive, like a swarm of piranha. It was all piling up, pressing down on his chest, making it hard to breathe, to catch his breath, making it hard to think. He was seeing the world through a thick, grayish-black fog, the light snuffed out. He wasn't sure how much longer he could last without her.

"Come on, let's get out of here before the press comes back," Seth urged.

The cars were parked up the street, out of the light, beneath one of the trees with the low-hanging branches, deep enough in the shadows that neither Chris nor Seth saw them. But the reporters saw him, and by the time he and Seth turned back to the car, they were there, camera lights flashing, questions being screamed at him from every direction.

Chris! How long have you been seeing Sofia?

Is she the first escort you've hired?

How long have you been having sex with hookers, Chris?

Are you addicted to sex?

They descended on him before he could get the door open, coming out of nowhere, eight or nine of them, their voices getting louder with every question, increasing the buzzing in his brain, like a swarm of bees, buzzing louder and louder with every beat of his heart. They blocked the door to the car, making it impossible to get it open, their voices drowning out the ones in his head.

Any truth to the rumors you've given up acting?

Come on, Chris, just answer a couple of questions!

It was the ratty guy from The Gossip Monger, the one with the sharp nose and big teeth. He was the one that asked the question that pushed him over the edge. His face was inches from Chris's, stale coffee breath blowing over him, ratty little eyes narrowed, an evil grin on his face.

"I see you didn't come alone," he sneered. "So, you share Sofia with your friends?"

"What did you say?" Chris snarled, laser-focused on the rat faced guy, his hands clenched so tight his blunt cut nails were digging into his palms. It was only later that he would notice the crescent shaped, blood filled wounds on his palms.

"I suppose that makes sense, her being a whore and all."

There was no thought, no pre-meditation, just Chris's fist connecting with the rat's face and the rat hitting the ground. Multiple cameras caught all of it, every brutal millisecond. Seth flew past the reporters, shoving them out of the way so he could grab Chris. He ripped open the door and shoved Chris in the car, his head hitting the edge of the roof, opening a two-inch gash on his temple, pulling his fingers out of the way before the door slammed closed. Seth vaulted over the hood of the car, pushing his way to the driver's side door, starting it while the door was still open, backing down the driveway, shouting for people to move, the door closing once he had the car pointed down the street.

"What the fuck were you thinking?" Seth shouted as he pulled away from the crowd of reporters, the engine of the BMW screaming. He shifted, gears grinding, earning him a dirty look from Chris.

"I wasn't," Chris grumbled. "Did you hear what the fuck he said about Sofia? He called her a whore. I'm fucking sick of everybody calling her a whore." He pressed a hand to his head, his fingers coming away covered in blood.

"Yeah, well, you screwed up, big guy." Seth shook his head. "That reporter is gonna press charges. I'll guarantee he's on the phone with the cops right now. Your ass is gonna end up in jail."

"I don't give a fuck," Chris muttered. "Take me home."

"You want me to what?" Chris grunted.

"One interview, an exclusive," Paul replied. "You go in, you answer their questions, you apologize to the goddamn reporter you clocked, and we salvage what we can of your career."

He shook his head before Paul finished speaking. He didn't want to apologize to the reporter. He didn't want to give any interviews. What he wanted was Sofia. None of that would bring her back.

"No," Chris said. The one word of rejection meant more than denying Paul his request. It meant standing up for himself, holding firm in his decision that the life he had, the fame, the fortune, the notoriety, none of it meant anything without the woman he loved.

"It's one interview." Paul rubbed a hand over his bald head. "Please think about it. You can't take another blow. You're close to losing the movie. The studio is postponing the new season of *Hunting the Criminal*. Everyone is out for blood. We can't rely on press releases anymore; we need to do some damage control. Call me and let me know what you decide." He waved goodbye over his shoulder, grabbing Seth and whispering furiously in his ear.

Chris grabbed the half-empty bottle of whiskey on the bar and took a long swallow, chugging it, not even bothering with a glass, drinking it straight from the bottle. He was drunk, had been since about five this morning when he and Seth had gotten back from their poorly executed trip to Sofia's condo. He went directly to the bar once they were back at his place, pouring a glass of whiskey, downing it in two swallows, chasing it with another. By the time Paul had arrived, bright and early at seven a.m., the bottle was half gone, and Chris couldn't stand upright without holding on to something. It was sheer luck that he'd had a halfway intelligent conversation with his agent.

Seth reappeared, shaking his head as soon as he saw the alcohol in Chris's hand. He stalked across the room and snatched the bottle away. "That's enough alcohol. Go get some sleep, Chris."

"I'm not tired," Chris slurred, gripping the edge of the bar as a wave of vertigo overtook him. "Why did Paul want to talk to you?"

"He's worried about you. Everyone is." Seth cleared his throat. "He asked about Sofia."

"What did he ask?" Chris growled. He could only imagine the things Paul had said about the woman he loved.

"He asked me if you loved her," Seth replied.

"Did you tell him the truth? Did you tell him I love her?"

"I did," his friend nodded. "Funny enough, I think he believed me. He's a good guy, Chris."

"Yeah, unless he's telling me to stay away from the only person who keeps me sane. Present company excluded." Chris sat on the barstool, his body too heavy to hold up any longer.

Seth shook his head. "Sofia keeps you sane. I try to keep you from doing stupid shit. Like drinking yourself to death. Now, you can't keep yourself upright, so even if you don't sleep, you need to go cool off for a while. Try to calm down." He leaned on the bar beside Chris. "Go."

"Fine," Chris grumbled. "But not because you told me to." He snatched the bottle from Seth's hand and spun around, fighting off a wave of dizziness as he stumbled down the hallway. It wasn't until he closed the door behind him that it all hit him full force, the force of it driving him to his knees. Until that point, he'd been flying on autopilot, just trying to get through each day without coming undone. But he had hit the end of the road. He was unraveling—the attack on the reporter, his career tanking, the anxiety, all of it.

But none of that hurt him as much as losing Sofia. He'd give up everything, all of it, if it meant he could be with her. The hope of that happening was fading and the knowledge had him spiraling into a dark hole he could not crawl out of.

Chris dragged himself across the room, pulled himself onto the bed, one foot hanging off the side, the bottle of whiskey tucked against his side. He pulled his phone from his pocket and pulled up her number.

He hit the button.

Chapter Twenty-Two
SOFIA

Sasha's Uncle Leo kept the cabin stocked: food, water, toiletries, anything and everything Sofia could need. He'd generously offered to let her stay however long she wanted, no questions asked.

The secluded cabin was deep in the mountains, far enough away from the city that no one would look there for her. Billy drove her all the way there and got her settled before he took his leave.

After ditching the reporters at the bus station by ducking into a bathroom and tossing the 'Sofia' costume they'd concocted into a trash can, Sasha drove up to the cabin. She'd offered to take a few days off, stay with her friend, but Sofia refused. Having her life turned upside down was bad enough. She didn't need to drag the only friend she had left down with her. It took some work, but Sofia convinced Sasha she should go back to her life. All Sofia asked was that she keep her phone close by. Sasha reluctantly agreed. She hugged Sofia hard enough to hurt before she climbed in her car and left, eliciting Sofia's promise to keep in touch.

Being alone sucked. Sofia hadn't realized how much until Sasha left, and there was no one around to distract her from the all-consuming thoughts of the man she loved. She missed Chris more than she thought possible; it was like a piece of her was missing, unaccounted for, torn out of her soul. Sofia knew she'd fallen in love with Chris, but she hadn't realized just how hard she had fallen. Being away from him ripped her apart; she couldn't stop crying, she couldn't focus on anything, and she couldn't breathe without him. Sleep was a long time coming, and she only got in a few hours, tossing and turning the entire time, waking up before the sun with the blankets twisted around her.

Once the coffee was brewing, she washed her face and brushed her teeth, then she sat down in the huge recliner that dominated the tiny living room. There was a small television in the corner, local channels only, no cable, no satellite, but she wasn't in the mood to watch anything.

She pulled her sketchbook out of her backpack and flipped the pages to the last thing she'd been working on—a sketch of Chris. Looking at the almost finished drawing brought tears to her eyes, blurring her vision. She'd started it a few weeks ago, drawn from a picture she'd found in a magazine—Chris at a press conference or something, a harsh look of irritation on his face. As she'd worked on it, usually after spending time with him, it changed, becoming something more. Sofia rubbed her finger along the edge of his jawline, smudging the pencil, the tiny gesture softening the harsh line of Chris's face, changing him from angry to contemplative. A sob tore out of her, and she slammed the book closed, tossing it to the floor beside the chair. She took a few minutes to calm down, then she dug her phone out of her purse and powered it on. It had been off since she'd left her house; after giving Billy the address to the cabin, she hadn't felt the need to keep it on.

She had a ton of missed phone calls, several voice-mails, and a half a dozen text messages, none of which she felt like dealing with, though she had to know if any of them were from Chris. With a heavy sigh, she opened her voicemail notifications. Her heart stuttered in her chest; Chris's number appeared halfway down.

Her hands shook as she pressed the button and put the phone to her ear, her breath catching in her throat at the sound of Chris's voice. It was thick, gruff, tired, like a man on the edge, a man with nothing left to lose. He sounded like she felt.

"Sofia, baby, call me, please."

Five words. It only took those five words to break her all over again. Sofia replayed the message over and over, silent tears sliding down her cheeks. She swallowed back the lump rising in her throat and took a deep breath, her finger hovering over the call button.

It rang in her hand, startling her. She almost dropped it, catching it before it hit the floor.

"H-hello," she stammered.

"Hey, Sof," Chris whispered.

A shuddering breath escaped her, and fresh tears leaked from her eyes.

"Hey."

Chris's deep voice filled her head. He'd been drinking, she could tell; he slurred his words, and he babbled incoherently. He let loose, a tidal wave of emotions and words falling out of him. She listened, wiping the tears from her face, a smile teasing the corners of her mouth. He tapered off after a few minutes.

"Sorry," he mumbled. "I'm babbling."

"You are," she laughed, "but I don't care. God, I miss you so much."

"I miss you, too," Chris whispered. "I'm so sorry about all of this...this mess I've gotten you into. You don't deserve this."

"And you do?" Sofia sighed. "Neither one of us deserves this."

"You're right. You know, it's killing me not to touch you, not to see you."

"I know—"

"Where are you? I went to your place, but it was empty."

"You went to my place? Really? You didn't have to do that."

"Yes, I did," Chris insisted. "I'm...I'm barely hanging on, Sof. I'm drowning under the voices screaming in my head. They're destroying me, pulling me apart at the seams. You're the only thing that shuts them up, the only thing that makes them better. I need you."

"Chris..."

"I love you, Sof."

"I love you, too." An indescribably heavy weight lifted from her shoulders. "More than I can ever tell you with words."

"Yeah, well, you may not want to associate with me after everything that's happened." He cleared his throat. "I hit a reporter."

"You what?" she gasped.

"I hit a reporter," he repeated. "It's a long story. I was defending your honor."

"I don't have any honor." She shook her head. "Haven't you heard? I'm a whore."

"Sof," he growled. "Don't say that."

"It's true," Sofia whispered. "Watch the news. They're quite clear about it. I take money for sex. That makes me a whore." Her voice broke, a sob she couldn't hold back breaking free. She put her hand to her mouth, shaking her head. "I'm sorry."

"Where are you?" Chris asked again.

"A cabin that belongs to a friend's uncle," she sniffled. "Hiding from the world."

"Tell me where," he demanded.

"Why?" she replied.

"I'm coming to see you."

It took him a few hours to work out how to get out of town without being seen by a gaggle of reporters. Neither of them wanted a bunch of reporters parked outside the cabin for obvious reasons. His friend

Seth, whom she'd never met, was more than willing to help. According to the last phone call from Chris, he and Seth were of similar build, Seth only about an inch shorter, and with his dark brown hair tucked beneath a hat, and sunglasses covering his face, he bore a striking resemblance to his friend. Chris promised her the plan was foolproof, that Seth would draw the press away while Alex snuck him out of the house under cover of darkness in the car's trunk. Sofia loved that he and Seth used a similar tactic to her and Sasha. It seemed appropriate. Thanks to the three-hour drive to the cabin, it would be after dark when he knocked on the cabin door.

Waiting for him was torture. Sofia couldn't sit still; she paced around the tiny living room, gnawing on the inside of her cheek, her fingers twisting together until her knuckles cracked. It reminded her of the first time she'd gone to his hotel to meet him: butterflies in her stomach, bouncing on her toes, fidgeting, her hands shaking, and her palms clammy. She wanted to throw up, to purge the anxieties. When the soft thuds sounded on the door after what felt like an eternity, she couldn't get there fast enough, tripping over the edge of the carpet as she stumbled across the room. She took a quick glance out the side window before throwing the door open.

Chris didn't say a word, just stepped across the threshold, his bag falling to the floor, his arms reaching for her. He wrapped himself around her, even as she seemed to melt into him, his face buried against her neck. He crushed her, squeezing her so hard she couldn't breathe, not that she cared; he was there with her. She was in his arms again. She forced herself to hold back the sob building in her throat. His hands slipped into her hair, cupping her head, their lips crashing together, the kiss fueled by raw, pure emotion. They both gasped for air when they broke apart.

"Hi," Chris said.

That one word broke her, her cries echoing off the brick walls. She collapsed against Chris, her face pressed to his chest; the sobs wracked her body, starting at her toes and rising through her to fight their way out. Chris held her, murmuring quiet assurances in her ear, his hands rubbing comforting circles on her back. He led her to the couch, pulling her into his lap as he sat down, peppering her face with gentle kisses.

"I-I'm s-s-sorry," she stammered, clinging to him, her tears soaking the front of his t-shirt.

"You need to stop apologizing," he told her. "All of this is my fault."

Sofia shook her head, opening her mouth to protest, but Chris cut her off.

"I did this," Chris argued. "Me. Being a celebrity comes with a lot of bullshit, and I knew this could happen, but I couldn't quit you. I've been denying my feelings for you for months, fighting them at every turn. If I'd pulled my head out of my ass sooner, none of this would have happened. We could have been a couple out in the open. But now, I wonder if I should walk away and give you back a normal life. I love you, and it would fucking kill me, but if it means you get your life back, I'll do it. In a heartbeat."

"No," she protested, her fingers tangling in his shirt, clinging to him. She couldn't believe the things coming out of his mouth. "Absolutely not. I can't live without you."

"Sofia, you don't want to live like this—in the spotlight, under a microscope twenty-four hours a day, seven days a week, year-round. It sucks." He pressed a kiss to the corner of her mouth. "I can't ask you to do that."

She took his head in her hands, her eyes locked on his. "We'll figure it out. You can't make me leave. You can't ask me to walk away, not when I know you love me. I love you too much to lose you. If you expect me to walk away now, you're crazy. We'll work it out." Sofia kissed him again. "Okay?"

"Okay," Chris murmured, his forehead resting against hers. "Thank you."

"For what?" Sofia asked.

"Not giving up on me." He hugged her close, his chin resting on the top of her head.

Sofia made dinner, a salad and some chicken she'd found in the freezer, but it was perfect, the first meal she ever made them. Chris helped her with the dishes afterward, then they cuddled on the couch, talking, trying to hash out the mess their lives had become.

"Paul wants me to do an interview," Chris told her. "No more press releases."

"Are you going to do it?"

"I don't know," he sighed. "What do you think?"

"I think you should," Sofia answered. "Maybe it's time the world heard your side of things."

CHAPTER TWENTY-TWO

"Yeah?"

Sofia nodded, her hair flying around her face. "Yeah."

"I'll think about it," he said. "It could mean a lot of pressure on you. Are you okay with that?"

"I've survived this long, haven't I?"

"Amazingly so." He pushed her hair off her face, tucking it behind her ears. There was a twinkle in his blue eyes. "Let's go to bed."

"What about dessert?" she whispered, her fingers dancing along his cheekbone.

"I want you first," he growled. "Dessert later."

She laughed and pushed herself off the couch, his hand in hers. "You know what, there's this great shower in the bathroom. What do you say we try it out?"

"Sounds fantastic." Chris grinned. He let her pull him from the couch, holding her hand tight as he followed her up the narrow stairs and down the hall to the bedroom.

She was only a few steps inside the room, the door swinging shut behind her before his arms were around her and his lips were on hers, his tongue shoving into her mouth, urgent, impatient.

Sofia giggled, the sound swallowed by Chris's mouth covering hers. "Impatient much?" she mumbled against his mouth.

"It's been too long," he grumbled, yanking at the buttons on her jeans.

He was right. It had been too long, even though it had only been a few days. Five minutes away from him was becoming too much, too long. Sofia was going to take full advantage of having him with her for as long as she could.

She kicked off her jeans and yanked her shirt over her head before falling back into Chris's arms. He dropped his clothes to the floor, a condom in his hand, as he pulled her after him toward the open bathroom door. His lips never left her skin even as he turned on the shower, set the condom next to the shampoo, and finished stripping her bra and panties. She held his head in her hands, kissing him deeply.

Chris tested the water, then he pulled Sofia into the roomy shower, pushing her against the tile wall, his body flush against hers, steam billowing around them, the water falling over his shoulders and cascading over both of them. He dragged his lips down her neck, over her shoulders and to her breast, suckling it gently.

Sofia ran her hands over his back and stomach, relishing the feel of him. Over the last six months, she had memorized every inch of him, every scar, every mark, everything. She knew he loved it when she ran her hands over his back, kneading the muscles, working away the tension; he loved it when she sucked marks into his torso, a reminder of their secret trysts he could hold onto for days. He also loved the feel of her hand sliding up and down his hard shaft; it always brought the sweetest sounds rumbling from his chest.

Chris moaned, just enough that she could feel the vibration under her lips as they skated across his chest. Sofia stroked him, taking her time, brushing her thumb over the tip of his cock with each upward swipe, drawing out the pleasure, savoring every gasping breath he took as she ran her hand up and down his length.

He held her against the wall as he licked water droplets from her neck and breasts. He reached to the side and grabbed something, then he stepped back, far enough away that he was no longer touching her. Chris brought his hands together, rubbing them together before placing them on her shoulders, scrubbing the soap up and down her arms, his eyes never leaving hers. His hands drifted over her breasts, plucking at the nipples, before continuing down her stomach and between her legs. His fingers drifted over her core, teasing her, a slight smile playing over his full, pink lips. He leaned over and kissed her, a deep, soul scorching kiss, even as his fingers slipped inside of her.

He caressed her, stroking her, his rhythm like the one she was using on him. They both moaned, gyrating and grinding against each other. Chris thrust into her fist, while Sofia pushed herself down on his fingers, trembling with every brush of his fingers against her sweet spot.

Chris's bearded chin brushed against her cheek. "Come for me," he growled in her ear.

His words pushed her over the edge, a loud gasp of his name falling from her lips as she came, her walls clenching around his fingers. Her head fell back against the tiled wall, and her eyes squeezed closed as she let the sensations take her away.

Chris hurried to put on the condom slid his arms around her, and he lifted her, lowering her onto his throbbing cock, filling her. He held her against the wall, legs spread for balance, one hand braced above her head, the other around her waist as he thrust into her. Sofia dragged her nails over his shoulders, leaving deep red marks on his skin. Chris attacked her neck, biting and sucking as he fucked her, his hips pumping at a maddening pace.

Sofia slipped her hand between their bodies, her fingers caressing herself, brushing against Chris's cock with every thrust in and out of her wet warmth.

"Jesus Christ, Sof," Chris growled, his voice wracked with lust. "That's fucking hot." He slammed into her several times, both of them moaning until he came hard, his forehead pressed to hers, his cock buried deep inside of her. She dropped her head to his shoulder, gasping as she joined him, reeling from another onslaught of pleasure.

Chris held her in his arms, lazily kissing her, a smile playing over his lips. He set her on her feet, allowing them both to finish cleaning up. After she stepped out of the shower, he wrapped her in one of the huge towels hanging on the wall, dropping a kiss to her cheek or her shoulder every few seconds. He moved her out of the bathroom and into the bedroom, pushing her down on the bed.

"I thought we were getting dessert." Sofia sighed as Chris kissed his way from her breasts down her stomach until he was hovering over her warm core.

"You're my dessert," he growled, pushing open her thighs and settling himself between her legs.

The first touch of his tongue to her womanhood caused a delicious tightening of the muscles in her stomach and a satisfied sigh to slip past her lips. When his mouth closed over her, his tongue dipping into her, she couldn't hold back the scream of pleasure, nor could she stop the obscene noises she made as he brought her to orgasm again and again. By the time he finished, she was shaking and breathless.

Chris rolled her to her stomach, rolled a condom down his throbbing length, and entered her from behind, thrusting into her hard and deep. Sofia pushed back against him, taking every inch of his substantial length, the pillow beneath her head smothering her cries, her hands fisted in the sheets.

When it was over, they both collapsed to the bed, limbs tangled together, face to face. Chris pushed her hair away from her face and pressed a kiss to her forehead. Sofia fell asleep beside him, his hand on her waist, her hand on his chest.

Chapter Twenty-Three

CHRIS

"I'll do it," Chris said.

"Really?" Paul asked. "You're sure?"

Chris glanced at Sofia sipping coffee on the patio, wrapped in a blanket, red hair pulled into a low ponytail at the nape of her neck. He itched to walk out there and kiss her neck. The voices were silent, had been since he'd shown up and pulled her into his arms, kissed her, made love to her, held her all night.

"Yeah, I'm sure," he replied. "Set it up. Text me the details." He disconnected the call and tossed his phone to the counter. He was almost to the door when he noticed a large sketchbook on the floor, half beneath the chair. Chris crouched down and grabbed it, holding it with one hand while he flipped through it. The drawings inside were gorgeous pencil sketches, some of them in color, while others were done with what looked like charcoal: page after page of beautiful drawings that looked as if someone had put their heart and soul into the work.

The last drawing in the book was of him. He glanced in Sofia's direction, but she was still staring over the porch railing at the lake. He closed the book and slid it back under the edge of the chair just as his phone went off. Paul had sent him one word.

Tomorrow.

Chris texted Alex, then he slipped quietly out the sliding glass door and bent over Sofia, his lips on her neck, right where he'd wanted them.

She tipped her head to the side, giving him better access, one hand coming up to grab the back of his head, a sigh escaping her.

"You're leaving, aren't you?" she whispered.

"I'm going to do the interview," he murmured.

Sofia tipped her head back, her sapphire blue eyes staring into his. He pressed a kiss to her lips, his hand on her throat, his thumb rubbing circles against her pulse point.

"I'm gonna make this right." Another kiss. "I promise."

"When?" Sofia asked.

"Alex will be here in a couple hours," he said, taking her coffee and setting it on the small wicker table next to her chair. "I need you, Sofia."

"Then what are you waiting for?" she asked, a teasing lilt to her voice.

Chris scooped her up and carried her back inside. They didn't make it up the stairs.

"Mr. Chandler, I appreciate you agreeing to this interview."

The reporter, Allison something—he couldn't remember what—smiled at him. Chris knew she was just trying to put him at ease. He fidgeted, crossed and uncrossed his ankles, straightened his tie, the cuffs of his shirt, and ran a hand through his hair. Even knowing that the reporter had a list of approved questions she could ask, he was sweating, his throat was dry, and his stomach was in knots.

Out of the corner of his eye, he could see Paul and Jack hovering, ready to jump in should Allison What's-Her-Name stray from the list of questions. Chris had been adamant he would only answer the questions on the list.

"You ready?" she asked.

Chris tried to smile, though he thought it likely appeared as more of a grimace and nodded his head.

"Let's start with an easy one, shall we?"

The first few questions were straightforward, set-up questions: how was he holding up, was he still planning on acting, was he worried how this would affect his career. He answered them as truthfully as possible, cringing at the answers he gave. God, he annoyed himself.

"Okay, the questions will get a little bit harder, but I'm sticking to the list like I promised." Allison cleared her throat. "Why did you hire an escort? You're one of the most sought-after bachelors in Hollywood, women all over the globe would give anything to date you, yet you hired someone to sleep with you. Why?"

Chris pulled in a deep breath. There it was. He sat forward, his hands clasped between his legs, speaking slowly, intentionally; he had to make sure it was clear why he'd hired Sofia, why he'd paid someone to sleep with him.

"It started as a way to keep my private life out of the press. I hired Sofia to hang out with me, be my friend. I wanted to spend time with someone outside of the limelight, outside of the constant scrutiny. The sex came later, and it seemed so easy—sex with no attachments, no romantic complications, just two people together for the sex. That's it. I was tired of the press dissecting every little thing I did, every relationship I had. I wanted something uncomplicated. Sofia gave me that."

"But couldn't you have done that with someone else, someone who say, wasn't a celebrity. Someone the press wouldn't care about?"

Chris shook his head before she finished the question. "See, that's the problem. When you're a celebrity, the press cares about everything you do, everyone you date. There is no such thing as privacy. It wouldn't have mattered whether I dated an actress or the girl next door that no one knew. The outcome would have been the same."

Allison What's-Her-Name was nodding as if she understood. "Always on the news, right?" she laughed.

He didn't see the humor in his life always being played out in the press, though apparently, the reporter did. He shrugged and sat back, hands resting on his thighs. "Something like that."

The next few questions were the same as the first—why, why, why? He suspected the reporter didn't like his answers, that she was trying to delve deeper into his thoughts and feelings. He kept giving her the same answer, and she kept asking the same question differently.

She must have sensed his irritation, his reluctance to give her a different answer because the next question came straight out of left field. It was definitely *not* on the approved list.

"What about Ginny, Chris? Aren't you concerned with how this has affected her? How it's affected your relationship with her?"

"What?" he snapped, looking toward Paul and Jack.

"According to a source close to Ms. Etling, the two of you were close. In fact, she claims your relationship was serious, so serious that she thought you might propose."

Chris couldn't stop his eyes from rolling back in his head or the sigh of frustration that huffed out of him. "That is not accurate," he snapped. He shot another look at his manager and agent, but neither of them seemed to be in a hurry to come to his rescue, even though the interview had veered off course.

Allison What's-Her-Name held up a tablet that had been sitting on the table beside her, turning it to face him. It was an Instagram post, a picture of him and Ginny, a picture of her hugging him in the middle of his living room, the caption "Back with my bae" beneath it. It was maybe twenty-four hours old, posted while he was with Sofia.

"This picture says differently," the reporter shot back. "This looks like Ginny was in your house, the two of you sharing a moment. So, how does your girlfriend feel about you having sex with an escort? How does she feel about you cheating on her? Does this photo mean she's forgiven you?"

Chris sat up straight, his hands wrapped around the arms of the chairs, squeezing so tight his knuckles ached. "Ginny Etling is *not* my girlfriend. Our relationship was never serious. It was all for publicity—"

"So, you're saying you don't love her anymore?" Allison interrupted him.

"I never loved her," Chris spat.

"That's not what she says—"

It was Chris's turn to interrupt. "She's lying," he growled. "I am not in love with her."

The reporter's eyes lit up, realization dawning in them. "You're in love with the hooker." It wasn't a question.

"This interview is over." Chris ripped the microphone from his tie and dropped it on the floor, then he rose to his feet and stalked from the room, both Paul and Jack hot on his heels.

"Shit, Chris, sorry," Paul muttered. "That got out of hand."

"Ya think?" Chris snapped. "You were supposed to stop the interview if it got out of hand, if she didn't ask the questions on the list. I didn't agree to answer questions about Ginny. In fact, I said she was off limits.

Instead of doing anything, instead of stepping in like you promised you would, you let her rake me over the coals over something that doesn't mean shit."

"You need to go back in there." Jack caught up with him and stepped in front of him, his hand on Chris's chest. "If you don't, that reporter will go on national television and tell the world you're in love with a hooker."

"Good," Chris said. "It's about time they knew the truth." He pushed Jack out of his way and called for Seth. He waited maybe two seconds, then he took off down a back hallway, the same way he'd come in, hitting the door so hard on his way out it slammed into the wall.

"Where are we going?" Seth asked, one hand braced against the dashboard, the other fumbling with his seatbelt.

The car was flying, going over ninety miles an hour as they shot down the California freeway, weaving effortlessly in and out of traffic. Chris drove, a vague destination in mind, propelled by the need to move, to get himself away from everyone and everything. The damn voices were back, an inaudible murmur in the back of his head, but soon they would jockey for his attention. He couldn't stop them; only Sofia could quiet them, and she was two hundred miles away.

Chris saw the sign out of the corner of his eyes, and he knew that was where he wanted to go. He changed lanes, cutting off an elderly man in a Dodge pickup, hitting the brakes so he could slide the car between a garbage truck and a black limo, shooting a glance over his shoulder before he hit the gas, shifted gears, and broke for the exit ramp, jetting across the double white lines, not slowing until thirty feet before the stoplight, brakes squealing as the car stopped on a dime, pausing only long enough to look for oncoming traffic before he turned right and hit the accelerator again.

"Chris?"

"What?" He'd forgotten Seth was in the car.

"Where are we going?" his friend asked again.

"Harry's," Chris mumbled.

"Why don't we go back to your place—"

"I'm sick of being cooped up in my house," Chris spat. "It feels like a goddamn prison. And since I can't go where I want to go, we're going to Harry's. Being my friend, he'll make sure the press doesn't bother me."

"I can't believe you have other friends?" Seth gasped, eyes wide, hand on his chest, feigning shock.

Chris glanced at him out of the corner of his eye. "Yes, I have other friends." He chuckled. "Can't spend my life with a loser like you as the only friend I got."

"I see your terrible sense of humor has returned." Seth grinned, shaking his head. "Maybe you should at least try and cover that stupid mug of yours up with sunglasses and a hat. That way no one will recognize you."

"Oh yeah, because that works every time," Chris scoffed. "Remember that time in Boston? You had to call the police to get us out of that dive we'd stumbled into. I believe your exact words were 'nobody'll recognize you in here, Chris.' An hour later, we needed a goddamn police escort."

"I underestimated your appeal." Seth shrugged. "I still don't understand what they see in you." He ducked as Chris threw a mock punch.

"Do me a favor and call Harry. Let him know we're coming."

Seth did as Chris asked, staring at his phone rather than the cars flashing by at unbelievable speeds. It took less than ten minutes to get to Harry's, thanks to Chris's insane driving. He parked in his usual spot and entered the bar through the back. Harry waved them over as soon as they stepped into the main room.

"Thanks for giving me a heads up you were coming," Harry said. "With all the heat you've been taking, I thought it would be best if I put the 'No Press Allowed' sign up and called in my security early."

"You've got a 'No Press Allowed' sign?" Seth laughed. "And security?"

"When you are friends with this guy," Harry shrugged, pointing at Chris, "you have to have 'em both. I use them for private parties, things like that."

"I'm not the only celebrity Harry rubs shoulders with," Chris explained. "There's a whole bunch of us that used to hang out here."

"Yeah, before you all got too famous for me." Harry grinned. "All joking aside, kid, how're you holding up?"

"Not so great." Chris sighed, sliding onto a bar-stool. "I'm sure you've heard everything. My life sucks right now."

"So, I've seen," Harry said, setting a beer in front of him. "But I'd like to hear it from the horse's mouth."

Chris gave Harry a brief rundown of the previous week, capping it off with the interview gone wrong. Harry listened—no comments, no judgment, just a sympathetic ear.

"Remember when you were up for the part in *Hunting the Criminal,* and you weren't sure what you should do?" Harry asked. "You came in here looking for advice, for someone to tell you what you to do?"

"Yeah," Chris murmured.

"What did I ask you?"

"You asked me if I thought it was worth it," Chris replied.

"So, I'm gonna ask you the same thing now." Harry leaned over the bar. "Is *she* worth it?"

Chris picked up the beer in front of him and took a long drink, wiping his mouth with the back of his hand once he finished.

"She's more than worth it."

———————————

The press stayed outside, thanks to Harry's sign and his security team, who refused to let anyone in that even looked like they might be a reporter. Chris and Seth set themselves up at one of the pool tables in the back, and Harry kept the drinks coming.

Chris had a decent buzz going on, and he was enjoying the hell out of beating his best friend at pool. He felt relaxed for the first time since all the bullshit had started. The only way it could have been any more perfect would have been if Sofia had been there. The voices were getting louder; Chris knew he wouldn't be able to be away from her for much longer. While the alcohol helped, nothing would ever compare to her touch, her voice, her presence.

By the end of their third game of pool, he'd achieved full blown drunk, but it was a good drunk, and he was still enjoying himself. Until the bar door blew open and Ginny strolled in, short skirt, low-cut blouse, heavily made up, her so-called squad in tow. She grimaced as she looked around the bar, her lips pursed, and her brows furrowed. As soon as her eyes landed on Chris, an evil grin spread across her face. She stalked across the room, shoving people out of her way, coming to a stop in front of him, her hands on her hips, her face now rearranged into a full pout.

Chris dropped the pool cue and sat on the edge of the table, his arms crossed. His head was spinning, the alcohol affecting him; sometimes there seemed to be two of Ginny—a frightening thought. He was having trouble focusing, and there was a low buzzing in between his ears.

"Ginny." He nodded at her.

"Do you want to explain what the hell you're doing?" she barked.

"Playing pool." Chris shrugged.

Ginny rolled her eyes. "I saw the interview, Chris."

"Really?" Chris glanced over his shoulder at the television hanging above the bar. "Must have missed that."

The reality-star-turned-actress closed the distance between them until they were only inches apart, so close Chris could smell her cloying perfume. God, he hated that smell. It was cheap, overpowering, what an actual street walking hooker might smell like. It made his stomach churn.

"You made me look like a fool." Each word emphasized with a finger to his chest, her too long, fake nails stabbing him, even through the thick cotton dress shirt he wore. "You called me a liar on national television."

"If the shoe fits—"

"Fuck you, Chris!" Ginny shouted, spit flying from her lips, hitting him in the face.

"You are a liar, Gin," he said, pushing himself to his feet, holding the edge of the pool table to keep himself steady. "Telling the fucking press that we were so in love you thought I would propose, posting a picture of us in my house, making it look like we're together—it's all lies. I can't believe you're so damn desperate to be in the spotlight, to be in the press, that you would lie to get what you want. Did you think it would make me want you, that I'd be willing to perpetuate the lie so we could be together? You're out of your fucking mind. Now, get the fuck away from me. And stay away from me."

He turned his back on her, prepared to walk away from her for the last time ever, but her next words stopped him dead in his tracks.

CHAPTER TWENTY-THREE

"Are you in love with that whore?"

Chris swung around, and in two steps he was beside Ginny, his hand wrapped around her upper arm. He yanked her close, his lips pressed to her ear.

"You aren't worth shit compared to her," he growled. "The woman you call a whore makes you look like garbage."

Gin's hand came up, batting at his chest, but he took a step back and released her, just as she tried to yank her arm free. Her arms pinwheeled and then she was falling, her ankle twisting in her stupid high heeled shoes. She hit the ground with a loud grunt, then she was crying, bawling, screaming that Chris had pushed her, shoved her to the ground.

"Did you see that?" she sniveled, fat, phony tears streaming down her face. "Did you see him push me?"

Chris had heard enough; he turned and hurried from the bar, digging his keys out of his pocket, ignoring Ginny's shouted curses. He could hear Seth running after him, calling his name, but he reached the car first, flinging the door open and diving inside. He backed out of the narrow parking space where they'd left the Beamer, tires spinning, gravel flying, then he was gone, slamming through the gears, Seth fading away in the rearview mirror.

The voices in his head weren't just screaming, they were rioting, drowning out every other sound, terrifying him as they battled for his attention.

Whore.

She's a whore.

Sofia is a whore.

You're in love with a whore.

They wouldn't stop; the voices wouldn't shut up, screaming, shrieking, pushing out all the good, reminding him he was no good, that he didn't deserve the life he had, but worse than all of that, the damn voices were trying to convince him that the woman he loved was no good.

"Shut up!" he yelled, his fist pounding the steering wheel. "Shut up, shut up, shut up!"

Chris squeezed his eyes closed, the wheel jerking in his hands, the car drifting over the double yellow line, the bile rising in his throat, his attention on the voices, not on the road, not where he was going.

He didn't see the other car until it was too late.

Chapter Twenty-Four

SOFIA

The pounding woke her up; it was loud, rattling the door in its frame. Sofia had fallen asleep on the couch, waiting for Chris to call her. She watched his interview, watched as he'd stormed out, watched as that reporter latched onto the idea that Chris was in love with "the whore" and ran with it, over-analyzing it, twisting it into something it wasn't. She turned the television off, disgusted at the things the press said about not only her but Chris as well. She hated that they acted as if they knew her, as if they knew Chris, making assumptions and unfounded accusations. She hated all of it. But more than anything, she hated that Chris hadn't told the truth, that he hadn't stood up to the reporter and proclaimed his love for her. If he had, maybe all of this would be over. Her head hurt from thinking too much. Exhausted, she closed her eyes and dozed off.

Whoever was knocking on the door got louder, more insistent, dragging her out of an already restless sleep. She sat up and pushed her hair out of her face with one hand before she staggered to the door, still half asleep, but awake enough to look out the window before opening it.

The door creaked on its hinges as she opened it. "Alex? What the hell are you doing here?"

"You're not answering your phone, Ms. Larson," Chris's driver replied, stepping inside and closing the door. "I've been calling you for over an hour."

Those words could only mean one thing, that whatever had happened had been bad, terrible. Sofia lunged over the back of the couch, snatching her phone off the table. Dead.

"Why have you been calling me, Alex? What's wrong?" Her stomach twisted into a knot of fear and worry.

"It's Mr. Chandler. He was in an accident. They asked me to come and retrieve you."

Alex's words echoed in her head. *An accident. Asked to come and retrieve you.* Shit.

"By whom?" She could feel the tears threatening, but she refused to let them take over; she needed to focus.

"A friend of Mr. Chandler's. Get your things, Ms. Larson." Alex pointed toward the stairs. "We have to hurry."

She didn't wait for him to say another word; she sprinted up the stairs and threw what few belongings she'd brought with her into her bag. It didn't take long, only a few minutes, but every second that passed felt like an eternity. Chris was hurt. She had to hurry.

"Let's go," she said, flying down the stairs, marching past Alex and out the door. Five minutes later the car was moving, pointed south, back to Los Angeles.

"Tell me what happened," she demanded. "Tell me as much as you know."

News vans filled the parking lot in front of the entrance to the private hospital. It looked as if there were fifty or more reporters milling around, waiting for information on Chris, some kind of update they could plaster all over the internet. Alex parked the crappy four-door sedan he was driving far enough away from the reporters that Sofia could see them, see what they were doing, but not so close they would recognize her. He pulled a cell phone from his pocket and made a call.

"Ten minutes," he said after hanging up, chancing a look at Sofia out of the corner of his eye.

Sofia stared out the window, every possible scenario running through her head, all of them bad, each thought growing worse, more catastrophic with each passing second. She was desperate to see Chris, desperate to know how he was, desperate to let him know she was there. Her fingers tapped against her legs, and she kept checking the time on her recently charged phone. Ten minutes after Alex made his phone call, a door at the back of the hospital opened, and a man she vaguely recognized stepped out. He looked both directions, then hurried across the grass to the sedan.

He leaned over the car, peering in the window at her, then he opened the door and held his hand out to her. She took it and let him help her from the car.

"Sofia," he said, "I'm Seth. It's nice to meet you."

"S-Seth," she stuttered. "You're...you're Chris's best friend."

"That I am. Come on, let's get you inside." He smiled. "Get you to Chris."

"Is he okay?"

"He will be," Seth replied. "Even better after he sees you." He leaned in the car window and smiled at Alex. "Thanks for this, man."

Alex nodded. "Anything for Mr. Chandler." He started the car and drove out of the lot.

Seth took hold of her elbow, guided her through the door he'd just come through, and up the stairs, three flights, each taking longer to climb than the one before. He pushed open the heavy door, striding through it, and down the hall, glancing over his shoulder every few seconds as if he was making sure she was still behind him and they weren't being followed. He stopped outside a room marked "Private."

"He's pretty banged up, Sofia," Seth explained, turning to face her. "His face is a mess, cut and bruised, he's got a severe concussion, and he had to have emergency surgery to remove his damaged spleen. He sprained his left wrist and his left leg is in a walking cast. Not that he's gonna be walking any time soon."

"Jesus Christ," Sofia whispered. Tears leaked from the corner of her eyes, her stomach in knots. She swallowed back the bile rising in her throat. "Alex said it was a car accident?"

Seth nodded and cleared his throat. "Yeah. He was, uh, he was drinking. We both were, at a bar, a place that belongs to his friend. I was going to call Alex to come and get us when we left, but then, Ginny fucking showed up. She and Chris got in a fight, a big one, huge. Chris ran out of the bar, and before I could stop him, he was in his car, driving away. A mile from the bar, he lost control of the Beamer, crossed the centerline, swerved to avoid an oncoming car, and flipped his car, rolling it several times. They had to cut him out. They will charge him with a DUI. The only reason he's not cuffed to that bed in there, under arrest, is because his manager is one smooth motherfucker, *and* no one else got hurt. Thank God."

By the time Seth finished speaking, the tears streamed down her face. Sofia pressed the back of her hand to her mouth, trying to hold the sobs in, trying and failing to keep it together.

Seth squeezed her shoulder. "He's been asking for you since the accident. Your name was the first thing he said when he came out of surgery. I don't quite understand it, but he needs you, Sofia. He's never needed someone the way he needs you. He's never loved someone the way he loves you. Trust me on that one." He held the door open for her, nodding for her to go in.

The door swung closed behind her, Seth staying in the hall. The room was dark, the lights out and the blinds drawn, the only light coming from the machines surrounding Chris, the only sound a low beep monitoring Chris's heart rate. Slow, steady. Alive.

Standing in Chris's hospital room seemed so surreal. Her life had taken a crazy turn; she felt off-kilter, out of whack, as if she'd just stepped off the world's most twisty, turning rollercoaster. Now that she was there, she didn't know what to do with herself.

Sofia dropped her sweatshirt and backpack on a chair by the wall, crossed the room, and slipped into the chair positioned beside the bed. Chris was asleep, his mouth open a little, his chest rising and falling, his skin pale, a deep, purple bruise on one cheek, his eye black, swollen, closed tight. There was a bandage on his forehead, blood sleeping through the gauze, an IV in his left elbow, and several wires snaking out from beneath the light blue hospital gown, running toward a machine at the head of the bed. She took his hand in hers and kissed his bruised knuckles, caressing them, her chin resting on the edge of the bed, her tear-filled sapphire blue eyes gazing at the man she loved.

"I'm here, Chris," she whispered. "I'm here."

"Sofia?" he muttered, the words thick and garbled. He shifted, wincing, one hand to his head, turning to look at her. "Hey, sweetheart."

"Hey, yourself," she replied. Sofia moved to sit gingerly on the side of the bed, his hand still in hers. She smiled as she leaned over and kissed his cheek. "God, you scared the shit out of me. When Alex told me what happened...I was so worried about you. Do that again, and I will kill you myself."

Chris squeezed her fingers, chuckling low in the back of his throat. He winced again. "Don't make me laugh," he grunted. He rubbed a hand up and down her leg. "I'm sorry, baby."

"For what?" Sofia murmured.

"Everything," he sighed, his eyes drifting closed again. "I'm sorry about everything."

Chris was in the hospital for a little over seventy-two hours, only stopped from checking himself out by the combined force of his doctors and Seth. He'd argued, pouted, even whined a little, but he couldn't win.

He spent most of the first day sleeping, drifting in and out of consciousness, thanks to the pain medication and the aftereffects of the surgery to remove his spleen. Each time he woke up, he would look for Sofia, calling her name if she wasn't nearby. She'd stayed close, the chair pulled right up next to the bed, his hand in hers. The doctors, a team hired by his management team, would swarm in every few hours, check him over, then as one entity, move back out again.

By the end of the second day, Sofia felt like a zombie shuffling around Chris's hospital room, running on autopilot, coffee, and force of will. There was no time to process anything that was happening, nothing she could do but attempt to keep her head above water. There seemed to be a constant flow of people in and out of Chris's hospital room—nurses, doctors, his management team. She wasn't sure how they expected Chris to get the rest they kept instructing him to get; it seemed an impossible task because of all the people in and out of the room.

Sofia dreaded the visits from Chris's management team, especially his manager, Jack. It was obvious he did not approve of her; in fact, she was sure Jack hated her. After their first visit to Chris's hospital room, she felt so uncomfortable that she made herself scarce whenever any of them showed up. She could not deal with the scathing looks they shot her way or the complete contempt radiating from them. Unfortunately, they seemed to be there several times a day.

On the morning of the third day, they arrived to talk to Chris before he checked out of the hospital. The second Jack stepped through the door, his typical "what the fuck are you doing here" expression on his face, Sofia grabbed her purse and excused herself, finding a quiet spot in the cafeteria two floors down. Seth found her there, sitting at a table in the corner, staring out the window.

"Hi." He slid into the seat across from her.

"You found me." She grinned.

"I knew you didn't go far. You've been sticking close to Chris unless Jack and Paul and Wendy are around."

"Chris's manager hates me." She shrugged. "Not sure his agent and publicist are any better. It's easier for me to just disappear when they're here." She took a sip from her watered-down coffee, focusing on a spot just over Seth's shoulder. "His management team thinks I ruined his life, don't they?"

Seth stared at her for a full minute, one eyebrow raised. He cleared his throat before he spoke. "They want to blame someone besides Chris. They want all of this madness to be someone else's fault. It's their job to make Chris look like the injured party, the good guy. If they can blame all of this on someone else, they will. No offense, but you are the obvious choice."

"I get that." She sighed. "I do." Sofia set her coffee on the table and blew out a shaky breath. "You know Chris told me he loves me?"

Seth sat back in his chair, arms crossed over his chest, smiling and nodding.

"Don't you think all of this would go away, or at least get better somehow if he told the truth?" Sofia asked. "Told *everyone* he loved me."

"He tried that—" Seth shook his head.

"No," Sofia cut him off. "When that reporter said he loved me, he said nothing, he didn't deny it, he didn't confirm it, instead he got up and walked away— ran away—without a word."

"It's complicated, Sofia."

"Love is always complicated, Seth. But you do what you have to do to make it work if you love someone."

"Chris loves you," Seth insisted.

"I know," Sofia said. "Maybe it's time he told the world."

Seth looked ready to argue, to defend his friend, except his cell phone chirped. Biting back the words on the tip of his tongue, he dragged it from his front pocket.

"The doctors are springing Chris." He smiled. "He wants to go. Now."

Sofia followed Seth back upstairs to Chris's room. They passed Jack and Paul leaving; Sofia felt the weight of Jack's accusing glare on her back, judging her, making her feel like something she'd never believed herself to be.

A whore.

There wasn't time to dwell on that because Chris was up and out of his hospital bed, waiting for them. He grabbed Sofia as soon as she stepped through the door, his mouth on hers. He hugged her to his chest, dragging in one deep breath after another, his heart pounding beneath her cheek.

"Let's get out of here," he whispered.

Getting out was easier said than done. Seth called Chris's driver, Alex, to pick them up, but they decided that to avoid the press with their inevitable speculation and probing questions, Sofia would not leave the hospital with them. While she wasn't on board with that plan—she was tired of hiding, tired of keeping her feelings for Chris hidden from the world—she'd do as he asked. This time.

Sofia watched from behind a potted tree in the lobby as they wheeled Chris out of the hospital to his waiting car, reporters pressing in from every side, shouting questions at him, clamoring for his attention. He made a brief statement, written by his publicist. It addressed the drunk driving charges, apologized for his behavior, but he avoided questions about Sofia, and flat out refused to discuss Ginny. Once he'd said his piece, Seth held the reporters at bay while a nurse ushered his best friend into the backseat of the black limo, then Seth climbed in after him. Chris caught Sofia's eye just before the door closed, winking and smiling at her.

Fifteen minutes later, Sasha arrived in her late nineties Honda Civic. By that time, the press had dispersed, following Chris's limo, allowing Sofia the opportunity to slip out of the hospital and into the burgundy sedan without being seen.

"Where are we going?" Sasha asked.

"Just drive," was Sofia's reply. "I'll tell you when to stop."

An hour later, after one stop for gas and two for coffee, Sasha parked at the bottom of a long hill, near a sidewalk that wound up through the multi-million dollar homes nestled there.

"What are we doing here?" Sasha murmured, peering out the car window.

"Chris lives at the top of that hill," Sofia explained.

"And you're going up there?"

Sofia was nodding before the words were out of her friend's mouth. "He begged me to, Sash. He needs me."

"If he needs you so much, why is he still hiding your relationship? I saw the interview, Sof. He had a chance to tell the entire world how he felt about you, but instead, he got up and ran. Maybe he doesn't need you as much as he thinks. Or as much as you think."

Sofia recoiled. Sasha's words stung, but only because it was her own thoughts echoed back at her. She wanted to scream her love for Chris from the top of the Hollywood sign. Why didn't he want to do the same?

"Sasha, please—" she tapered off. Her head hurt.

Her friend put a hand on her shoulder, squeezing it. She cleared her throat. "You sure you don't want me to come with you?" she asked.

Sofia shook her head. "No, I'm good." Sasha shot her a skeptical look. "Really, Sash, I'll be fine."

She hugged her best friend, her only friend, snagged her backpack off the floor, and climbed from the car, disappearing into a stand of trees near the sidewalk. She followed the directions Chris had given her, directions that had her traipsing through the neighborhood, coming out in an alley between two rows of homes. It took her almost five minutes before she found the black wrought iron gate leading into Chris's yard and slipped inside. A few seconds later, she was standing at Chris's sliding glass door at the back of the house, staring into an enormous living room with hardwood floors and cozy looking modern furniture. It was now or never; she could turn and walk away, change her number, take the money she'd saved the last three years and disappear. It would hurt like hell, but it might be the best thing for both of them.

Sofia tapped on the glass. A giant blob of black and white fur appeared at the door, tail wagging, head cocked to one side, tongue hanging out of the side of its mouth, staring at her. The dog let out a bark so loud it seemed to rattle the glass, then it licked the closed door.

"Oliver, cool it!" Chris laughed, limping as fast as he could across the room. He bent over beside the dog, wincing as he did, patted the furry animal, and whispered something in its ear. Whatever he said sent it rushing out of the room.

Chris yanked the door open, grabbed her hand, and pulled her inside. She stumbled, falling against him, though he caught her easily, despite his injuries. His arm slid around her waist, his head falling to her shoulder.

"I'm glad you're here."

Sofia wrapped her hands around him, absentmindedly scratching at the hairs at the back of his neck. "Me too," she replied.

Their kiss, which could have turned into so much more, was interrupted by a four-legged beast pushing between them, almost knocking Sofia on her ass, and dropping a ball between her feet.

Chris chuckled. "Sofia, this is Oliver. Ollie, that's Sofia."

She crouched in front of the excited dog and let him smell her hand. After a few seconds, he tentatively licked her face, then sat, staring at her.

"I think he likes you." Chris smiled.

Sofia rose to her feet. "As much as his owner?"

"Nah," he grunted, pulling her back into his arms. "Not quite that much. His owner loves you."

She ran a hand down the side of his face, tracing the line of his jaw, his cheekbone, her fingers dancing over the bruises covering him. A million questions tried to push past her lips, but she forced them back.

"You look exhausted," she said instead.

"I am," he sighed.

"Why aren't you in bed sleeping?"

"I was waiting for you." Chris shrugged. His eyes were half-closed, his words slurring, a side effect of the pain medication the doctor gave him. She wasn't sure how he was still standing.

"Come on. Let's get you to bed." She took his hand in hers and took a step toward a large archway leading out of the living room before realizing that she had no idea which way to go.

"Um, where's the bedroom?"

Chris stepped around her, laughing as he led her through the house to a vast bedroom. He dropped her hand and shuffled to the bed, easing himself onto it, lying down with his foot propped on a stack of pillows. He gestured for Sofia to join him.

Her backpack fell to the floor at the end of the bed, and she kicked her shoes off, crawling up the bed to join Chris. His eyes were already closed, his breathing slowing as he drifted toward sleep. He pulled her into his arms, hugging her close, his lips just grazing hers before he dropped off into a deep slumber.

It took Sofia a lot longer to fall asleep; she laid there staring at the ceiling for quite some time, her head spinning. It was the first time since she'd found out about Chris's accident that she had time to think, to replay and process everything that had happened. The sheer amount of changes that had occurred over the last few days overwhelmed her. Never in a million years did she think she would be in Chris's house, lying in his bed, tucked under his arm as he slept. That had always been a pipe dream, the ultimate dream. It was everything she'd wanted for months.

So, why wasn't she happy?

Chapter Twenty-Five

CHRIS

Chris's grandfather, the world's biggest pessimist, always said, "Things could always get worse."

Chris didn't want to believe that; he believed things could only get better. Having a woman in his life, a woman he loved more than anything, only made him believe that more. His life had taken a left turn, going in a direction he'd never expected. He couldn't blame anyone but himself for the shitstorm his life had become. Everything that happened was his doing. The accident, the DUI, all the crap Sofia was going through, it was his fault. He prayed every day that there wouldn't be anything else. He didn't want to put Sofia through anything else.

Since coming home from the hospital, he'd spent every day with Sofia. She was a staple around the house. He'd grown accustomed to having her around.

In fact, he liked it so much that making it a permanent thing had crossed his mind more than once. Today was the first day he hadn't seen her, the first day they'd been apart. All he wanted was to get inside, get Sofia on the phone, and get her over here. He needed her.

He'd spent the better part of the last three hours discussing the DUI the police had charged him with after the accident. His lawyer was a miracle worker; Chris would get off with nothing more than community service and a hefty fine. While that made his management team happy, he couldn't stop dwelling on the fact that he could have killed someone. The thought made his head hurt and his stomach churn.

His cell phone rang as he unlocked the door. "You home?" Seth asked before Chris uttered a word.

Seth had left two days earlier, gone home to take care of his flourishing construction business in upstate New York. Chris felt like a complete asshole keeping him away from home and his business. Even though Seth never complained, Chris felt awful, demanding too much of the people he cared about and giving them nothing in return.

"Just got here. Why?" he responded.

"There's something you need to see," Seth said. "Turn on the TV."

"What now?" Chris sighed. "What channel?"

"It doesn't matter," Seth said. "It's on every channel."

Chris grabbed the remote and turned on the television. He found the entertainment channel, the one that had been running a multitude of stories about him. Ginny's face popped up on the screen, streaked with makeup and tears. Under the glaring lights on set, Chris could see where the extensions attached to her real hair and splotches where her fake tan wasn't evenly applied. It was as if everything fake about her was on full display. Not that anything about Ginny was real.

A squeaky sob erupted from the television, loud enough to make Chris cringe. Ginny talked to a reporter offscreen, and the story she told was enough to make Chris drop to the couch, nauseous, his hands shaking so much he dropped the remote, her words ringing in his head. Drunk, cheater, abuser. If there was something bad one person could do to another, Ginny claimed Chris did it to her.

"You should see the bruises on my arms," she sniffled, touching her sleeve covered arms. "I'm so embarrassed. I can't believe I let him hurt me." Some sympathetic sound came from the reporter, which only egged Ginny on, sending her on a rant about Chris pushing her in the bar, knocking her to the floor for everyone to see. When she sobbed again, he grabbed the remote off the floor and shut off the television. He spun around, the remote flying across the room, hitting the corner of the glass door, cracking it, and drawing a startled bark from Oliver.

"When is it going to fucking end?" he screamed, dropping his head into his hands, his phone falling to the floor. His ears were ringing, his eyes pulsing, feeling as if they were bulging in their sockets, trying desperately to pop out, his head locked in the vise grip of a debilitating headache.

"Chris? Chris, can you hear me?" Seth shouted.
He disconnected the call without responding.

Chris tried to get some rest, the headache now bad enough he might vomit, but he couldn't sleep. He picked up his phone several times to call Sofia, but what was he supposed to say? He was running out of words, running out of ways to apologize; he wasn't sure how much more Sofia would take, how much more could happen before she called it quits.

After trying to sleep for an hour, he moved from his bedroom to the living room and stretched out on the couch, a baseball game on TV, his phone on the table, off. Five innings into the game, a sharp knock on the sliding glass door had Oliver barking and him dragging himself off the couch, the headache so bad he couldn't see straight. Sofia glared at him from the other side of the glass, her brow furrowed, her shoulders stiff, lips pursed.

He opened the door and leaned against the jamb. "Hey."

"You turned off your phone," she snapped.

"I was trying to sleep," he groaned, wincing, a hand to his head.

Sofia pushed past him, stopping long enough to pet Oliver before continuing to the couch. She perched on the edge, her back ramrod straight, her hands folded tightly in front of her.

"Seth called me."

Chris lowered himself to the couch beside her and took her hand in his. "He ratted me out?"

"He's worried about you," Sofia said. "So am I."

"I'm fine," he grumbled, though the painful twinge behind his eye said otherwise.

"What are you going to do about Ginny?" she asked.

"I don't know," he muttered. "Hope someone hits her with a car? Or maybe she'll drown in all those fake tears she's been crying. I know I don't want to talk about it. Not right now." He returned to his previous position, stretched out on the couch. "Come here." He held out his arms, grateful that Sofia didn't hesitate to crawl into them, wrapping her own arms around him and letting him pull her down beside him, curled against his side.

Sofia put her hand on his cheek, tracing the cheekbone and the fading bruise around his still swollen eye. "You can't hide from your problems, Chris. They won't go away on their own. You need to stand up to her or she wins."

He closed his eyes, his forehead resting against hers. "I know, baby, I do. But I'm not sure how much longer I can fight. I'm drained."

The faint brush of her lips against his quieted him, pushed all thoughts of Ginny out of his head. It was soft and gentle at first, but growing more intense with each pass of her mouth over his. It wasn't long before his hands were beneath her shirt, their legs tangled together, both of them panting. His entire body thrummed with need. He rolled her beneath him, his thigh pushing her legs open, his hands caressing her flushed skin, his kisses becoming more demanding, his aching head forgotten, all of his injuries forgotten. Only Sofia mattered.

He didn't know how long they laid together, bodies intertwined, their desire ramped up to immeasurable heights. Chris had his hands on the button of her jeans, opening them, but Sofia pushed him away, easing herself out from beneath him, her breasts heaving with every breath she dragged in, her cheeks tinged pink, her lips kiss swollen.

"Enough," she said. "You're supposed to be resting, not raising your blood pressure. Doctor's orders."

"All right," Chris sighed, shaking his head. "All right." He laid back, hands beneath his head, feet crossed. He closed his eyes, the sounds of the baseball game and Sofia's steady breathing filling his ears. Sleep came easily when she was near.

"Chris?"

He grunted and pulled the pillow over his face, trying to block out the light hitting his face. He'd been dreaming, a pleasant dream, a dream filled with light, love, perfection—Sofia. The dream was losing its realness, its solidity, fading quickly. He reached for it, tried to hold on to it, wanting to keep it for as long as he could.

"Chris? Wake up! We need to talk."

This time he opened his eyes, pulled the pillow from his face, squinting at Sofia. She had moved at some point, freeing herself of his arms to sit near his feet. The remote was in her hand. He chanced a glance at the TV, startled to see Ginny's overly made-up face frozen on the screen.

"I don't want to watch this again," he groaned, hiding his face beneath the pillow. "I can't stand the sound of her voice."

"I need to show you something," Sofia insisted. "I have to ask you a question. An important one."

Chris rolled off the couch and dragged himself to the bar on the other side of the living room. He felt Sofia's eyes on him as he opened the small refrigerator beneath the countertop and pulled out a water. He drank the entire bottle before returning to her side. His headache was back, throbbing behind his eyes.

"All right, what is it?" he asked, rubbing the center of his forehead.

Sofia hit play on the remote. "Do you know that woman with Ginny? That one in the purple dress."

Chris studied the woman in the purple dress. "Um, shit, I think her name is, uh, Tanya? Tammie? Yeah, that one's Tammie with an *i* and an *e*. She's one of the girls that Ginny calls her 'squad.' Why?"

Sofia hit pause and set the remote on the table. "I know her. And Ginny, too."

"What?" That wasn't what he expected her to say.

"I don't know why I didn't tell you," she mumbled, staring at her hands folded in her lap. "I guess I thought it didn't matter. After the press got my name, I wondered if it could be her who told them."

"Wait? Why would it be her? How would Ginny know you were an escort?"

Sofia exhaled, her shoulders shaking. "She worked for Private Lives. She started as an escort, but she couldn't cut it, so they moved her to the office. It wasn't long, maybe six, seven months, less than a year for sure. Then one day, she was gone, like she'd never existed. I knew she was on some reality show, but it wasn't important. It didn't matter until my name came out. But deep inside, I always wondered if Ginny had something to do with it. I convinced myself that couldn't be true, that she wouldn't, *couldn't*, do that to another woman, that she wouldn't dare violate her non-disclosure agreement. Then I saw this interview." She gestured at the TV. "That woman in the purple dress? Tammie? She's Georgia's secretary."

Chris shook his head. "Georgia? The lady who owns Private Lives, right?"

Sofia nodded, grimacing. "I did not know Ginny and Tammie were friends. I doubt Georgia even knew."

A smile spread across Chris's face. For the first time since everything had happened, he thought things might go their way. He leaned over and kissed Sofia.

"Babe, I think you should call Georgia," he grinned. "I'm gonna need to talk to her."

Chris was tired of meetings, tired of sitting like a bump on a log, listening to everyone around him tell him how he should live his life. Today was no exception, though he thought it might end differently than anyone expected.

Jack started in on Chris as soon as he came through the door. Right off the bat, he brought up Sofia and the rumors they'd been spending time together since he'd left the hospital. Not that they were inaccurate rumors, but Chris knew no one had seen her; they'd been too careful. It was speculation by the press, nothing more.

"I thought we talked about this before you left the hospital. About you not seeing that woman?" his manager chastised. "What were you thinking?"

"I'm getting really tired of that question, Jack," Chris sighed. "Exhausted, in fact."

"And I'm tired of putting out your fires," Jack snapped. "Speaking of fires, what the fuck are we going to do about Princess Ginny's latest bombshell?"

"Keep in mind who forced 'Princess Ginny' on me, Jack," Chris growled. "None of this shit with Ginny would have happened if you hadn't pushed me to date her to advance my career."

"May I suggest something?" Wendy interjected, stopping the argument between them from continuing. "We release a statement saying that Chris is under a lot of stress, a lot of pressure, that a simple misunderstanding escalated into something it shouldn't have. We don't admit guilt, we don't admit he hit her—"

"I'm fucking done with statements. You and Jack have done a shit job of controlling Ginny's statements about me, so forgive me if I don't trust you." He shifted in his seat, glaring at his management team one by one. "And for the last time, I didn't hit her,"

"But you pushed her." Wendy shot him a condescending look, her finger wagging in his face.

"No, I didn't," Chris said. "She's lying. Again."

"We can't prove it." Jack shook his head.

Chris didn't bother to remind them that a bar full of witnesses could prove it. He scrubbed a hand over his face. "I'm so pleased that two-thirds of my management team believes a bunch of lies about me," Chris huffed. "Paul? You've been awfully quiet."

Paul shrugged and gave Chris a wry smile. "I don't for a second think you hit or pushed that girl," he said. "And I was never on board with the whole 'date Ginny for publicity' idea. I went along with it because I thought it might work out for the best. Obviously, I was wrong. I never trusted Ginny, for good reason. She has an ulterior motive and has since day one. She will not be happy unless she tears you down."

"Jesus, why didn't you say something sooner?" Chris grumbled.

"I never thought it would get this far." His agent shrugged. "I should have said something, and believe me, I regret keeping quiet. I'm sorry. I can only hope she doesn't destroy your career before we can rein her in."

"I don't think we have to worry," Chris replied. "I'll take care of Ginny." That line from the *Wizard of Oz*— and her little dog, too—popped into his head, and he had to stifle the insane laughter bubbling out of his chest.

Chris's lawyer, Albert, opened the door, and ushered in the conversation's subject, along with her two ever-present friends, Tanya and Tammie. Ginny had a smug look on her face, the proverbial cat that swallowed the canary. She slid into a chair across from Chris, her hands folded in front of her. She wore a sweater and slacks, more covered up than he'd ever seen her. Apparently, it was harder to hide the lack of bruises when she was wearing her normal, skin-baring clothes.

"What am I doing here, Chris?" Ginny asked, a decided snarl in her voice. She avoided making eye contact with the other people in the room, her focus on Chris and Chris alone.

"I thought we should talk," he explained.

Then, and only then, did Ginny look around at the group assembled in the room. "Is that why these people are here? So, *you and I* can talk?" she brayed like a donkey. "If you're going to talk me out of pressing charges, you're out of luck." She smirked. "I have bruises. Lots of them." She patted her cloth-covered arm where his hand had been in the bar, where he had grabbed her in his enraged, drunken stupor.

Chris ignored her attempt to drag him into an argument. He knew she was baiting him, trying to get him to explode again. He'd made that mistake once. He had no intention of making it again. Out of the corner of his eye, he saw Wendy open her mouth, hellfire in her eyes, but he put a hand up to quiet her.

"I'm not here to discuss that, either." He shook his head.

"Then why am I here?" Ginny spat.

Chris nodded at Albert, who opened a door on the opposite side of the room, this one leading to another conference room. A sharply dressed older woman gathered the papers scattered in front of her and crossed the threshold between the two rooms.

Ginny's eyes widened, her heavily made-up lips falling open. Tammie shrank in her chair, eyes downcast, her face as white as a ghost.

"Ginny, I think you know Georgia Pierce," Chris murmured. "Owner of Private Lives?"

Ginny nodded, just a tip of her chin, almost imperceptible, but it was there. Georgia stopped beside the reality star and handed her a stack of papers, then she turned and shoved a similar stack into Tammie's hands.

"Ladies," Georgia barked, making both women jump in their seats. "Those papers are copies of the non-disclosure agreements you signed with Private Lives. Legally binding non-disclosure agreements. NDAs that you have both violated."

Ginny's mouth opened and closed like a fish in a fishbowl. Her eyes flitted around the room as if she was looking for escape. Tammie licked her lips and shifted uneasily in her chair.

"I don't know what you're talking about," Ginny muttered.

Georgia crossed her arms and glared at the platinum blonde. "I suspect that you leaked Sofia's information to the press. Her name, my company's name, all of it. You or your best friend over there." She nodded in Tammie's direction. "And while I can't prove you leaked that video of Sofia and Mr. Chandler, I believe you were responsible for that as well. I already have staff working on the paper trail, and from what they are telling me, it appears to lead back to you and Tammie releasing private information about my clients and staff. An obvious violation of the NDA you signed with Private Lives."

"You...you can't expect..." Ginny blew out a stuttering breath. "You can't expect us to abide by those. My agent said—"

"Whatever your agent told you is wrong, Ms. Etling," Georgia said firmly. "I can and will go after *both* of you for violating those NDAs. Every dime you earn for the next ten years will be mine. If not longer."

Ginny crushed the papers in her hand and looked around as if she wanted to escape. "What do you want?" she murmured.

"I want you to set the record straight," Chris spoke up. "Stop telling lies about me. You tell the truth— we were never in a relationship, I never hurt you, we weren't about to get engaged, and whatever else you might have fabricated gets put right. Then you get out of my life. Forever."

"No. No way." Her fake blonde extensions whipped back and forth as she shook her head. She threw the papers on the table. "You will pay for what you've done to me. You will not treat me like this, like...like I'm not as good as you." Her volume kept increasing until she was screaming, her face red, her eyes bulging. "You fucked a whore. A goddamn whore. While you were supposed to be my boyfriend. Do you know how that makes me look? Do you know how foolish I feel? You did that to me, Chris, and I will not stand by and let it happen. Not after what you did to me."

Behind Ginny, Tammie's eyes went wide, and her hands shook. What little color she had left in her cheeks drained away, as if her digested lunch might make a comeback. "Gin, please," she begged weakly. "It's not worth it."

With a roll of her eyes, Ginny turned toward Tammie. "They're not gonna do anything, Tam. They don't have the balls. Chris doesn't have the balls," she sneered, laughing, a sharp, barking laugh.

"Let's get something straight. I have done nothing to you, Gin." Chris shook his head. "Not yet. But I guarantee you, if you don't do as I've asked, I will expose you and your lies to every media outlet imaginable. I will make sure the world knows what an insane fake bitch you are. You won't be able to get a job acting in a third-rate D movie once I'm finished with you."

Georgia spoke up, her eyes flashing as she glared at Ginny and Tammie. "I was kind the last time we saw each other, Ginny. Kind, despite the problems you caused Private Lives. I could have done so much more than fire you. I will not do that again." She perched on the edge of the table, staring down at them. "You agree to do what Mr. Chandler has asked *and* you tell us who released those photos and videos—"

"That wasn't us," Tammie squawked. "It was one of Sofia's clients, Patrick—"

Ginny spun around, glaring at the other woman. "Tam, shut up!"

"Ms. Etling," Georgia smirked, her tone calm. "This is your last chance. You agree to what Mr. Chandler said, and I will consider forgetting that you violated an ironclad non-disclosure agreement."

"You…you've got to be kidding me," the reality star sputtered. "This is ridiculous…and…and unfair."

"No, it's not." Chris shook his head. "What's unfair is you trying to destroy the lives of two people because you're a greedy bitch."

"Fine!" Ginny hissed. She rubbed her forehead, glanced at Tammie over her shoulder once more, and scooped up the stack of papers sitting in front of her. "If I agree, then nothing happens with this?" She waved the papers in Chris's direction.

"That's not up to me," Chris shrugged. "But I won't make it worse." He leaned back in his chair, his arms crossed over his chest, and nodded in Georgia's direction. "I can't promise she won't do anything, though."

"You're a bastard," Ginny whispered. "I hope you know that, Chris. You're an absolute bastard." She slumped, defeated. "What do I need to do?"

Chris's team descended on her, his lawyer shoving papers in her face, uttering instructions to the dejected actress. Chris sat back and watched, relieved, a million pounds lifted from his chest. He was free.

———

Sofia sat on the couch, waiting, Oliver's head in her lap. She didn't move when he came in, only stared up at him, smiling, a sheen of tears in her eyes. He didn't say a word, just crossed the room and took her in his arms. He wanted her, wanted her like a thirst he couldn't quench, a hunger he couldn't quell; he needed her too much. He was desperate to have her, to feel her in his arms, to make love to her.

Their clothes hit the floor the minute they were in the bedroom, then they were in the bed, drunk with excitement over what had happened. Chris floated on a high he thought he'd never come down from. Not that he wanted to.

Afterward, they laid in the dark, buried beneath piles of blankets in Chris's bed, Oliver sleeping on the floor, his soft snores echoing through the room. They hadn't talked much since he'd returned from his meeting, just his whispered reassurances that things were better.

"It's over," Chris whispered, his nose buried against the side of her neck. He pulled her closer, her naked body flush against his. "We're free."

Sofia stiffened in his arms, her head shaking. "It's not over, not yet. Maybe the stuff with Ginny is, but you and me, the shit about us, that's far from over."

"What do you mean?" Chris asked, pushing himself up on one arm to look down at her.

"We're not free, Chris," Sofia muttered, struggling to free herself from his arms. She pushed off the blankets and stumbled out of the bed. "Not yet. Not until you admit you love me."

Chris shoved himself up on the bed, unable to ignore the surge of pain deep in his gut. "Sofia, you know I love you. I *told* you I love you."

She groaned and raked her hands through her hair. "You don't get it! I know you love me, Chris. But, what about everyone else?" She snatched her clothes off the floor and yanked them on. "You know that you've never said it publicly, that you've never actually told anyone with the press you love me? As far as the world is concerned, I *am* just a whore you fucked."

He cringed at her words. "Screw everyone else! I don't give a shit about anyone but you!" Chris wasn't shouting, not yet, but he was close, teetering on the edge, the anger building and building, like the water in a forgotten tub, close to spilling over and ruining everything. He wasn't angry with Sofia—it was everything else, all that had happened. He was still holding onto the hope he could have it all—the girl, the career, the happily ever after. They'd reached a turning point, or so he thought, the dream within his grasp. He didn't want to think about the alternatives.

Chris pushed himself out of the bed, stumbling and twisting on his wounded ankle. He took a deep breath, a poor attempt to squelch his anger before he let it loose on the woman he loved.

Tears streamed down Sofia's face, and he wanted to go to her, to pull her into his arms and tell her that everything would be okay, that he would fix it. But as soon as he took a step toward her, she backed away, her hand up, shaking her head. It couldn't have hurt more if she'd stabbed him in the heart.

"I know you love me," she repeated, holding the edge of the bed to keep herself steady as she shoved her feet into her shoes. "But where do we go from here?" She swiped at the tears sliding down her face.

"I'm a secret, Chris, a dirty little secret you've held onto for over six months. Plain and simple, I'm a whore—"

"Don't say that. You're the woman I love."

"That may be true, but that's not how I feel. You sneak me in and out the back door. You hide me away from your manager, your publicist, your agent, from the world. You pretend I don't exist to protect yourself."

"That's only because I can't watch the entire world tear you apart," Chris snapped, pushing a shaking hand through his ruffled hair. "I've seen what they're saying about you. I read the blogs, the news stories, the snide comments. They're so cruel, tearing you down, reducing you to something you're not. I hate it. I despise it. Babe, I'm trying to protect you."

"I don't need you to protect me. I'm not some damsel in distress, and this isn't a fairytale, Chris!" Sofia cried. "This isn't one of your movies." She pushed past him, heading for the back door. Oliver followed her, his tail wagging, looking back over his shoulder at Chris, curious why his owner wasn't following this new human that had become a staple in their home during the last couple of weeks.

Chris followed her down the hall and through the living room, but all he could do was watch her go. Nothing he said would change her feelings; nothing would make her feel better. They'd been going around and around for a week, even before meeting with Ginny, back and forth, not quite arguing, but closer than they'd ever been before. Now that everything with Ginny had come together, he'd hoped maybe the rest would fall into place. He thought maybe the rest of the world would forget how he and Sofia had met and leave them alone to live their lives. He foolishly hoped they could ride off into the sunset and live happily ever after.

Maybe he was being foolish, foolish to believe he could have the dream come true, foolish to think he could walk away with it all.

That would not stop him from trying.

Chapter Twenty-Six
SOFIA

"I need time, Chris," Sofia sighed.

"It's been a week," Chris said. "Sof, I...I need you."

She didn't like the desperation she heard in his voice. The guilt wrapped around her heart like a vice and squeezed. She hated herself; she shouldn't feel guilty because she needed time to think, time to process, time to figure things out.

As for Chris, well, he shouldn't need her, shouldn't want her. No one ever had. No one ever would. She wasn't worth loving; the people in her life had taught her that—her mom, her boyfriend, her friends. It was just a matter of time before he realized it, too. She had to prepare herself for the inevitable.

"You don't need me," she insisted. "You want me. There's a difference."

"Sofia, I love you." His voice broke.

"I know," she replied. "I just wish you could admit it to someone besides me." She dragged in a deep, shaky breath. "I have to go. I'll talk to you later."

It was the same argument they'd been having all week. While things were better for Chris, the horrible rumors about her intensified. She went into hiding, a prisoner in her own home. Every time she went out in public, it felt as if everyone was staring at her, talking about her, judging her, pointing their fingers, those vile names on the tips of their tongues. The press still hovered, hanging around outside of her condo, bombarding her whenever she stepped out the door. She couldn't check the mail or put out her trash or recycling cans. They were always there. Each time she looked out the window and saw them sitting there, it reminded her that Chris hadn't been able to do the one thing she needed him to do.

Sofia closed the box stuffed with clothes and sealed it with packing tape. She'd spent the morning packing her clothes, her "work clothes" into boxes. There was no need to keep all the dresses and shoes, so she'd picked through them, keeping her favorites, getting rid of the others. When she pulled the peacock blue dress from the closet, everything hit her like a punch to the gut, and she burst into tears, staggering backward until her knees hit the bed. She cried until her head hurt, her nose ran, and she couldn't breathe.

It was cathartic.

"You want another glass of wine?" Sasha stuck her head in the door, the bottle of chardonnay in her hand.

"Yeah," Sofia nodded, sniffling.

"You okay?" her friend asked. "You look like you've been crying. Again."

"I have." She shrugged, smoothing her hand over the dress laying across her lap. "I miss him." Those three words were harder to say than her admission of love. She hated being the desperate, needy damsel in distress.

Sasha came all the way into the room, picked up Sofia's glass, filled it to the brim, and forced it into her hand. "There's no doubt you miss him. You love him. He loves you. It has to hurt like hell that you haven't seen him."

"You're supposed to be making me feel better," Sofia complained, swiping at the tears sliding down her face. "Not reminding me why I'm miserable."

"Sorry." Sasha shook her head and laughed. She sat beside her friend, grabbed the edge of the dress, and rubbed it between her fingers. "It's gorgeous."

"This was the dress I wore the night Chris told me he loved me for the first time."

"Oh sweetie, it's okay." Sasha put an arm around her, hugging her close. "It's all gonna work out."

"I don't know. I'm not sure about anything anymore." She wrenched herself away from Sasha and threw herself backward on the bed, staring at the ceiling. "And what if it does? Even if everything works out, and we get the happily ever after, I will still always be the whore that the famous actor fell in love with; it will follow us for the rest of our lives. This isn't some movie, Sasha. Chris won't climb the fire escape and sweep me off my feet."

"Well, yeah," Sasha interjected, "you don't have a fire escape."

Sofia burst out laughing, doubled over, holding her stomach, tears streaming down her face. Leave it to her best friend to lighten the moment, to make her feel better. Thank God for Sasha.

"Come on. Let's finish boxing all this stuff up, then we can watch that new movie, the one that looks hilarious." Sasha set her wine glass on the table, grabbed a stack of clothes, and kicked a box to the middle of the room.

"Fine," Sofia sighed, joining her friend in the center of the bedroom. "As long as it's not a romance."

The knock on the door startled her, her coffee spilling on the counter. It wasn't even seven a.m., but she was awake, had been since about four. She'd unsuccessfully tried to go back to sleep, finally giving up. Now she was on her second pot of coffee.

"What the hell?" Sofia muttered to herself. She stalked down the hall, sliding to a stop in front of the door.

It had been a while since the reporters had been ballsy enough to knock on her door. Perhaps it annoyed them that she was becoming a non-story, and they thought they'd stir things up. She hit the button on the camera covering her front door, a recent acquisition thanks to Billy. He installed it while she stayed with Chris.

Sofia didn't recognize the man standing at her door at first; it wasn't until he pushed his hat back from his face and peered into the camera that she knew who it was. She yanked open the door a couple of inches.

"Alex? What are you doing here?"

"Morning, Ms. Larson," Alex said. "May I come in?"

"Yes, of course. Sorry," she responded. When she opened the door, she noticed that the street seemed to be empty of reporters, only two or three cars out front.

"Is Chris okay?" She couldn't help but think of the last time Alex had shown up at her door—the night Chris had rolled his car.

"He's fine," he assured her. "But Mr. Chandler sent me. He was wondering if you'd be able to join him this morning."

"I..I... I don't know," Sofia stammered. "I shouldn't...I should...I should stay here."

Alex scraped the toe of his shoe along the edge of the carpet. "May I talk to you for a moment?"

She nodded and opened the door all the way to let him in. "Coffee's in the kitchen." She gestured for him to follow her.

Alex sat on a barstool at the kitchen counter, a faint smile on his face. "I've never been much for beating around the bush, so I'll get straight to the point. I've been Chris's driver and bodyguard for a long time. I've never known him to be happier than he's been since you came into his life. He loves you. You know that, right?"

Sofia paused, set the pot down with a shaking hand, and pushed the half full cup across the counter.

"Yes."

"Do you love him?"

"Yes." She wiped away the tear sliding down her cheek. "Yes, I love him very much."

"Then do me a favor and just trust him, okay? Come with me and see what he wants. That's all he's asking."

As much as she wanted to stand her ground, she also wanted to know what was so important that Chris sent his bodyguard to retrieve her. Alex said Chris loved her. She wanted to believe him.

"Where?" she asked.

"I'm afraid I can't say," Alex replied. "He, well, he wants you to trust him. He'll explain everything as soon as he can."

She leaned against the counter and stared out the window, her heart and her head fighting over what she should do. After a minute, she stood straight and turned to Alex.

"I need time to get ready." Sofia pointed to her pajama pants and sweatshirt.

Alex chuckled. "Take your time."

Forty-five minutes later, she was in the backseat of a dark blue Escalade, driving into the heart of Los Angeles. Alex wasn't forthcoming with what was happening or where they were going; he would only tell her that things would make sense soon, and Chris would explain everything when they arrived.

They pulled into the parking garage of a high-rise building smack in the middle of the city. Alex helped her from the vehicle and led her to the elevator where they met a matronly woman in her fifties.

"Thank you, Alex." The woman smiled at the driver. "Mr. Chandler will call you when he's ready to leave." After Alex nodded his understanding and headed back to the car, she turned her attention to Sofia.

"Ms. Larson, my name is Anita," she explained, extending her hand, which Sofia shook warily. "I'm sure you're curious about what is going on."

"You could say that," Sofia said, just as the elevator pinged and the doors opened. She followed Anita inside. "No offense, but who are you?"

"Sorry," the woman chuckled. "I'm Albert Goldberg's administrative assistant. Mr. Goldberg is Mr. Chandler's lawyer. We're going to his offices on the upper level."

Chris's lawyer. Sofia's stomach dropped, and she broke out in a clammy sweat. If she wasn't worried before, she was now.

"Why?" she asked, her hands crossed in front of her, her nails digging into the palms.

"I'm sorry, but Mr. Chandler asked to be the one to explain everything," Anita said. "Don't worry. You'll understand soon enough."

The elevator doors opened to a back hallway, concrete walls and no windows. Sofia followed Anita, her heels loudly clicking on the uncarpeted floors.

"I apologize that we had to bring you in this way," Anita explained. "It's to avoid the press." She took a key from the pocket of her jacket and unlocked a heavy metal door, gesturing for Sofia to go in first.

Sofia stood in an overly decorated room with an enormous conference table surrounded by chairs. Seated at the far end of the table was Chris, along with his manager, agent, and publicist, and an older gentleman she didn't recognize; she assumed it was his lawyer. As soon as the door opened, whatever conversation the group had been having abruptly stopped. Chris rose from his seat, ignoring Jack's hand on his elbow as he hurried the length of the table, reaching Sofia in just a few strides of his long legs, pulling her into his arms and kissing her.

"God, I missed you," he breathed.

She choked back a sob. She hadn't realized how much she missed him until she stood there with him. "I missed you, too. So much."

"Thank you for coming."

"You're welcome." She smiled. "Now, do you want to tell me why I'm here?"

"Come here." He dragged her after him, sitting her in a chair beside him. The weight of his manager's and publicist's hateful stares sat heavy on her shoulders while his agent looked confused. The only person in the room who seemed calm, aside from Chris, was the older gentleman no one had introduced.

Once she sat down, Chris made formal introductions all around. He kept a tight grip on her hand, which earned them dirty looks from Jack. It was Wendy who asked the question on everyone's mind.

"Why are we here, Chris?" She stared pointedly at Sofia.

The older gentleman rose to his feet. "Ms. Larson, I'm Albert Goldberg, Mr. Chandler's lawyer. He called a press conference—"

"You can't do that," Jack blurted, his cheeks turning bright red.

"I can and I did," Chris responded. "I have something to say, and I want it to be *my* words, *my* thoughts, *my* feelings. I'm not letting anyone else speak for me anymore."

Wendy shook her head, her lips pursed. She opened her mouth, snapped it shut with an audible click, then she rose to her feet, picked up her bag, and left without a word.

"Well, that saved me a conversation," Chris muttered. He sat up straighter and turned to his manager. "You might as well follow her, Jack."

"What?" Jack snapped. "What are you talking about?"

"You're fired, Jack. The only best interests you have in mind are yours, not mine. Every turn I've made has had you forcing me to do something I didn't want to do—Ginny, previous statements to the press, not speaking to Sofia—those were all things I didn't want. If I had told the truth from the beginning, if I had stood my ground when you were forcing Ginny on me, a lot of things would be different. It's too late to fix it now, but you can bet your ass from now on, things will be a lot different."

"This is bullshit," Jack sputtered as he sprang from his seat. He tapped his knuckles on the table as he spoke. "You are out of your goddamn mind. If you could see past the end of your dick for five seconds, you'd know you're making a mistake. A terrible mistake." He turned his angry gaze on Sofia. "You must suck one hell of a cock."

Chris jumped out of his seat, his face red, his jaw clenched, fists up, ready to swing, but Albert put a reassuring hand on his shoulder, pressing him down into his seat before nodding at Anita, who took Jack by the elbow and escorted him from the room without a glance back.

Paul cleared his throat. "I guess that just leaves me. Am I out of a job, too?"

"Not yet." Chris shook his head. "I need to keep somebody. While you weren't always supportive, you tried harder than Jack or Wendy. There will be some changes though, that's for goddamn sure." He checked the watch on his arm. "It's time for the press conference."

"I'll wait right here," Sofia said, squeezing Chris's hand.

"Oh no, babe." Chris shook his head, dragging her to her feet. "You're coming with me."

———

The press packed the room, every face turned toward them, every eye looking at her, judging her as she stepped onto the raised dais and took a seat, Chris right beside her. The lights were blinding, the camera flashes caused bursts of color to erupt at the edges of her vision. Unable to take it any longer, she squinted and looked down.

Chris grabbed her hand beneath the table, holding it so tight it hurt. His lawyer said a few words, but Sofia couldn't hear him over the murmuring of the crowd. Once Albert finished speaking, Chris pulled the microphone in front of him.

"Thank you for coming out today," he said. "As Albert said, I will make a brief statement. I will not be answering questions afterward. As I'm sure you all know, the woman sitting next to me is Sofia Larson. She was an escort. Six months ago, I hired Sofia to work for me, to enter into a mutual agreement, one that eventually became a sexual relationship. I did this because I wanted something easy, no strings attached, something you guys wouldn't and couldn't scrutinize. As you can see, that worked out well." Chris smirked at the crowd of reporters.

Nervous chuckles drifted around the room and a few of the reporters became very interested in their shoes, their phones, or whatever they were writing in their notebooks. Most of them refused to make eye contact with either Chris or Sofia.

"I never expected to fall in love."

There was a collective gasp from the assembled press. Sofia's heart thumped uncontrollably in her chest.

"I fell in love with Sofia. And by the grace of God, she fell in love with me. I thought everything would be perfect, but everything got screwed up. Out of control. I let my management team tell me what to do, dictate what I should do, say, and to an extent, what I should feel. I never should have done that. The only words you should have ever heard were the ones I said to the woman beside me. I love Sofia Larson."

The first tear slid down Sofia's cheek, and she had to stop herself from jumping into Chris's arms and plastering his face with kisses. That would have to wait until later. Her heart pounded, jumping out of her chest, like a cartoon animal in love. He'd done it; he'd told everyone he loved her. She wanted to jump up and down, scream, laugh, and dance around the room, but she nodded, silently agreeing with and accepting everything Chris was saying.

"I've fired my manager, Jack Winslow, and my publicist, Wendy Trenton. My agent, Paul Tucker, and my lawyer, Albert Goldberg, will handle most aspects of my business from now on." Chris cleared his throat. "Starting immediately, I will take some time off to focus on my personal life and the people I care about." He slipped an arm around the back of Sofia's chair, his hand on her shoulder, his strong fingers digging into her skin. With a contented sigh, he pressed a lingering kiss to her temple; she could feel the smile on his face.

"I love you," he whispered.

Sofia could only nod, the tips of her fingers pressed to her mouth, stifling the sobs she felt rising in her throat.

"Hey, it's okay," Chris consoled her. "Everything is gonna work out." He wrapped his other arm around her and hugged her to his chest.

For a minute, Sofia forgot reporters surrounded them until the camera lights flashed, and the crowd roared, every reporter in the room shouting questions. Not that she cared; she only cared about Chris.

She took a second to get her breathing under control, to gather her thoughts, to stop wondering if this was all real. Once she got herself somewhat under control, she looked up at the man she loved and spoke for the first time since entering the room.

"You climbed the fire escape."

Chapter Twenty-Seven

CHRIS

Chris knew the press didn't like the "no question" rule, but he didn't care. The only person who mattered was Sofia and how she felt. Making her happy was all that mattered.

As he and Sofia left the room, hand in hand, he could hear the bloggers, the reporters, and the other gossip mongers shouting questions.

You're really going to have a relationship with a whore?

Sofia, how do you feel about Chris giving up his career for you?

Chris, have you been tested for sexually transmitted diseases?

What happens when this relationship is over? Then what?

Paul slammed the door, cutting off the roaring press. Chris sent Alex a text asking him to get the car ready. Sofia sank into the nearest chair, her head in her hands.

"Are you okay?" Chris murmured, crouching beside her.

"Can I get some water?" she asked.

As if by magic, Anita appeared, a bottle of water in her hand. She put it in front of Sofia and sat beside the younger woman, a soothing hand on her back. She leaned in close and whispered something that made Sofia smile.

"Christopher?"

Albert was standing at the opposite end of the table, gesturing for Chris to join him. He kissed the top of Sofia's head, earning himself a smile, then hurried to join his lawyer.

"Are you sure about this, Christopher?" Albert asked.

Chris loved Albert Goldberg. The man had been his lawyer forever, a grandfatherly man who could be serious when it was necessary, and was always open and honest, even when Chris was being an arrogant asshole. He almost always called him Christopher.

"Yes," Chris sighed. "One hundred percent."

"All right," Albert said. "I'll take care of any details you need me to take care of. But going off the grid—"

"It is risky, but this is what I need to do," Chris interrupted. "Just for a while. It will be okay. I promise."

Albert nodded, shaking Chris's hand. "I'll be in touch."

Sofia appeared at his side, her hand on his arm, her head on his shoulder. He hugged her, rubbing his hands up and down her back. He kissed her forehead.

"You okay?" he whispered.

"I am now." She smiled up at him.

"What did Anita say to you?"

"She said she can tell you love me. In the twenty years she's worked for Albert, she's never seen anything like this. 'Actors are a finicky bunch, Sofia,' she said. 'But that Chris is a keeper.' I guess I better hold onto you. Anita approves." Sofia laughed, the sound like bells. "This is surreal."

"A little." He chuckled. "But good, right?"

"The best." She nodded.

Ten minutes later, he and Sofia were in the car, Alex at the wheel, ready to take them wherever Chris instructed. An hour after that, once they'd stopped at Sofia's and then Chris's, they were on the road again, heading to Sasha's uncle's cabin.

They spent the ride snuggled together with Oliver on the floor near their feet, his head resting on his master's leg. The Escalade wasn't as private as the limo had been, so Chris kept his hands to himself, though he couldn't stop kissing her. Having her back in his arms after a week was like coming home after a long absence. He couldn't wait to get her alone.

Once they arrived, Chris refused Alex's help getting their bags; he yanked them out of the back of the Escalade while Sofia held Ollie's leash. They stood outside for a few minutes, watching the taillights receding, the realization that they were alone hitting them both.

Chris took their bags upstairs, dumped them in the master bedroom, then hurried back down to the living room where he found Sofia in the kitchen, filling two glasses with wine.

"Where's Ollie?" he asked.

"I put him in the backyard. He's rolling around in the grass and staring at the birds. He doesn't want to come back in." Sofia laughed.

"City dog." Chris chuckled, chancing a glance out the window, smiling at his dog sunning himself on the wooden porch.

"What do you want to do now that we're alone?" Sofia asked, drawing his attention back to her.

He crossed the room in two quick strides, trapping Sofia between the counter and his body, one hand on her ass, the other cupping her breast through the thin cotton blouse she was wearing. He leaned over her, so close his lips grazed hers as he spoke.

"You." His kiss was bruising, demanding, and intense, all the pent-up feelings he'd been holding back for a week exploding out of him in that moment of contact. The voices were quiet; they'd been nothing more than murmurs for the last few hours, but they were silent, banished forever.

Chris grabbed the bottom of her skirt, his fingers dragging up her thigh, the calloused tips scratching her soft skin. He yanked it above her waist and twisted his fingers in the panties she was wearing, pulling them down just enough to get his hand between her legs, delving into her warm core.

"Chris," Sofia gasped. "What are you doing?"

"I can't wait any longer," he growled, nibbling at her lower lip until she opened her mouth, his tongue sliding over her teeth, exploring her mouth as if he'd never kissed her before. He slipped a single digit into her wet heat, pumping it hard and fast, pushing her underwear down with his other hand, until they were sliding down and pooling around her ankles. Another finger slid in beside the first, drawing a moan from her, her legs falling open as she ground down on his fingers.

Chris broke off the kiss, grabbed her around the waist, and turned her around, leaning her over the counter. Her hands came down on either side of the kitchen sink, her head down, long, silken strands of red hair hanging in her face. He pulled a condom from his pocket, ripped it open, and slid it down his hard shaft, then he pressed against her, his chest to her back, one arm around her waist, a hand on her shoulder as he entered her, sending her hips into the edge of the counter. Sofia gasped, pushing back against him, begging him for more.

"It's gonna be quick, baby," he breathed, his warm breath blowing against her ear, goosebumps rising to the surface of her perfect skin. The hand around her waist slid down her stomach and between her legs, finding the sensitive nub, circling it with the tip of one finger. "But I promise it'll be good."

Sofia nodded, her nails digging into his wrist as he thrust into her, hard and fast. She squeezed the edge of the counter, unable to do anything more than hold on as he slammed into her.

The feelings rolling through him were overwhelming, blocking out everything—every sound, every sight, every little thing. It was just him and Sofia and his need for her. He could feel her body responding to him, her walls clenching around him, the pleasure building to a frenetic force that couldn't be stopped. Her cries grew louder and louder until she was coming, screaming his name.

Chris's thrusts became harder, more erratic, his hips pumping at a maddening pace as he pounded into her, his hands clamping down tight on her waist as he climaxed, a deep groan rumbling through his chest.

He leaned over her, both of them spent, her body flush against his, his hands caressing her, his touch meant to soothe as he peppered her neck with soft kisses. He wanted to hold her in his arms forever.

A sharp bark and long nails scratching at the back door interrupted his musings. Both he and Sofia laughed. He pressed one more kiss to the back of her neck, stepped back, discarded the condom, and tucked himself back into his dark blue dress pants before taking a cursory pass at straightening Sofia's skirt.

"I guess Ollie decided he wants in," Sofia laughed.

Chris hugged her, her lips drifting along the edge of her jaw. "Let's get him in here. I'm sure he's as hungry as I am. Is there a pizza place in this town?"

"Oh my God, Chris, I'm freezing!" Sofia laughed, her arms wrapped around herself. She was bouncing on her toes, her cheeks flushed pink, the tip of her nose red. "Let's go back!"

The temperature dipped overnight, hovering in the low fifties, colder in the mountains than down in the city, something neither of them expected. Chris didn't think either of them had expected to stay for almost three weeks, either.

They went for a walk around the lake, the urge to explore coming over Chris after a late lunch. They put Oliver on his leash, threw on light jackets, and set out a little after three. Chris didn't realize it would be so cold once the sun dipped below the horizon.

"Come here," he chuckled, drawing Sofia into his arms. He hissed when her icy hands slipped beneath his t-shirt and touched his bare skin. "Damn!"

"Let's go back to the cabin," Sofia begged.

"All right, just give me two seconds." He yanked his phone from his pocket, jogged fifty yards down the path, and snapped a picture of the sign he'd spotted through the trees, then he returned to Sofia's side.

"What were you taking a picture of?" she asked, peering over his shoulder.

"Thought I saw a deer." He shrugged. "I think I missed it, though. Come on. Let's go." He took her hand and they set off, heading back at a quick pace. It took them over an hour to get back to the cabin.

Chris pulled blankets from the cabinet and grabbed a movie from the stack on the table. Over the past few weeks, he and Sofia had fallen into a routine, one he'd grown comfortable with: sleeping late, cooking together, walks around the lake, movies in the evening. It was all very domestic, and he loved every minute.

Once he had everything ready for the night, he grabbed his phone and stepped out onto the patio overlooking the lake.

"Christopher," Albert answered, his tone warm and friendly. "How are you?"

"I'm doing well," Chris replied.

"And that lovely young lady of yours?"

"Perfect. Thank you for asking." He glanced over his shoulder, but Sofia was in the kitchen, making hot apple cider. "I've got a question for you, Albert. A request."

"All right." Albert sounded all business. "Tell me what it is."

Chris rattled off what he wanted Albert to do and promised to send the picture he'd taken as soon as he hung up the phone. His lawyer promised to get back to him as soon as possible, hopefully with good news.

"Thank you, Albert. For everything."

"You're welcome." He could hear the smile in the man's voice. "You deserve happiness, Christopher. I'll talk to you soon."

Sofia tapped on the glass door, a question on her beautiful face. Chris smiled at her, slid open the door, and stepped inside.

"Sorry, babe," he said. "Talking to Albert."

She held out a steaming mug, the heat rising from it warming his hands. He followed her to the couch, settled in beside her, and pulled the blanket over them. Oliver jumped up beside them, digging and pawing at the corner of the blanket before laying down with a heavy sigh.

"This is about as close to perfect as it gets," Sofia whispered, her head resting on his chest.

Chris kissed her temple, his hands sliding down her back, cupping her ass, and dragging her up his body until she laid on top of him. He took her head in his hands, tipping her head back so he could kiss the long lines of her neck.

"You're perfect."

Sofia sighed, wrapped her arms around his neck, and caught his lips in hers. She stretched out, her foot hitting the dog at the end of the couch. Oliver jumped to the floor with an irritated huff and gave them a dirty look before padding across the room and laying down in front of the fireplace.

"Oh, hell, Ollie. Sorry," Sofia giggled.

Chris rolled to his side, trapping Sofia between himself and the back of the couch. The fingers of one hand tangled in her hair, and his other hand slid under the edge of her t-shirt to rest on the bare skin of her back. He kissed her until they were both panting, and he felt like he might combust.

"How did I get so lucky?" he asked. "How did I find the one woman in the world who was exactly what I needed? Who is everything I need?"

"You need me?" Sofia whispered, her blue eyes wide with wonder.

"I've always needed you," he replied, burying his face against the side of her neck. "But for a long time, I couldn't bring myself to admit it. Not even to myself. I'm sorry about that." A shiver raced through her, making her tremble in his arms.

"Cold?" he asked.

"No," Sofia answered, shaking her head, her hair falling over her face. She kissed the hollow of his throat, then the edge of his jaw, and his lips. She pushed her hands under the edge of his shirt, flattening them on his hard stomach muscles.

Sofia tugged at his shirt, stopping the kiss just long enough to tug it over his head. Her lips returned to his, kissing him with a desperate determination that surprised him. She sat up and pushed him to his back, straddling him, her legs on either side of his hips, her hands holding his head as she kissed him.

Chris drew in a deep breath, his hands tightening on her waist. Her hand drifted farther up his chest, her touch cool against his hot skin. He moaned low in the back of his throat when the tip of her thumb brushed over his nipple, the tiny nub hardening.

"God, Sofia, the things you do to me," he whispered against her lips. He ran his fingers through her hair, playing with the silken strands, then he was kissing her, his tongue swiping across her lips before slipping inside her mouth.

Chris slid his hands up her waist until he was cupping her breasts, caressing them. But it wasn't enough; he wanted her bare skin against his. He ripped her shirt off and hurried to unhook her bra, freeing her breasts. She leaned over Chris, pressing herself against his naked chest, and licked his throat, drawing a moan from him. His hands slid up her back to her shoulders, pulling her down onto him, his hips grinding against hers.

Sofia moaned, her nails digging into his scalp, tugging on the short strands. Chris fumbled with the button on her jeans, then he yanked the zipper down and pushed her jeans just past her hips. He slid his hand down the front of her underwear, one finger dipping inside of her, a low growl rumbling low in the back of his throat. His stomach muscles tightened as he pushed himself up and leaned against the back of the couch, watching Sofia as she stood up and stripped off her jeans and underwear. Once she was free of her clothing, she grabbed the waistband of Chris's jeans and yanked them down as he toed off his boots. He kicked off his jeans and held out his arms to her.

She returned to him without hesitation, her lips finding his. Chris cradled her in his arms as he pulled her down on the couch beside him. His hand moved between her legs, massaging her, teasing her, kissing her. Sofia wiggled against his hand, silently begging for more even as he slipped a finger inside of her, pumping it in and out.

Sofia palmed him, rubbing her hand along his length, before grasping the base of his cock and slowly tightening her grip as she slid her hand up the shaft and back down again. She swiped her thumb over the tip, squeezing him a little.

Chris grabbed her, his lips crashing into hers, the kiss hard, demanding. He bit at her lip and shoved his tongue in her mouth, the two of them moving and grinding against each other.

"Oh, God, Chris, please," she begged.

Chris rolled Sofia to her back, nestled himself between her hips, and took her breast in his hand, kneading it as he sucked the nipple into his mouth, swirling his tongue around it. He moved down her body, placing gentle kisses every couple of inches until his head was between her legs. He pulled her legs over his shoulders as he flattened his tongue and licked her, his tongue flicking at her sensitive bud.

Chris glanced up at her as she let out a shaky breath, then he reached up and took her hand as his tongue sank into her body. His other hand slid beneath her, pulling her against his mouth. Sofia squeezed his hand, her back arching, loud moans coming out of her perfect mouth.

She rocked against Chris, her nails digging into the palm of his hand, a breathless scream leaving her when he slipped a finger inside of her. She wrapped a hand around Chris's head, holding him to her as she came, her entire body convulsing.

Chris worked her through it, not stopping until she lay spent on the couch. He kissed the inside of her thighs, working his way back up her body, his lips settling at the junction where her shoulder and neck met. He released her long enough to snatch his jeans from the floor and yank a condom from the pocket.

"Always prepared," she giggled.

"Like a Boy Scout," Chris replied, groaning as she took it from him and slid it down his length.

He guided himself to her entrance and eased into her. Sofia wrapped her legs around his waist, pulling him into her as she moved her hips up to meet his, encouraging him to move with her. His lips slid up her neck to her mouth, kissing her as he thrust inside.

Sofia held him, her arms wrapped around him as they settled into an easy rhythm, their bodies moving in sync, hands and lips everywhere, her quiet moans and his low grunts filling the room. Her fingers dug into Chris's ass as he pounded into her, harder and harder, the rhythm lost as they both drew closer to orgasm. Chris stiffened, his entire body tensing as he came, the orgasm so intense he forgot everything: the past, the pain, the grief, all the heartache they'd suffered. At that moment, the only thing that existed was the woman he loved.

Afterward, they lay entwined in each other's arms on the couch for a long time.

Chapter Twenty-Eight

SOFIA

"I should be back in three or four hours," Chris said.

"Promise?" Sofia asked, holding the phone between her cheek and shoulder as she opened the back door for Ollie. Again.

"I promise," Chris chuckled. He cleared his throat, and his voice dropped a notch, lower, sexier, the sound shooting straight to the apex between her thighs. "I miss you."

God, this man was too good to be real. "I miss you, too," she breathed. "Hurry back."

Chris had gone into L.A. early, something about clearing up some important business. They'd decided together, as a couple—something she had a hard time wrapping her head around—Chris would go alone; it was easier than fighting off the press and their endless, awful questions. He promised to be back by nightfall. It felt like an eternity.

They'd been at Sasha's uncle's cabin for three weeks. They spent their time getting to know each other. It surprised her the things they *didn't* know about each other; it was painfully obvious their relationship had been strictly business. They discussed their vastly different childhoods, how Chris had become an actor, how Sofia's life had done a huge one-eighty, forcing her to become an escort to survive. They talked about anything and everything, then they talked some more. If it was possible, Sofia was more in love with Chris now than she'd ever been.

The next few hours lasted an eternity. She took Oliver for a walk, hoping the dog would burn off some of his restless energy, then she changed the sheets in the master bedroom, even tried to read a book, but she resorted to sitting on the patio with a mug of hot cider in one of Chris's sweatshirts, watching the road, her sketchbook on her lap. She tried drawing Ollie sleeping in the sun until she saw the black Escalade coming through the trees. She set aside the sketchbook, rose to her feet, whistled for the dog, and hurried outside.

Sofia sprinted down the driveway and threw herself into Chris's arms, smothering him in kisses. He laughed, crushing her to his chest.

"I was only gone for a few hours." He smirked.

"It was too long," Sofia giggled. She peered over his shoulder at the SUV in the driveway. "Where's Alex?"

"I left him in L.A." Chris shrugged. He kissed the tip of her nose. "I wanted the Escalade. Come on. Let's take a drive."

He didn't wait for her response, just spun on his heel and yanked open the car door, whistling for Oliver to get in. Sofia followed the ball of black and white fur, laughing as he plopped himself on her lap and waited for her to roll the window down.

Chris held her hand as he drove, his fingers intertwined with hers, his thumb rubbing over the knuckles on the back of her hand. Oliver stuck his head out the half-open window, tongue out, tail wagging. Sofia felt the sting of tears, good tears, happy tears. She rested her head against the back of the seat and closed her eyes. Everything was changing. Most days she still had a hard time believing this was her life, that she was lucky enough to be with the man she loved, that somehow they had come out the other side of a storm of insanity whole and in one piece.

"Where are we going?" Sofia opened her eyes and leaned forward, trying to see around the dog in her lap.

"It's a surprise," Chris answered, squeezing her hand. "You'll see."

Five minutes later, Chris turned down a familiar dirt road, one they'd walked down only a few days ago. They drove for a few more minutes, then Chris took a right into a stand of trees, the dirt road there obscured by the tall grass and low hanging branches. He came to a stop in front of a locked gate, rolled down the window and punched a code into the box hidden behind a large bush. The old vine-encrusted gate swung open.

They drove up a long drive, one in desperate need of upkeep. There were branches strewn across the road, weeds growing up on either side, and the lawn needed a trim. Despite her constant questions, Chris would only smile and nod. They stopped in front of a sprawling two-story cabin with a long porch spanning the length of the house. Huge pine trees surrounded it, and a large hill sloped down to the lake.

Chris cut the engine, came around the front of the Escalade, and opened the door. Ollie jumped out and took off before Sofia could grab him.

"Oh crap! Ollie!" she yelled.

"He'll be fine," Chris laughed. "Let him explore."

"What are we doing here?" Sofia asked. "What is this place?"

Chris scooped her up, lifting her from the SUV and carrying her up the porch stairs before setting her on her feet. "This is our future," he answered, pressing a kiss to her forehead. "If you want it."

"What are you talking about?"

"I bought it," Chris said. "For us. You and me." He scratched his fingers through his beard, his eyes flitting around. He was gnawing at his lower lip, watching her, trying to gauge her reaction.

It took a minute for the words to sink in, for Sofia to understand what Chris was saying. He wanted a future with her; he'd bought them a home, a place to call their own, a place for them to start fresh.

She must have scared him, silently staring at him, speechless. He started babbling, his words spilling out of his mouth as if he was trying to cover up the silence surrounding them.

"It has three bathrooms, four bedrooms, one of them a huge master bedroom with one wall of windows overlooking the lake. There's a game room downstairs with a pool table, and we could put whatever else we want in there, I guess. There's room off of the living room, I, uh, think it's supposed to be an office or something, but I thought it could be a great studio for you. You could draw, paint, whatever you want to do in there. There's a lot of light, natural light coming through the windows. And, um, there's a dock leading to the lake, our own private access, along with a gazebo and a fire pit, and the property is huge, and gorgeous. I think you'll love it if you give it a chance." He bounced on his toes, running his fingers through his hair, then tapping them on his legs. "Say something, baby."

Sofia took a step closer to him, leaving only a millimeter of space between them. She reached for him, put her hands on his cheeks, and guided his lips to hers, kissing him. "Show me the bedroom."

———

"That box goes upstairs, third door on the left, the guest bedroom," Sofia called over her shoulder.

Seth nodded her general direction, made a sharp left turn, and jogged up the stairs, the box balanced on one shoulder. Sasha paused, leaning over the box she was unpacking to watch Seth.

"Sash?" Sofia giggled, her eyes wide, astonished at her friend's bold behavior.

"What?" Sasha feigned innocence, returning to the box of utensils she was placing in the kitchen drawers.

"I saw that," Sofia said. "You totally eyeballed Seth."

"He's cute." Sasha shrugged.

"And sweet," Sofia added helpfully.

Sasha smiled, a genuine, sweet smile, one that Sofia didn't see often. Unfortunately, she knew the instant the memories came back. Sasha's eyes dropped to the floor and her hands shook.

"Don't play matchmaker, Sof," she said. "I don't know if I'm ready for that."

"He's not Liam," Sofia argued.

"Who's Liam?" Chris interjected, setting another box on the kitchen counter. He slipped an arm around Sofia's waist and pressed a kiss to her temple.

"Nobody," Sasha said, shaking her head. "Just my ex. That's all."

Sofia could see how nervous Sasha became at the mention of her ex-husband's name; she felt the waves of worry and irritation rolling off her best friend. Sofia changed the subject.

"Are you guys almost done? Unloading the truck, I mean?" she asked.

"Yep." Chris grinned. "All that's left is a few boxes and the big stuff. Couches, chairs. The bed's already upstairs." He winked, his laughter following him out the door.

"You two are disgustingly cute," Sasha said, pretending to gag. "Must be nice to get your happily ever after, huh?"

"You'll get yours, Sasha." Sofia hugged her friend. "It'll happen. I know it will. Never in a million years did I think Chris and I would be together, that I'd get that happily ever after. But, look at us, two people that the world fought against every step of the way, planning our future, figuring out how we can make it work. And we will make it work. I believe it'll happen for you, too."

Sasha smiled and hugged her friend back. "I'll go grab another box," she said.

Sofia watched her go. Seth met her at the front door and held it open for her, both of them smiling and laughing. She worried about her best friend, more than Sasha knew, but her preoccupation with the chaos of her own life the last couple of months had left little time for her friend. She needed to remedy that situation.

It would start tonight—dinner and drinks under the stars, with a roaring fire to keep them warm, her way of saying thank you to Sasha and Seth for helping her and Chris move in. She'd already made them both promise they'd stay for a day or two, already made sure that both guest rooms were ready for company. If Sasha and Seth hit it off, who was she to stop it? It wasn't like she hadn't noticed Seth flirting with Sasha most of the day, and her friend found him attractive. A little matchmaking wouldn't hurt anyone.

"What are you plotting?"

Startled, Sofia jumped, knocking a stack of silverware into the sink. She giggled and shook her head.

"How did you know?" She took Chris's hand in both of hers, her fingers intertwined with his. The ring he'd put on her finger three days earlier, the day after he'd shown her their new home, scratched against her palm.

"You've been watching them all day, grinning every time they're within arm's reach. You convinced both of them to stay for the weekend, and you planned this huge dinner, even though we haven't unpacked yet. I know you're up to something." Chris ducked his head and kissed the corner of her mouth. "Spill it, Sof."

"Does Seth have a girlfriend?" Sofia whispered. She knew the wicked grin Chris referred to was back, but since the cat was out of the bag, she figured she might as well go all in.

"No, he doesn't," Chris chuckled. "But I think you're going to fix that, aren't you?"

"Maybe." Sofia laughed. "We'll see."

"I love you." He grinned. "You know that, right?"

She rested her head against his chest, a blush coloring her cheeks. She'd never tire of hearing those words come out of his mouth. "Yeah, I do, but tell me again."

Chris put his arms around her, picking her up and setting her on the counter. He stepped between her legs, his nose drifting along the line of her throat, his beard tickling her. Sofia sighed and leaned into him, her hands on his shoulders, digging in, pulling him closer.

"I love you," he breathed.

The End

About the Author

I'm a northern girl transplanted to the much warmer southwest. I've always been a voracious reader and ever since I was a little girl, I've had some kind of story playing in my head, daydreams that I turned into intricate stories. After my three children grew up and started their own lives, I decided it was time to chase my dreams.

I love writing contemporary, romantic fiction, which I stumbled into when I started writing fanfiction for my favorite obsessions. One of my favorite series is JR Ward's Black Dagger Brotherhood series. I long to have people love my books like I love hers. She is an inspiration to me and my writing.

When I'm not busy writing, I love to binge-watch new shows, fawn over my favorite Supernatural monster hunters, rewatch my collection of Marvel movies, crochet, and spend time with my husband of twenty-seven years and our dogs.

4 HORSEMEN PUBLICATIONS

ROMANCE

EMILY BUNNEY
All or Nothing
All the Way
All She Needs
Having it All
All at Once
All Together
All for Her

FANTASY/PARANORMAL ROMANCE

BLAISE RAMSAY
Through The Black Mirror
The City of Nightmares
The Astral Tower
The Lost Book of the Old Blood
Shadow of the Dark Witch
Chamber of the Dead God

VALERIE WILLIS
Cedric: The Demonic Knight
Romasanta: Father of Werewolves
The Oracle: Keeper of the
Gaea's Gate
Artemis: Eye of Gaea
King Incubus: A New Reign

BEAU LAKE
The Beast Beside Me
The Beast Within Me
The Beast After Me
The Beast Like Me
An Eye for Emeralds
Swimming in Sapphires
Pining for Pearls

J.M. PAQUETTE
Klauden's Ring
Solyn's Body
The Inbetween
Hannah's Heart
Call Me Forth
Invite Me In

V.C. WILLIS
Prince's Priest
Priest's Assassin

EROTICA

4HorsemenPublications.com